A BLACK
EAST WIND

JACK GRANFERS

Matador
Unit E2 Airfield Business Park,
Harrison Road, Market Harborough,
Leicestershire. LE16 7UL
Tel: 0116 279 2299
Email: books@troubador.co.uk
Web: www.troubador.co.uk/matador
Twitter: @matadorbooks

ISBN 978 180313 325 6

British Library Cataloguing in Publication Data.
A catalogue record for this book is available from the British Library.

Printed and bound by CPI Group (UK) Ltd, Croydon, CR0 4YY
Typeset in 11pt Minion Pro by Troubador Publishing Ltd, Leicester, UK

Matador is an imprint of Troubador Publishing Ltd

This book is dedicated to Charlie, Evie, George and Leo – have a great life.

Prologue

Morning of Friday 2nd June 1944

H E'S SCARED. NO, NOT SCARED. TERRIFIED.
As terrified as he was on his first day of assault training ten months ago. Ten long treacherous months that have done nothing to dissipate his dread of being on the open sea.

The sea has always been his nemesis, and the weather today is only making matters worse. Much worse. Thunderclouds whipping across a brooding sky. Wind howling. Menacing. Breaking waves tossing the craft around like a toy. Torrential rain soaking everybody and everything to the core.

His icy fingers grip the steel rail of the landing craft, his knuckles white from the cold. And the fear. It feels more like a bleak, freezing day in February, not an early summer's morning in June.

Nausea engulfs him.

It's all right for the military brass, perched above the beach, cocooned on their viewing platform, congratulating themselves on how well equipped their troops are for D-Day. Little do they know!

He despises the hypocrisy of it all; wants to shout out obscenities, scream in anger at the hundreds of lives already lost in a war that has damn all to do with him. And they haven't yet left for France.

A dress rehearsal for Normandy? More like a goddam suicide mission!

He'd never been so fearful of not seeing her again. The deep blue of her eyes, the curl of her lips as she smiled up at him. He feels her closeness, breathing her scent, tracing the outline of her mouth with his fingers as they enveloped one another. She loves him. She wants to marry him. He'll take her home Stateside. Keep her safe. Far away from the limey soldier who beat her up, made her life a misery.

A massive wave hits the craft broadside, almost knocking it over. Saltwater pierces his face, tears at his skin. The British major in charge is shouting at him. 'Corporal, something's wrong! We're slipping off course. Get back to the helm. Alert the cox'n or we'll be on the rocks.'

He fights his way back, hand over hand along the rail. Too late. The craft is thrown unceremoniously onto its side. Men and equipment flung into the raging sea, crashing against the granite rocks.

Someone's behind him.

He turns. What's he doing here? He's not part of the crew. As he stares into the hate-filled eyes his head explodes as the vicious blow knocks him overboard into the icy water.

Waves cut through him like shards of glass, water filling his mouth, lungs burning, desperate for air. Powerful hands dragging his body deeper and deeper below the surface.

He can't defend himself.

He can't keep her safe.

Goodbye sweetheart.

Everything goes black.

'I have full confidence in your courage,
devotion to duty and skill in battle.
We will accept nothing less than full victory!
Good Luck! And let us beseech the blessing
of Almighty God upon this great
and noble undertaking.'

Eisenhower's message to his troops on D-Day
6th June 1944

Part One
North Devon Coast

August 1943

Chapter 1

First Lieutenant Jim Ridd

J IM RIDD SAT HUDDLED TOGETHER WITH TWO FELLOW
US Army officers in the back of a requisitioned British
Army sedan driven by a female corporal on its way to
Woolacombe, North Devon. The journey from London
had been tedious, not helped by the poor state of the roads
and the absence of any road signs, taken down in case of a
German invasion.

The eight-hour journey had given Jim time to reflect
on how his life had changed since his country had entered
the war. One minute a reporter on The Patriot Ledger, the
newspaper of Quincy, Massachusetts. The next, enlisted
and posted to London as one of the US Army's first public
affairs officers, or PAOs, to serve in the UK where he would
put his journalistic skills to use in public relations for the
war effort.

His repeated requests to join a combat unit had
fallen on deaf ears and, despite reassurances of just how
important the work of a PAO was, Jim felt ashamed that
he was not destined for action in France. He'd spent the
last eighteen months in London pushing paper around as

part of a PAO team charged with ensuring the US Army in Britain was viewed in a positive light.

There was one small consolation. His fellow travellers' reconnaissance mission to Devon was to assess the beaches along the coast and determine their suitability for the amphibious training exercises planned for the D-Day preparations. If Woolacombe was considered appropriate, the US Army's Assault Training Centre, the ATC, would be established there under the command of a Colonel Webb, and Jim would be working with combatant units at the forefront of the planned invasion.

His companions were engineers from the Engineer Amphibian Command at Camp Edwards, Massachusetts. They had told Jim the most suitable D-Day training areas had already been claimed by the British months ago. All that was left was a stretch of notoriously wild and rugged Atlantic Coast, renowned for its strong waves and unpredictable undercurrents that made landing assault craft safely hazardous in the extreme.

Jim's task on this trip was to determine how much disruption the ATC would cause to the life of the local population when ten-thousand GIs descended upon them for ten months. As the car meandered slowly across the English countryside, he took a card out of his pocket to remind himself of his likely day job in this remote part of the West Country.

Your role as the ATC's PAO in XXX (redacted for security reasons) is to create a working relationship with the media, develop a community relations programme, keep regular contact with government agencies and gain the support of local government officials and people of influence within your region. You must establish confidence in the US Army and its readiness to conduct operations in war. You will help raise and maintain troop morale and will report and be accountable directly to the ATC Commanding Officer.

Much better than being stuck in London, Jim thought to himself.

Jim's car finally stopped outside a large detached house, and the driver announced they'd arrived in Woolacombe. The men who greeted them were members of the local commando group who introduced them to their host Mrs May.

'You'll be billeting with me at The Lookout for as long as you're in the area.'

At least, that's what one of the locals told Jim she'd said. It took several weeks for her guests to understand her broad Scottish accent and, likewise, for her to make any sense of their North American dialect.

The engineers spent the best part of a week assessing the local terrain and producing their report. They inspected the largest beaches along the coast and learnt as much as they could from the Coast Guard about the notorious currents, tidal movements, and strong winds. Their conclusion was that the beaches *were* suitable for amphibious training exercises, despite the ferocity of the Atlantic surf. Their report highlighted that the wide expanses of beaches at Woolacombe, Croyde and Saunton were almost identical to those the invading forces would encounter in Normandy.

Jim's week was taken up meeting local dignitaries and officials to explain the implications for the surrounding population, and the necessity for strategic tracts of land and prominent buildings to be requisitioned. His presentations were met with bemusement and bewilderment, as if the locals couldn't quite believe what they were hearing, or that their small rural community could soon be the epicentre for the US Army's invasion of Europe.

He concluded that whilst there would inevitably be disruption, the GIs and locals could co-exist with give and take on both sides and well-conceived public relations. His negotiations were helped by explaining his strong family connection to the area. His great-great-grandfather Jack Ridd had been born in nearby Mortehoe village before emigrating to Quincy some one hundred and twenty years before.

Colonel Webb wasted no time informing his superiors that the ATC HQ and its five hundred staff would be based in the Woolacombe Bay Hotel, adjacent to the seafront, with the first of the ten-thousand combat troops arriving in three weeks' time.

The friendly invasion was about to begin.

Jim wrote his first letter home to his wife Susan from The Lookout. His bedroom window had panoramic views over the bay, where, as the engineers had explained, multiple training exercises would take place with thousands of GIs endangering their lives every day, learning the rudiments of landing assault craft safely in the wild surf.

He explained the guilt that ate away at him inside, telling her that, if *any* opportunity presented itself to join in the training, he wouldn't hesitate to take it.

Keeping the locals happy was not something he'd envisaged doing when he had enlisted. He'd wanted so much to fight against the tyranny overshadowing Europe, to do his duty, and make his wife and baby daughter Amy proud.

Fat chance of that he thought. Public relations was a soft option and Jim had not once, in his twenty-five years, opted for the easy life. Serious-minded and carrying the weight of the world on his shoulders, he knew his conscience would not rest until he could find an opportunity to prove himself to his peers. And to his younger brother Billy.

Jim knew Billy was in combat training at an unspecified location in Scotland and was expected to move south in a few weeks' time. God willing, it would be to the ATC in Woolacombe.

Chapter 2
Billy's arrival

JIM'S PRAYERS WERE ANSWERED. BILLY RIDD, A corporal with the National Guard Infantry Division arrived in Devon three weeks later. His train pulled into Barnstaple after a fifteen-hour journey from Aberdeen. Billy sighed with relief, eased his numb backside off the hard bench and stretched out his long frame, keen to get moving at last.

Eighteen months younger than Jim, Billy's care-free approach to life made him popular with the GIs in his unit, just as it had with his fellow workers in the family's ship building business in Quincy, where he'd happily laboured by day and partied hard by night.

The two brothers could not have been more dissimilar: Jim, lean and academic. Billy, tall, muscular, and good with his hands, he lived for the moment with little regard for the consequences his devil-may-care attitude might have, especially where the opposite sex was concerned. Despite their differences, Billy loved his elder brother dearly and appreciated the guardian role Jim had adopted at times to get him out of more scrapes than he cared to remember.

8

Billy and all the soldiers in his infantry division, known as the 'Blue and Grey', had no experience of fighting a war. They were tradesmen, who until recently had been plying their craft in the towns and villages throughout Virginia, Maryland, and New England. After basic training in Scotland, they were now headed to a makeshift camp near Braunton to join the other ATC combat troops arriving daily by the thousands from the four corners of the UK.

As Billy's train slowed to a stop, a volley of instructions rang out ordering soldiers to collect their kit bags and disembark. Within minutes, he was standing with hundreds of other GIs, their greatcoat collars turned up to shield the easterly wind that greeted their arrival.

'Where the hell is Barnstaple?' asked one of Billy's buddies, peering at the temporary sign.

'We're in North Devon, England, not far from where my forefathers emigrated. This, my friend, is a lucky omen.'

They joined the throng of GIs boarding the line of army trucks transporting them the six miles to their camp. Billy smiled broadly. Jim had intimated in his last letter how close he was to where their family originated from. They would soon be re-united.

The unit had to brave the October weather as they began their brutal training programme, and were relieved to move from their damp bell tents into the Nissen hut encampment before the worst of the winter weather had set in.

Billy shared his 'home away from home' with thousands of GIs, none of whom had any idea how long they'd be spending their days in and out of the sea preparing for amphibious warfare. As the training progressed, members of his unit were selected for different roles that made up the team on each of the landing craft. Billy was appointed assistant section leader.

His job was to support the section leader, a commissioned officer, in looking for enemy fortifications and identifying ways to breach the defences blocking their route up the beach. Covered by the fire of riflemen, he had to move his men forward to clear a path for the infantrymen and equipment following behind.

He had to be first off the landing craft. Boots sinking in clinging sand; currents tugging at your legs; waves breaking over your body; sodden clothing and equipment forcing you down into the freezing water; cries and screams filling your ears as bullets raged overhead. Frightening. Intimidating…

Especially for someone like Billy, terrified of water.

He was under no illusion. The work was treacherous; the training relentless; every day fraught with danger. He determined from the outset to make the most of his downtime – beer in hand and a pretty girl on his arm. *Life's too short.*

Chapter 3
Family comes first

WHILE BILLY MADE THE MOST OF HIS BACHELOR lifestyle, Jim spent time away from his PAO duties contemplating his life in Devon and sharing these thoughts in letters to Susan. He knew from the tone of her replies she was desperately lonely without him, despite doting on their first-born baby girl and being kept busy with her art classes in the Quincy gallery.

Jim's letters could say nothing about the military operation going on around him. Instead, he described the local landscape, aiming to bridge the three thousand miles that separated him from his wife. Life here was akin to many parts of New England, with farming and fishing two threads of familiarity that bound the places together.

One early October evening, when most of his colleagues were drinking in the village pubs, Jim sat on his bed in The Outlook.

Dearest Susan

It's Friday evening here and most of the guys are out in the village pubs challenging the locals to darts and chatting up the girls, with Billy no doubt the centre of attraction as usual!

The animosity that greeted us when we first arrived, and the jibes from the young farmers exempt from conscription, are less frequent now. Life appears to be slowly settling down and I guess we're gradually becoming accepted.

The locals are getting used to army vehicles speeding along their narrow lanes, holding up the farmers' tractors and spreading mud everywhere. Less so, the culture shock of our trans-Atlantic accents and uniforms. But we've money to spend in the shops and at the weekly dances in the village halls to keep the tradespeople happy, and many of the guys have taken to the Devon cider served up in copious quantities in the pubs.

We have lots of supplies they don't have, especially chocolate, gum, and nylons and although some locals refer to 'the American invasion,' most are keen to befriend us and appear grateful for our contribution to the war effort – even if they think it's 'too little and too late.' The children have certainly acquired a taste for ring doughnuts and Hershey bars!

I met a farmer my age last night and he told me how little had changed for the locals over the years prior to our arrival. Most of his friends had enlisted and he was very put out that his reserved occupation had prevented him from joining up. He said the seasonal cycle continues as it always has in this part of the world, far removed from the devastation happening in places like London and the channel ports. Food rationing is a hardship but nothing like as bad as in the big cities.

Jim enquired about the folks back home and requested new photos of Amy. He read everything through carefully and suspected some sensitive words might fall foul of the censor's pen.

Writing the letter left him feeling more homesick than he'd felt for a long time. Susan was not the only one to be lonely. Then he remembered he was meeting Billy tomorrow to find the Ridd family grave in Mortehoe. He smiled at the thought of spending some quality time with his brother.

The brothers had been close since toddlers and had grown up sharing many of the same friends and adventures. Billy had always been the bigger and stronger of the two; the adventurous risk taker compared to his more cautious elder brother. But they'd always looked out for each other whether in the school playground or on the sports field.

When the challenges of adolescence arrived, the bond between them grew ever stronger. They played in the same football teams and shared many happy times playing a three-ball at the nearby golf club with their father. As Jim reminisced, his mind flashed back to an incident in their teenage years; an incident that reinforced the bond between them and left Jim forever in his brother's debt.

When Jim was fourteen, he was old enough for membership of the long-established local basketball club.

A club that prided itself on selecting only the very best players in Quincy. Prospective members had to excel in a series of demanding mental and physical challenges. Jim was a talented point guard, the 'de-facto' leader of the team on the court, and he excelled in all the challenges thrown at him. All that was left was the initiation ceremony.

The ceremony was very much a rite of passage. It consisted of a bizarre ritual in which prospective members were stripped to their jockeys, locked in the club's storeroom, an underground bunker where they had to remain in the cold and dark until released by the club captain.

Unknown to Billy, the club captain had decided Jim was ready for his initiation and had locked him in the bunker earlier in the day, planning to get the team together later that afternoon, release him and welcome him into the club. No one except Billy knew he suffered from allergic asthma and, after an hour breathing in the bunker's dust, Jim was wheezing badly, his chest tightening, struggling for breath. He fought the panic that threatened to overcome him as the tubes carrying air to his lungs became more inflamed. Suffocation creeping closer and closer.

The club captain, oblivious to Jim's condition, had driven downtown to see his girlfriend, taking the storeroom keys with him. He planned to return a couple of hours later and, with team members alongside, hand over the much-prized club shirt to Jim and carry him aloft to the nearby basketball hall.

Had Billy not bumped into a team member that afternoon, his brother would have died. He sprinted the two miles to the bunker and, using a steel pipe from the building works nearby, broke the lock on the store door and carried his brother outside into the fresh air.

Billy knew all about the Holger Nielson Method of resuscitation from the first aid classes their father had insisted his sons attend. Jim was soon recuperating in Quincy Medical Center. He made a full recovery and went on to captain the team for five successive seasons. Billy's quick thinking and athleticism had saved his brother's life.

Chapter 4
Tips for US Servicemen

'HERE YOU GO GUYS, SOME BEDTIME READING.'
Billy's sergeant had told him to distribute some booklets to the men in his hut.

'Make sure they read them carefully Billy,' he had said. 'The information just might keep you and them out of trouble.'

After handing them out, Billy jumped on to his bunk and scanned the front cover.

'*Over There – Tips for American Military Personnel Serving in Britain.*'

'If this helps us sweet talk the girls, I'm all for it,' Billy said. 'But, now my friends, it's Saturday night and time to party. There's always something going down at the Red Barn in Woolacombe and it's about time you lot loosened up a bit.'

'Don't you ever tire of being the life and soul of the party, Billy?' his neighbour asked. 'And what's the Red Barn when it's at home?'

'It's my name for the Club. It's big, it's red and it's shaped like some of the barns back home. And so, from now on, the Red Barn it is.'

Billy's Red Barn was the American Red Cross Service Club, in the centre of the village. Previously called The Bungalow Café, it had been requisitioned by the US Army for food, recreation, and to billet Red Cross nurses.

When Billy arrived with two of his buddies, a GI band was playing a repertoire of popular songs. The dance floor was packed with soldiers and land girls, forgetting the strains of wartime life for a few precious hours. Billy escorted a pretty nurse to the floor and showed off his dancing prowess to the music of Glenn Miller and The Mills Brothers.

Jim walked in some thirty minutes later and sat in a corner, drink in hand, enjoying the music and reminiscing of Susan and how much she loved to dance. Had she been there, she'd have cajoled him onto the floor and not let him stop until the last sounds faded. Billy came over as the band finished their last number, Miller's 'That Old Black Magic', and introduced him to his dancing partner.

'Betty, this is my brother Jim. He's the serious one in the family and, unlike me, always on his best behaviour!' Betty laughed, shook Jim's hand, and ran off to the cloakroom for her hat and coat.

Billy said they were going to a local pub where the ten pm closing hour was overlooked as long as there was a ready supply of customers with cash in their pockets. Jim declined the invitation to the 'lock in' and told his brother to stay away from any trouble. Billy laughed, pulled the booklet out from his pocket and handed it to Jim.

'See what you make of this big brother.'

Back at his digs, Jim studied the booklet further. The more he read, the more he realised that, despite the officious language, it held sound advice that most GIs would benefit from. Especially as few of them had travelled outside their own state, let alone to a foreign country.

It needed a wordsmith's hand and Jim set about summarizing the relevant points.

Assault Training Centre's 'Commandments'

1. *Understand the British are reserved but not unfriendly*
2. *Do not invade their privacy if not invited*
3. *Learn about their sports, especially cricket and football*
4. *Be frank as long as what you are saying is friendly*
5. *Do not make fun of British speech or accents*
6. *Do not eat too much if invited to dine with a local family*
7. *Do not, whatever you do, make fun of their warm beer*
8. *Never be impolite or criticise your hosts*
9. *Never criticise their King and Queen*
10. *Be aware that you earn far more than the average British soldier*

Jim took the liberty of adding two more, unaware of just how sagacious his thinking was.

11. *Do not fraternise with women who are married, engaged, or going steady*
12. *Never antagonise your allies.*

He hoped his revised version would help safeguard relations with the locals.

Perhaps it would. But not for Billy.

Chapter Five
Eisenhower's visit

J IM WAS MAKING PROGRESS BUILDING BRIDGES between GIs and locals, but the same could not be said for his efforts to improve troop morale. The daily grind of exercises in the brutal winter was taking its toll in the worst way possible. As the men grew exhausted, safety measures were overlooked; the number of casualties accelerated, and fatalities increased. Every GI's death sapped troop morale. Jim knew he had to find a solution, and quickly.

At the end of a long day, he was in his office scanning the latest casualty report. It did not make pretty reading. Two GIs had been killed in a beach-side bunker that had been booby trapped by the local Home Guard six months earlier. Two more infantrymen were killed clearing mines from Woolacombe beach, and a soldier drowned when his landing craft capsized in particularly rough conditions. Jim could only pray his recommendation to the CO for a visit by Eisenhower would raise morale and bring about a significant reduction in casualties.

He got his wish.

On the morning of 5th December 1943, Ike gave a rousing

speech to hundreds of GIs packed into the recreation hall. Loudspeakers were set up outside for thousands more. The men were told their training in Devon was pivotal to the war effort. The Normandy landings would mark a turning point in defeating the enemy.

So far so good, Jim thought as he joined other senior army personnel in the ATC Officers' Mess waiting for the general to brief the officers. Jim's orders were to sit in on the briefing and prepare copy for the world's media. What he heard did not bode well.

'The truth is, gentlemen, the training conditions for our soldiers are just not realistic enough. The landing crafts aren't doing well in the surf, and there is too much congestion on the beaches. We need to toughen up the men for the real thing and get them used to the sight, smell and sounds of live ammunition and explosives.'

What was already a fraught situation had just gotten a hundred times worse. Later that evening, Jim heard that Churchill had given the same order to British troops carrying out assault training on the South Devon coast. As he walked home to his digs, the sentiment resonating amongst the officers hit home.

The Sunday school picnic is over. Welcome to the real war.

An immediate effect of Ike's order was to increase the resentment felt by the locals. The noise of live ammunition from the constant barrage of mock battles could traumatise the farmers' precious livestock. Jim's efforts to bring the locals back on side had come to nothing.

And then the tide turned in his favour, but for all the wrong reasons.

Despite efforts to keep the ATC's work secret, the talking point in the pubs just before Christmas was the deaths of two GIs using Ike's much-vaunted live ammunition. One soldier was killed when a quarter-pound block of TNT exploded in his hand, blowing an arm and leg clean off. Suffering severe burns and with major internal injuries, he was rushed to hospital but died of shock four hours later. Another infantryman was killed by a flying steel fragment as he rested between exercises in the sand dunes, unaware he was in a restricted area.

These fatalities proved a turning point. The locals' animosity towards the GIs all but disappeared, replaced by a deep appreciation of the sacrifices they were making to help win the war. Snide comments about the GIs being *too loud and larger than life* stopped overnight.

Even with the Germans hundreds of miles away across the Channel, it was abundantly clear to the locals that their quiet corner of rural Devon was now fully engaged in the theatre of war. But it was the tragic incident on New Year's Eve that finally opened their eyes to the bravery of their American allies.

On his way from his office to the mess, for some much-needed light relief before seeing in the New Year, Jim was summoned, along with some fellow officers, to report to Colonel Webb.

The man had aged ten years overnight. Jim had never seen his CO so distraught. His once brown hair was flecked with grey, and his forehead resembled the furrows of a newly ploughed Devon field. His voice was hoarse, the words slow and strained.

'Tragic news has just come in.'

Jim stood rigid. Colonel Webb told them that seven GIs had been killed and ten seriously wounded by machine-gun fire on Saunton beach. The gun had sunk into the sand. Instead of firing over the soldiers' heads, it had fired too low, killing the men instantly and injuring the others.

'A detailed investigation is underway, and I will inform the men's families.' He paused and took a sip of water to clear his throat.

'Apparently, compared to other assault units, we are fortunate not to have suffered more losses at this stage in our training.'

Jim shuffled his feet and turned his eyes to the ceiling. Anger welled up inside him. He wanted to scream out loud; hit out at someone, anyone.

'That makes it alright then does it, sir?' He could not contain his fury. 'We're supposed to be grateful only seventeen men are to be coffined home to their families?'

The silence was deafening. This was the first time he, or any fellow officers had challenged Colonel Webb. The CO stared at Jim, unsure whether to reprimand him or empathise. He chose the latter. His words might have sounded heartless, he said, his tone resembling a parish priest ministering to his flock, but he believed them to be true.

'Shit happens and we'd all better get used to it. Tomorrow's training is cancelled to give the troops time to come to terms with what's happened. But then we continue with renewed vigour and I'm looking to you *all* to play your part in rebuilding the men's confidence. Don't let me down.'

Jim walked home alone that night, any thoughts of celebrating the New Year long gone. The training exercises were going to get a hell of a lot more dangerous, and his brother Billy was in the vanguard of that danger. Despair, not hope, seeing in the New Year.

Welcome to 1944.

Chapter 6

Glenn Miller comes to town

TWO WEEKS AFTER THE TRAGIC MACHINE-GUN incident, it was clear as day to Jim that the benefit of Ike's visit had been short lived. Troop morale was at its lowest since the first GIs had arrived five months before. No one knew how much longer they'd have to endure the daily grind of hazardous training before departing for Normandy.

Jim knew many of the men were in the pubs early most nights, drinking hard until curfew, their behaviour becoming more raucous, and the military police kept busier than ever. The locals accepted the GIs' exuberance with good grace, and Jim continued to be amazed at how well they put up with the rowdy behaviour.

He'd been wracking his brains for how to relieve the pressure the men were under; a release valve to help reduce their dependence on alcohol as the short-lived palliative he knew it to be. A solution, as it turned out, was just around the corner. When Jim arrived at his office on Monday morning, an office orderly summoned him to the CO. He entered the room to find several female orderlies around the conference table. Colonel Webb gestured him to take a seat.

'Jim, best you take a few minutes to read this note from military HQ.'

Jim scanned the contents quickly.

The Glenn Miller Army Air Force Band will be performing at 1800 hrs on 2 February at XXX (deleted for security reasons) with as many of the ATC troops attending as possible. This performance is one of several at US bases in the UK with three objectives – to raise the soldiers' morale, showcase American music, and create good will in the local community.

Signed General D Eisenhower – Supreme Commander of the Allied Expeditionary Force

Jim waited until given the nod by the CO.

'That's only five days away Colonel; a mighty big task for someone.'

'And that someone is you Jim, assisted by the team you see around this table.'

Colonel Webb told Jim he'd have all the support he needed, and he looked forward to reporting back to Ike's office on how the concert had lifted the troops' spirits.

'Whether this is Ike's idea or not, you can bet your life he'll want to take the credit for it when it goes well. Keep me posted Jim, and let's make it a night we'll never forget.'

One hour later, Jim and his team had mapped out a

skeleton plan with everyone assigned specific tasks. He looked at the plan with mixed emotions. The concert was just the tonic. His input would be pivotal to its success. No small task given the logistical issues. But there was no denying the voice inside his head – *nothing but a glorified entertainment officer!*

He closed his eyes and pictured Billy. Explosions all around him, his face scorched by the heat, holes punched in his assault vehicle from mortar fire, his body weary from the relentless waves that soaked the bazooka he gripped as if his life depended upon it. *Because it did.*

And what did his life depend on? Making sure the stage was big enough, finding thousands of chairs from God knows where, organising food and drink for the VIPs. Work that would really make his family proud!

How he envied Billy.

On the day of the concert, Jim was in the recreation hall checking his snag list. The hall had massive roll-back doors, a polished wood dance floor, and a stage with dressing rooms behind. Sound engineers tested the sound system, ready for the band to rehearse in a few hours time. Everything in place for a successful evening. His only concern was what might happen when the band finished playing. The CO had insisted that at 20.00 hours, the GIs could dance to records and drink for a further three hours. The curfew, normally rigorously imposed at 10 pm, was to be extended by one hour.

'The men will soon be fighting for their lives, Jim. The least we can do is to give them the chance to let off steam before that happens.'

A temporary bar, stocked from floor to ceiling with Devon cider and local beer, was set up in the large marquee alongside the hall. Transport was laid on to collect girls from the surrounding villages and the land girls who'd arrived from every corner of the country. The GIs had taught the girls the Jive, Lindy Hop and Scuttlebug. And they loved to dance, much to the annoyance of the local men, most of whom stood around watching, getting more and more riled. Their anger made worse by the streams of cigarettes and black silk stockings the GIs had at their disposal.

By 18.30 hours the performance was in full swing. All the invited VIPs had turned up and were enjoying the spectacle. Troops and guests alike were in raptures with the catchy beats and sentimental tunes. As the concert drew to a close, Glenn thanked everyone for being such good sports and told the enraptured audience he would finish with favourites, 'Moonlight Serenade' and 'In the Mood'. The GIs went wild. Jim's concerns melted. He was on his feet clapping madly as the curtain finally came down with Miller's rendition of 'American Patrol' and the band's famous synchronised routine. He mentally penned a memo to Ike's office in his head.

Troops happy; morale boosted; local goodwill enhanced. Job done!

Goodwill was furthest from the mind of the British soldier lurking in the shadows near the dance floor. He couldn't tear his eyes away from the girl dancing with the tall, fair-haired GI. The girl who smiled up into the guy's eyes. The girl who attracted looks from the yanks ogling from the edge of the dance floor. The girl, *his fuckin' girl,* who was now smooching with that bastard.

She'd pay. He knew exactly what she needed, and he'd make sure she got it.

And the yank? He'd get it too. Not now, not here, but soon.

Chapter 7

Billy and Elsie

BILLY COULD DANCE. HIS NATURAL RHYTHM WAS the envy of his buddies when it came to the jive. When he was not at the bar knocking back pints of cider, he was on the dance floor with a pretty girl, jiving as if his life depended upon it. Not just one girl. He danced with as many of the best-looking girls as he could. But there was one girl called Elsie, who had really caught his eye. He'd danced with her several times and when the smoochy songs started, he knew the evening would soon come to an end. He made a beeline for the petite brunette, determined to walk her home or escort her back to her village on one of the army trucks.

Elsie smiled broadly as Billy approached the small circle of girls, handbags at their feet. The air was ripe with anticipation, the girls excited at the opportunity of a slow dance with these handsome young Americans.

Billy bowed ceremoniously. 'Would you like to dance?'

If the cider had slurred his words, Elsie didn't seem to notice. Why would she? She loved the distinctive accent, so different from the melodic tones of her home county.

She'd probably sipped more cider that evening than on any previous occasion. She was lightheaded in a carefree sort of way, far removed from her humdrum waitressing and the daily tedium of rationing.

She nodded graciously, determined not to let on how she'd been longing for this moment since their first dance together. Billy guided her arm gently to the dance floor for a slow ballad, joining the couples entwined in each other's arms, desperate to squeeze every last drop out of the evening.

At the signal for the last record, Miller's Moonlight Serenade, Billy held Elsie tightly and mimicked the lyrics of Carlotta Dale's recording.

I stand at your gate and the song that I sing is of moonlight.
I stand and I wait for the touch of your hand in the June night.
The roses are sighing a moonlight serenade.
The stars are aglow and tonight how their light sets me dreaming.
My love, do you know that your eyes are like stars brightly beaming?
I bring you and sing you a moonlight serenade.

They were the last couple to leave the floor. The music had finished a minute or two before, but they kept dancing, the rhythm of the music still alive in their ears, Elsie high with the euphoria of the moment. Reality finally kicked in and they walked arm in arm outside, towards the waiting trucks. Elsie pointed to the truck with a Woolacombe sign on the windscreen. Several GIs were sitting at the back and as Billy helped Elsie up, she saw some of her friends holding hands with their new sweethearts.

Cigarette smoke drifted aimlessly from the open truck as it wound its way along the country lanes towards the centre of the village, the night punctuated with frequent giggles and the girls' voices telling their partners to behave. Glints of light bounced off the sea from the full moon. Elsie looked up at a crystal-clear sky embroidered with hundreds of stars.

'That's Sirius, the Dog Star,' she whispered to Billy, pointing out the brightest star of all, its beauty all but taking her breath away.

'It's our star then,' said Billy. 'And every time I see it, I'll think of you.'

She snuggled closer, willing him to kiss her but just a little bit afraid. The truck stopped abruptly and, as the couples clambered off, the driver's curt instructions made it clear he'd be headed back to camp in five minutes sharp to beat the curfew. They stood close together, making the most of their last precious moments. He put his hands on her shoulders. Turning her face to his, he brushed his lips gently against hers. Barely a touch but she tingled inside, her heart pounding at the most sensuous encounter of her life. How could a man so big and strong be so serene? So, so different from the local men.

The truck driver's shout rang out; a rude awakening for the couples hidden in the darkness; the noise of his engine disrupting the still night. Billy pecked Elsie on the cheek and whispered he'd meet her on this very spot at seven the following evening. He sprinted to the truck, jumping on as it pulled away. Elsie walked slowly up the steep hill to her parents' house, her head dizzy, a warm glow percolating her body, the music of the night echoing in her head.

Something to smile about at last.

As she approached her garden gate, footsteps pounded behind her. For one sublime moment she thought it was Billy. She turned, but was grabbed from behind and manhandled to a nearby wall. A vice-like grip held her throat and then pulled hard on her hair, forcing her face next to her attacker's. She recoiled at his rancid breath, his rasping voice in her ear.

'I saw you dance with that Yank. I saw him kiss you in the shadows just now. That's never going to happen again, cos if it does, I'll kill him, you hear me? This is what bints like you need.'

He pulled her around, shoving her up against the wall, his hands groping her as he tried to kiss her on the mouth. Elsie kneed him where it hurt. As he bent in pain, she slapped him as hard as she could across the face.

'You little bitch,' he said, rage welling up inside. He swung his fist into Elsie's face and as the blood gushed out of her nose, he grabbed her again.

'Remember this Elsie Taylor, if I can't have you, nobody else will. I'll see you and your fuckin' Yank dead first.'

He pushed her away and walked off down the hill.

Chapter 8
Despair and disappointment

'Jesus, Billy, if it's this bad in training, what kind of hell is Normandy gonna be?'

Billy and his men were in the shower block, recovering from another six hours of simulated landings and assault training. Training as close to the real thing as it could ever be. It had been one of those days. A bitter north-east wind blew across the beach as the dull grey crafts cut through the angry sea pitching towards the beaches. Soldiers crouched low to avoid the bullets that ricocheted around them, some gripped by seasickness, others by morbid fear.

Young men, soaked, scared and very cold, who'd never fired at an enemy or been fired upon, faced the daily threat of being killed by their own troops. Today was no exception. Machine-gun fire had rained down from their emplacements high up on the rocks, causing chaos and confusion on the smoke-filled beach. The noise of battle relentless, sodden uniforms dragging men down into the wet sand, their hands and faces bleeding from the barbed wire stretching before them. The dunes full of booby traps, ready, given half the chance, to shred skin and bone.

Casualties had been heavy and inevitable in the rush to prepare for Normandy.

Throughout the day as the firing ceased and coloured flags were raised to denote the end of the exercise, hundreds of weary men would pick themselves up and march slowly back to their craft. And then begin the wretched process all over again. The men knew they were being pushed to the limit day after day. Departure for France was only weeks away.

In the final days, a joint training assault had been planned for Woolacombe beach. American and British landing crews would combine in a massive PR exercise to demonstrate how prepared allied forces were to secure a foothold on mainland Europe in what could be a major turning point of the war. Billy knew he would secure promotion to Sergeant, if he was selected.

No big deal.

Not when, after months of training, he was resigned to his low – very low – chances of surviving D-Day. He accepted his fate in the knowledge that, unlike Jim, he didn't have a wife and child to mourn his death. He was a free agent. Far better someone in his position perish than leave a widow and an infant without a father.

But Billy was petrified of dying. He loved life, loved his brother, loved his buddies. He lived up to his reputation as this carefree, live-for-the-moment guy, always on the lookout for the next drink, next dance, and new girl.

And why not? If he had to risk his life every day, why the hell shouldn't he make the most of what the evenings had to offer? He would drink all he could and make love as often as possible until the day came when his number was up.

He knew, deep down, that this bravado was his way of coping with what military life threw at him. He looked at the rugged face in the shaving mirror. And he realised that meeting Elsie had triggered something dormant in him. How could such a chaste kiss under the moonlight have made this impression? His brother Jim would have said he was finally growing up, understanding that one-night stands provided only the most temporary of fixes.

Thinking about seeing Elsie again, his pulse raced. His heart beat faster as he pictured the pretty face that had looked up at him on the dance floor. Had it been a one-off, served up by the cocktail of cider and Glenn Miller's romantic music? Or perhaps, just perhaps, he'd met someone special enough to make him change his ways?

If so, tonight's rendezvous would witness a very different Billy. He'd be courteous and content just getting to know Elsie better, not trying his luck at the first opportunity. After taking her somewhere quiet to eat, he'd walk her home, perhaps steal a gentle kiss, and tell her he cared for her. What happened next would be very much of her making.

An hour later, as a church clock struck seven, he stood on the agreed spot. It was a lady's privilege to be late. He puffed on a cigarette, shifted his weight from one foot to the other, looking around anxiously to try and spot Elsie at the earliest opportunity.

Ten minutes later he was beginning to think the worst. How naive to think his feelings had been reciprocated. And then, he recognised one of Elsie's friends from the dance coming down the hill towards him. She'd been in the lorry on that journey back the night before.

There was no laughter in her eyes this evening.

'Elsie's not coming,' she said in a croaky voice, her eyes flitting left and right, anywhere but meeting his.

'She asked me to say thanks for last night but she's sorry, she doesn't want to see you again.'

Billy stared at her. Bewildered. His mind in turmoil. Trying hard to make sense of what she'd just said. As the girl began to walk away, he reached out gently for her arm, his eyes pleading with her to explain.

'Please,' he said. 'Please don't go. I thought she liked me cos I sure as hell like her.'

The girl looked at him properly for the first time. Her eyes held his as she struggled not to tell him more, her face resolute, as if she wanted to open up, but was constrained by something Billy could neither see nor understand. After hesitating a moment she made her decision.

'Elsie's my neighbour and best friend. We grew up together; have always looked out for each other. Except last night, I didn't. I let her down and I can't let her down again by betraying what she's asked me to do. Believe me Billy, if it's your love life you're worried about, don't be. There'll be a queue from here to the beach and back.'

Billy realised he still had hold of her arm. He let it go and asked her softly if he could buy her a drink and talk for a few minutes.

'I'm not hitting on you. I'm confused and just want to understand what's happened because I really thought there was something special between us. It's been one hell of a day and I would hate to drink alone.'

Susan looked him four-square in the face to check if he was being sincere.

'Just a quick drink as I want to call in on Elsie before heading home.'

A few minutes later they were sitting in the snug bar of the Mill Inn with two halves of cider, cigarettes, and a packet of Smiths crisps. Billy opened the little blue paper, poured the salt on the crisps and shook the packet before offering them to Susan. Not quite the evening meal he'd envisaged.

As Susan talked, Billy began to understand why Elsie and Susan were such good friends. They had grown up in the same street; attended the same primary and secondary schools and shared a love of sunbathing on the beach and long walks on the coastal path.

'Elsie's got such stamina. She thinks nothing of walking ten miles at a stretch, is a great dancer – but you already know that – and is great fun to be with. It's a pity she's not so lucky in love.'

Susan realised she had said more than she should have. She finished her drink, stubbed out her cigarette and said she must go. Billy offered to walk her home, hoping the conversation could continue where it had left off.

They walked for a good five minutes, but not a word passed between them. Billy thought it best to let Susan speak in her own good time. He sensed she was building up to say something and he didn't want to spoil the moment. She stopped walking, told him her house was just up ahead and beckoned for them to sit on an old bench.

'Elsie's been out with this bloke a couple of times. He's local, went to the same school as us and is now a private in the Army. He's been posted back here with his regiment before going off to France. She only went out with him to appease her mother who is good friends with his parents. On the surface he comes across as the perfect gentleman. Underneath he's a manipulative, two-faced bully. He's possessive, considers Elsie his property, and boasts to his army mates that he'll be 'getting his end away' with Elsie soon and will make sure she marries him.'

Susan paused, took a deep breath and carried on explaining how this man had tried to avoid conscription by pretending to have poor eyesight, and how the Army medic had not fallen for his ruse. Just before he left for basic training, he warned Elsie that if she went out with anyone whilst he was away, he would make her life a misery on his return. She thought he must have been watching for the trucks to bring them back from the dance last night.

'He saw you together, waited until you'd gone and then accosted her. He hit her, Billy. He punched her hard in the face, breaking her nose and giving her two black eyes. He threatened her with much worse if she as much as looked at you. Said you were dead meat if she did.'

Tears welled up in her eyes as she mumbled how Elsie had begged her to put Billy off somehow and now, she'd messed it up. Billy gave her a brotherly hug and tried to console her, doing his best to suppress the rage growing inside him. She wiped her eyes and warned Billy to be careful.

'I've never met anyone so jealous before. It's frightening.'

Billy paused to take this in.

'Susan, I have to tell Elsie my feelings for her. I have to let her know that I'll protect her. And don't worry about me; I've dealt with bullies like him before.'

They arranged for Billy, on his next evening off, to come to Susan's house when Elsie would be there. Susan would make herself scarce for them to have some time alone.

They said goodbye at Susan's gate. As he walked away, he realised he didn't know the soldier's name.

'Ritter,' she said. 'The bastard's name is Fred Ritter.'

Chapter 9
It's good to talk

S USAN WAS AS GOOD AS HER WORD. TWO DAYS LATER, she and Elsie were in her house eating a meagre supper of spam with a few precious potatoes. Meals these days were endured, not enjoyed. Susan's parents were visiting relatives in Bude overnight so she and Elsie had the house to themselves. After supper, Susan applied some make-up to mask the bruises on Elsie's face. When she'd finished, the black and blue swelling was less obvious, but there was little to be done with her red nose.

'I look terrible,' she said. 'No man will ever look at me again.'

There was a knock at the front door and Elsie thought for one awful moment that Ritter had come to give her another beating. Susan looked sheepishly at Elsie as she showed Billy into the hallway. She quickly made her excuses saying she had to pop out for a couple of hours. Elsie stood frozen to the spot, trying to take in what was happening.

'Don't blame your friend,' Billy said softly. 'I pleaded with her to let me see you again and she agreed when she realised how much I care for you and how angry I was hearing what that bully had done.'

His kind words were too much for Elsie. Tears streamed down her face and Billy wrapped his arms around her in a tender embrace.

Eventually, they broke apart. Elsie showed Billy into the kitchen and said she'd make them both a cup of tea. Billy had the good grace not to say anything. He'd vowed, after sampling the beverage for the first time a few weeks ago, to never imbibe again. What was it about this British obsession with tea? Why couldn't they make a decent cup of coffee? Then guilt kicked in as he realised how precious the allowance of tea, sugar and powdered milk would be to Susan's family.

Elsie sat opposite him across the small hand-scrubbed white-wood table and handed a mug to Billy, her hands shaking slightly, words deserting her. She wondered, for the briefest of moments, how surreal it all felt. What was she doing with a face the colour of a coal scuttle, sitting in her best friend's kitchen opposite this good-looking American soldier she hardly knew?

There were no intoxicating music or drinks of cider to loosen her inhibitions this evening. Elsie watched as Billy took a tiny sip of tea, doing his utmost to disguise the grimace on his face. and could not help herself. She burst out laughing.

'It's pretty disgusting isn't it?' she said. 'I suppose we've got used to it now. That tea has probably been used three times already today!'

Billy pushed away the mug with its offending contents

and smiled at her; a smile that made all the dancing and alcohol in the world redundant.

'I'll bring you and Susan some coffee from the canteen next time I come.'

'You think there'll be a next time, do you?' ribbed Elsie.

'I do hope so!' said Billy.

With the ice well and truly broken, they sat and talked about everything and anything, no props needed. Billy regaled her with colourful stories about his life in the shipyard back home. His words painted vivid pictures in Elsie's mind of white clapboard houses, golden red autumn foliage (or 'fall' as he called it) and lobsters and clam chowder for sale everywhere along the coast.

Elsie was not to be outdone. She too loved where she'd grown up. Her enthusiasm captivated Billy as she described wandering freely, with only the sound of the sea and wind for company, amongst the purple heather that covered Morte Point headland. She described the white horses of breaking waves like hundreds of hooves thundering along the shore; pretty villages with thatched cottages nestling in the valleys; and, best of all, exploring the half-hidden path that meandered along the coast to Ilfracombe harbour with its fleet of fishing boats, dancing a jig on the incoming tide.

There were two things they didn't talk about. The elephants in the room – Billy's assault training that wore him out like an old coat weighed down with stones, and his imminent departure for France, with bloodshed and misery his likely companions.

When Susan opened her front door two hours later, she could sense from Elsie's voice just how happy her friend was. She coughed aloud to let them know she was home, and alerted Billy to the imminent curfew.

Elsie walked him to the front door. They stood, arms around each other, broad smiles on their faces, whispering about their next rendezvous; Billy's tender goodnight kiss as romantic as Elsie could ever have imagined.

Ten minutes later Billy sat in a daze as the truck took him back to base. What was going on? What was it that made Elsie so different? Talking with her felt so good. So natural. No need for booze to loosen their tongues. No working up to the expected grope or quick sex that had punctuated most of his relationships. This felt different, felt better.

He wanted this relationship to last and there was something important he had to do to make that happen.

Chapter 10
Finding Ritter

I NEED YOUR HELP TRACKING DOWN A BRITISH *soldier. Please meet at the Red Barn 1900 hours tonight.*

Billy knew the best person to help him track down Private Ritter was his brother. As an officer based at HQ, he would have access to information channels that were a world apart from Billy's. And, much as he disliked asking his brother for favours, he didn't have much choice.

He managed to get the short message delivered via the ATC's messenger who spent his days travelling between the training sites and HQ. The Red Barn was a regular haunt for all ranks, not least because it was the base for the Red Cross nurses.

Later that evening, Billy explained why he wanted to confront a British private. Jim was sceptical. Much as he sympathised with his story, Jim said he should report it to the police. Elsie's injuries were a civilian matter, and the last thing Billy should do was take this into his own hands.

'The police can arrest him for assault if Elsie brings charges. Then he can be dealt with by the Special

Investigations Branch of the British Military Police. You need to stay out of it, Billy.'

Billy finally persuaded Jim that he would go to the police – but not before he had confronted the bully face to face.

'I owe her that, Jim. If I'd not kissed her, she wouldn't be sitting at home nursing a face beaten black and blue.'

The following afternoon, when Billy returned to camp after another gruelling day in the dunes at Braunton Burrows, he found an envelope on his bunk.

Private Fred Ritter is in the Devonshire Regiment returning this afternoon from training at Slapton Sands. My contact tells me that The Devons frequent the Jubilee Inn in Woolacombe. Find and report him, Billy. Nothing else! Jim.

'Fat chance of that,' Billy said to himself, more determined than ever to teach Ritter a lesson he'd never forget.

There was usually good-natured banter in the pubs of an evening, with British soldiers and GIs taking it in turns to mock the way everyday words were pronounced or different names used altogether. *Cookies for biscuits, flashlights for torches* and so on...

This bonhomie, however, barely masked an undercurrent of friction. The GIs were paid so much more than the Tommies. They had access to a seemingly never-ending supply of hot beef sandwiches, sweets, and gum. The GIs responded to the now all-too-familiar jibes with their usual retort of *under paid, under sexed and under Eisenhower.*

The biggest gripe from the local soldiers was how much

the land girls enjoyed being with the Americans, making the most of their generosity and lapping up the drinks and cigarettes.

This physical attraction was mutual. The GIs joked amongst themselves that the girls were wearing a new style of pants dubbed *one Yank and they're off.*

But when Billy set off for the Jubilee Inn that evening, the last thing on his mind was banter or sex. He was determined to find the bully who'd attacked Elsie and beat the living daylights out of him if he did not agree to leave her alone.

Billy had never been afraid of a fight. Whilst Jim, slight of build and good with words, took after their mother, Billy was his father's son, inheriting the same strong frame and southpaw stance. And, like his dad, he was happier working with his hands than sitting behind a desk.

He'd not forgotten the advice his father had drummed into him from an early age.

If you're going to pick a fight, make sure it's for a good reason. Pick your moment and strike when your opponent least expects it. Hit him hard enough to knock him out or at least knock him down.

When Billy entered the Jubilee pub, the atmosphere was far removed from the usual self-deprecating humour. It was more akin to a powder keg about to explode, an undercurrent of tension pervading the public bar. Half a dozen British soldiers stood around in a circle at one end, while three of Billy's buddies sat in the corner as far away from the Brits as they could. As Billy walked over to the GIs, a stream of vitriolic abuse came from one of the soldiers.

'Jesus Billy, the guy in the middle of those limeys has got a real problem. It's as if he hates us for no damn reason when all we did was buy our cider and sit here quietly. He's been egging on his buddies with language that would embarrass our Sergeant Major.'

Billy walked to the end of the bar, as far away from the British as he could be. He ordered four pints of cider as if he did not have a care in the world. The landlord put the drinks on a tin tray, gave him his change, and whispered to Billy that it would be wise if they drank their pints and got out sharpish.

'Things could get pretty nasty if you stay, Billy.'

Billy sensed the barman was embarrassed; he knew what good customers the GIs were and how far bar takings had gone up since their arrival.

'Who's the ringmaster – the guy with the weasel-looking face?' asked Billy.

The barman kept his eyes on Billy.

'That nasty piece of work is Fred Ritter.'

'Of course it is,' said Billy. 'Who else would it be?'

He faced his buddies and in the mirror above the fireplace saw weasel-face on his feet moving quickly towards him. Billy's timing was spot on. He dug his feet in hard and only tottered forward a little when the push came.

He bent down low, put the tray on a nearby table, pivoted on his right leg, turned quickly and punched Ritter hard on the chin with a clean uppercut. He went down like the proverbial sack of spuds, and stayed there.

Whether Ritter had been knocked out or just decided

to lie low Billy did not know. But as he rubbed his left fist, pandemonium broke out. Ritter's mates were charging down on him with pint mugs held high, faces white with rage. Billy and his buddies gave as good as they got, chairs and tables were overturned and shattered glass rang loud amidst a melee of shouts and bloody confusion.

The military police or AMPs appeared out of nowhere. With truncheons at the ready, they made short work of separating the GIs from the Brits. Billy had heard tell of the uncompromising way they set about their business, the bruises on his head and back testament to their brutality. A few minutes later, he and his buddies were bundled unceremoniously into an open truck on their way to the glasshouse. As Billy turned to look back, he saw Ritter stagger out of the pub door, soldiers struggling to hold him upright. Their eyes locked.

If looks could have killed.

* * *

Billy hurt. Not from his sore left knuckle. Nor from the bruises on his upper back courtesy of the AMPs' truncheons. And not because he'd kissed goodbye to his promotion prospects. The pain gnawing away at him was his failure to warn Ritter to his face to stay away from Elsie. He couldn't do that languishing in the glass house; and his brother's visit was not helping him come to terms with the error of his ways.

'Jim, he was badmouthing me, the US Army and the whole frigging U S of A. This is the bastard who beat up my girl and threatened to kill me. What d'you expect me to do, kiss his ass?'

'You were meant to reason with him,' Jim said. 'Warn him never to touch Elsie again, not knock him out in front of all his buddies. If he was sore with you before, he's going to be baying for blood now. And who's going to protect her when you leave for France?'

Billy banged the table. He knew he'd messed up. Would this coward really have taken any notice if he'd tried reasoning with him? Bullies relished the power they had over their victims; like an addictive drug, getting worse and worse until somebody or something turned the tables and gave them some of their own medicine.

'Hopefully, I'll be out of here in a few days and can sort this mess out. I'm just not sure how.'

Chapter 11
The media arrive

J IM HAD HIS OWN ISSUES TO DEAL WITH. THEY HAD
nothing to do with affairs of the heart. Eisenhower had
insisted on showing off the ATC's preparations to European
and US journalists, and Jim was tasked with planning the
three-day visit. A visit that seemed ill-judged to him, given
that the training regime was supposedly cloaked in secrecy.
Jim's CO signed off his programme and told him in no
uncertain terms to ensure his media release was used word
for word by the invited journalists.

'We don't want anyone going rogue on this one, Jim.
Ike will be studying everything that gets printed and I don't
need to tell you what'll happen if he doesn't like what he
reads.'

No pressure then, thought Jim. The last thing foreign
correspondents would agree to was to be spoon-fed copy.
Freedom of the press was sacrosanct to these free-thinking
men and women. He finalised the visit itinerary, paying
special attention to the social side. Journalists enjoyed
a drink or three and he wanted to ensure there were no
complaints on that score. If he was lucky, he might even

persuade them to leave the comfort of the officers' mess to watch the GIs in action!

Jim knew he had a difficult balancing act. Ensure a degree of secrecy on the rationale for the assault training, whilst giving the media sufficient information to create good public relations for the US and their allies. With the likes of Pathé News and Associated Press involved, he would have his work cut out.

The ten representatives of the media arrived in good time to freshen up for the welcome reception at six that evening: seven men and three female correspondents including Lady Margaret Randall-Harris-Adair, a thirty-three-year-old English aristocrat. The gossip gleaned from Jim's Reuters contacts in London was that she was extremely attractive and *devoured men for breakfast.*

As the grandfather clock in reception struck four, a silver-grey Bentley Mark V pulled up outside the Woolacombe Bay Hotel. A black-coated chauffer moved quickly to open the nearside door for his passenger.

Hotel footmen hovered around to carry the five-piece, monogrammed leather luggage into the hotel lobby, as the manager greeted his latest guest on the steps as if she was royalty. It was not every day an English aristocrat visited the hotel and Jim escorted Lady Margaret to the VIP lift leading directly to the penthouse suite and her customary bottle of chilled vintage champagne.

Two hours later the hotel ballroom was full. Reception invitations had gone out to the great and the good. The opportunity for free cocktails and hors d'oeuvre had attracted an impressive gathering. Jim did the rounds, making a point to speak one-to-one with all the invited journalists and to introduce them to local dignitaries.

With the welcome speeches over and most of the food and drink gone, the room thinned out fast and Jim hoped he could soon escape back to his digs and do a final run-through of tomorrow's programme. With free liquor on offer, the media were, as ever, the last to leave and they had gathered around the grand piano where someone was playing a medley of Cole Porter tunes.

Jim hovered some distance away, the music reminding him of life back home; of the intimate moments with the woman he loved; of long walks together along the beach with Amy, their bundle of joy strapped to his back, and of old friends gathered around the dinner table talking well into the night about everything and anything.

Loud clapping brought Jim back to the here and now. The music stopped and the group dispersed to reveal Lady Margaret sitting at the piano, looking pleased with herself. He had to admit the accuracy of this aristocrat's reputation for beauty. She could be mistaken for a Hollywood film star, her face flawless with beguiling eyes, and long auburn hair enhancing her shapely figure. Nor was he in any doubt she knew the tantalising effect her looks had on the opposite sex.

'I hope you enjoyed that, Lieutenant.'

'I did, Lady Margaret, very much. Thank you for bringing the evening to such a pleasant close. You play extremely well.'

'One of the benefits of an upper-class childhood. I was literally tied to the piano before I could walk. Nanny was always on hand to make sure I practised for the statutory hour a day. I cursed it growing up, but it's a useful party piece – especially as I very much like being the centre of attention. Does that sound very conceited of me?'

'Not at all. If someone's got a special talent, they should use it. Especially if, like yours, it can bring so much enjoyment.'

Lady Margaret got up from the piano and moved closer to Jim.

'I wonder what your special talent is, Lieutenant. Or can I call you Jim?' Her hand brushed the back of his as she turned to face him.

'Jim will do fine. And if I have any talent, I guess it's writing. I plan to become a full-time author after the war. And now, Lady Margaret, if you'll please excuse me, I need to finalise the preparations for tomorrow.'

'Not so fast, Jim. Surely you know in British society it falls upon the host to buy the last guest a nightcap at the bar. Or, if you prefer, we could enjoy one in my room and discuss our mutual love of the written word. And whilst I am here, do call me Maggie. All my *intimate* friends do.'

The mischievous look she gave Jim left him in doubt as to her intended meaning. Before he could protest, she'd taken his arm in hers and headed towards the bar, empty save for the barman, desperate for his bed and none-too-pleased that one of these latecomers appeared intent on doing justice to the hotel's best single malt.

The more Lady Margaret imbibed, the more tactile she became. Jim's attempts to fend her off failed miserably, his admonishments dismissed out of hand. The whisky mellowed his mood. He couldn't remember the last time he'd relaxed in such sensuous company, nor when he'd drunk so much, so quickly. As the flirting intensified, so did Jim's temptation to accept the offer of a final nightcap in the penthouse suite. Especially when the barman announced loudly, in his dour Celtic accent, that the bar was definitely closed.

Jim struggled to his feet, just about managing to stay upright, and mumbled something about having to leave and finish his preparations for the morning. Lady Margaret pecked him on the cheek, reminded him they had two more days to get to know each other better, and moved gracefully to the door, her perfume leaving behind the merest hint of her presence.

Jim loosened his tie, his stomach in knots as he contemplated what the next forty-eight hours could have in store.

Chapter 12

Seduction

JIM'S MOOD THE FOLLOWING MORNING WAS NOT helped by the pounding in his head. It served as a constant reminder of his late-night session with Lady Margaret. As he rushed from lecture hall to beach and back again, one member of the visiting media was conspicuous by her absence. Whilst all the other journalists engaged wholeheartedly in the programme of seminars and training demonstrations, Lady Margaret deemed not to appear. The only evidence she was still in Woolacombe being the note she'd had delivered to Jim's office:

Dear Jim, I'm sure you haven't forgotten what you promised me last night. I look forward to meeting up later. Don't disappoint me! Maggie xxx

Jim stared at the note, a look of dread on his face as he racked his brains to try and remember what words had passed between them. When he tracked down the female orderly assigned to her, it transpired Lady Margaret preferred talking to the locals in the surrounding villages to attending lectures from the US military. She was apparently keen to gauge the impact American troops were having in this quiet corner of North Devon.

The human angle, local colour and perhaps even some gossip, darling.

The orderly had failed to coax Lady Margaret inside the lecture hall and Jim needed to find out for himself what her agenda was. Adverse publicity could negate all the goodwill generated and leave Ike's public relations initiative and Jim's reputation in tatters. At the end of the second day, he asked the hotel receptionist to call Lady Margaret and ask her to join him in the lounge.

'Lady Margaret insists you go up to her room in five minutes, Lieutenant. The VIP lift will take you directly to the top floor.'

Jim paced anxiously back and forth by the lift and then decided the stairs would give him the breathing space he needed to rehearse what he had to say. He cursed himself for getting into this predicament, only too aware that Lady Margaret had considerable influence in Parliament and was best friends with Prime Minister Churchill's wife Clementine.

He needed to ensure she stayed 'on-message' and adhered to the rules of engagement all the journalists had signed up to when accepting the ATC's invitation.

Abide by the secrecy rules and do everything in your power to support the Allied cause.

Most of the journalists recognised the importance of safeguarding national security but it would only take one wayward report to put that at risk. He decided to be friendly but firm, keeping the conversation well away from anything personal.

Checking himself in the mirror at the top of the stairs,

he adjusted his tie, tidied his hair and took a deep breath, feeling like a schoolboy outside the headmaster's study. He knocked gently and when the door opened, Lady Margaret had a drink in one hand, cigarette in the other and looked ravishing in a silk dressing gown with next to nothing underneath. She brushed a loose hair off her face in a seductive manner and gestured for him to come in.

'Jim, I'm so pleased you found my note. Help yourself to a drink and freshen this one up, please. It's the decanter by my bed.'

He poured her drink and set it down on the bedside table.

'Aren't you joining me? You appeared to enjoy the single malt last time we were together.'

'I did, Lady M… Maggie, but I'm on duty and only here in a professional capacity. We need to discuss tomorrow's conference and it would be more appropriate if we continued our conversation downstairs in the lounge.'

Lady Margaret looked at him for what seemed like an eternity.

'I'm perfectly happy to talk here, Jim, and am suitably dressed for what I have in mind, once our little tête-á-tête is over. You do remember what you whispered in my ear last night?'

A pink blush spread over Jim's cheeks.

'Now, come and sit here and tell me what it is that's so important.'

Jim moved to the window, keeping as big a gap between them as he could. His mumbled words and incoherent message sapped away at his confidence. He came to the point with as much assertion as he could muster.

'Maggie, please respect the protocol you signed up to when we open up the floor for the Q and A session tomorrow morning.'

Lady Margaret stubbed out her cigarette and took a long pull on her malt, crossing her legs slowly on the bed. The response, when it came, was defiant, reinforcing the rebellious personality her editors respected and her fans cherished.

'That rather depends on what's in it for me, Jim. I have a duty to ensure my readers comprehend what life has been like for the locals, with little America dumped on them, regardless of this spurious PR exercise Ike has dreamt up. I'm sure we can come to a mutual understanding. You be especially nice to me and we continue where we left off last night, and I'll write a story to make your CO proud.'

With that, she picked up her glass and came over to stand next to him.

'Now my gorgeous man, I'm sure we have a deal, so let's get that uniform off and put this king-size bed to good use. I need some fun and I'm sure as hell you do too. What Maggie wants, Maggie gets, so, don't disappoint me!'

With that, she pulled on Jim's tie, turned his face to hers and brushed her lips sensuously against his. Their first kiss chaste; the second long and passionate, exploring each other's mouths, born out of Jim's two years of not so much as looking at another woman. They fell onto the bed, their bodies locked as one, lust plunging them recklessly towards the inevitable conclusion. The pause, such as it was, just enough for Lady Margaret to jettison the gown, exposing her pert white breasts, as her hands, desperate for exploration, pulled eagerly at his belt buckle.

The realisation of what he was about to do hit Jim like an electric shock. His body froze, his brain working overtime to compute how the hell he'd gotten into this situation. What was he thinking? He leapt off the bed, averting his eyes, desperate not to make the situation any worse than it was.

'Maggie, I'm so sorry, I should not have come to your room. I can't betray my wife, I just can't.'

He moved swiftly to make his exit, Lady Margaret's vitriolic screams of frustration echoing around the room as she threw her whisky tumbler at his head.

It missed, but not by much.

Chapter 13
The media conference

SUNRISE THE NEXT MORNING FOUND JIM HARD AT work at his desk, preparing for the conference and finalising the media's briefing packs. Sleep had evaded him for most of the previous night, the ramifications of his contretemps with Lady Margaret leaving its mark. A guilty conscience and fear of retribution his two bedfellows.

His copy-writing skills had deserted him as he hunched over his typewriter, struggling to draft the upbeat portrayal of the ATC's endeavours Ike and his CO would demand. Two hours later, with his media release as good as it was going to get, he knew the least industrious journalists would accept this version and use it for their articles. The majority would find an interesting angle and put their own spin on what they'd seen and heard.

Thirty minutes before the conference got underway, Jim was locked in the anteroom with the CO and senior staff rehearsing likely questions. He had decided not to alert his fellow officers to the risk of Lady Margaret causing trouble. How could he possibly explain away his altercation without casting a long shadow over his professionalism?

His behaviour was inexcusable. If exposed, he only had himself to blame for being so naïve and prey to her seduction. Surely it was in her interests to keep quiet and not ask questions that would undermine the ATC's contribution to the war effort.

His prayers appeared to have been answered. As the Q and A came to an end, with no intervention from Lady Margaret, the CO made his concluding remarks.

'We are at a crucial stage in the war, ladies and gentlemen, and the invasion will subject our soldiers to merciless enemy fire, the like of which they have never experienced before. Be assured, we are doing everything in our power to get them battle-ready.'

Strong nods of agreement from the audience augured well, and Jim relaxed his shoulders in anticipation of a successful conclusion to what had probably been the most stressful days of his military life.

'I have some questions that demand answers.'

The challenge came from Lady Margaret, now on her feet, notepad at the ready.

'It is clear from my research that your presence is having a negative impact on the local community and on the British troops stationed nearby. I would be failing my readers if I did not highlight the distress you have inflicted.'

The CO looked across at Jim, a perplexed expression on his face and body language that made it abundantly clear he expected him to step up to the plate. Jim groaned inwardly, shrunk down in his chair fearing the worst. The first two questions started harmlessly enough, but Jim sensed Lady Margaret was building up to a finale. He racked his brains trying to second guess what that might be. Her third question, answered by the CO, concerned GIs borrowing tanks and driving them up and down Croyde High Street endangering civilians.

'This was an isolated incident, Lady Margaret, and the soldiers responsible were severely punished. It will not happen again. The men apologised to the villagers and distributed sweets and Hershey bars to the local schoolchildren.'

'You mean currying favour with the locals to cover up the misdemeanours,' retorted Lady Margaret.

It was evident that she'd spent the past two days talking to the locals to document as many grievances about the Americans as she could. There are always people who love a good moan. She appeared to have found more than her fair share.

'And what do you say, Colonel, about how worried the farmers are with the fraternisation between your men and the land girls? I hear the beaches are regularly covered with condoms?'

Jim could not help but give a wry smile as the CO responded, keeping as straight a face as he could.

'Lady Margaret, our demolition squads attack the pill boxes we constructed to simulate the conditions in Normandy. Condoms provide good water protection for their fuses.'

If she was put off her stride, Lady Margaret did not show it.

'And is it true artillery noise is causing considerable distress to farmers' livestock, endangering food supplies, and tanks are driven across fields destroying much-needed crops?'

Colonel Webb motioned for Jim to respond, a look of complete exasperation on his face. But before he could, one of the US media representatives shouted out.

'For Christ's sake, Maggie, men are dying here every day to help protect your country and you're worried that the cows aren't producing their usual quota of milk. Give us a God damn break!'

Lady Margaret ignored the outburst, determined to finish what she'd started.

'This brings me to my final and most worrying point. You've made big play of the imminent training exercise between GIs and British soldiers – the only time, as I understand it, the troops will train together before Normandy.'

Tiny beads of perspiration appeared on Jim's forehead, his pulse rate increasing by the minute. He knew where Lady Margaret's statement was leading.

'Can you explain then why your GIs are beating up British troops in the local pubs? And, before you answer, my media colleagues should know the incident concerns Lieutenant Ridd's brother, Corporal Billy Ridd, currently locked up in the glasshouse for knocking a brave local British hero senseless without any provocation.'

Colonel Webb looked across at Jim. Lady Margaret's revelation could undermine all the goodwill garnered in the past forty-eight hours. Jim walked slowly to the front of the stage, knowing he had to choose his words carefully. This spiteful accusation had nothing to do with Billy, and everything to do with his rebuff the night before.

'Your Ladyship, ladies and gentlemen, our troops have been stationed here for the past eight months and, to the best of my knowledge, there has only been one fracas involving our men and British troops stationed nearby. That one incident *did* involve my brother and he was guilty of knocking down a British soldier.'

Jim paused until the mutterings of the journalists had died down.

'But let's be very clear. Billy did not knock a brave British hero senseless without provocation. He hit him because the man had verbally and physically abused the girl my brother Billy is sweet on, punching her hard in the face and leaving her with a swollen nose and two very black eyes.'

Anger reverberated in Jim's voice. Using his brother's misfortune to get back at him was demeaning and unjustified. Wasn't Lady Margaret infamous for supporting the underdog? Pride had a lot to answer for.

'Next, the soldier you refer to, Lady Margaret is not a hero. He's a coward and a bully who hides behind his friends, and takes his jealousy out on innocent young women who can't fight back. I don't condone Billy's violence, but I do understand why he did it. For what it's worth, I would have probably done the same.'

Jim walked back to his chair to applause from his audience. With one obvious exception.

As Jim and his colleagues enjoyed well-earned drinks in the mess later that evening, courtesy of the CO on a job well done, he couldn't help wondering if defending Billy had made matters better or worse in Lady Margaret's eyes. He didn't have to wait long. There was an envelope addressed to him on his desk the following morning. Inside, a hand-written note from Lady Margaret with a copy of her article, due for publication the next day.

Holding his breath, he scanned the copperplate writing.

Lady Margaret Randall-Harris-Adair
16 Audley Square
Mayfair
London
Telephone Mayfair 465

Dear Jim

Never let it be said that I am not gracious in defeat, just as I would have been humble in victory (well, perhaps not so humble!). This is the first time in my life I've been rejected by a man, and it hurt!

I should not have let my damaged ego get the better of me and here's something I've rarely said in my life before – I'm sorry. I respect you for taking the stance you did to defend your brother's honour. In different circumstances, I would have liked to get to know you better. Stay safe through this ghastly war and get home in one piece. Perhaps we'll meet again one day when you have resumed your writing career?

Tell your brother Billy to watch his back. I did some digging on that British soldier yesterday and you were right. He's a nasty piece of work.

Yours truly,

Maggie

PS. I hope you like the article.

A broad smile spread across Jim's face.
'Hats off to our brave American allies.'

Chapter 14
Jim Crow segregation

All public houses in your area should impose a colour bar from 1800 hours tomorrow. Black GIs will only be allowed to leave their base and enter these establishments on Monday evenings between 1800-2100 hours. Military police will arrest and imprison any soldier ignoring this instruction.

The timing, Jim thought, could not have been worse. He read, with incredulity, the notice from US Military Command HQ in London. How could they be so short-sighted? No – worse than that. How could they have such entrenched attitudes at a time when racial tension between white and black troops in the UK was reaching a tipping point?

Jim picked up the Reuters' report from the day before, and scanned the salient points.

The 100,000 Black American troops in the UK far outnumber the local black population…major clashes between white and black GIs on the increase…

Lancashire dubbed 'Battle of Bamber Bridge'... a bloody confrontation, one black soldier killed and many injured by white military police ...more a mutiny than a battle.... racism ingrained in a highly segregated army...black GIs having experienced the freedom of integration on British streets now demanding the same treatment inside their bases... this is only the beginning...growing tension will tear apart the US military in this country and diminish our war effort in Europe.

Jim knew the American journalist who'd filed the report. He empathised with his conclusions. He was aware from previous reports that black soldiers were, by and large, welcomed by the Brits, with discrimination rare in British non-segregated society. They could drink, dance and shop in mixed company and George Orwell's recent quote had struck a chord – *the general consensus is that the only American soldiers with decent manners are negroes.*

The black GIs Jim had come across in Devon were polite and as loyal to the Stars and Stripes as any white soldiers, despite being prohibited from combat duties. They were restricted to ancillary roles as labourers, cooks, quartermasters and drivers.

The humanity shown by the Brits had opened black soldiers' eyes to a different reality to the one they faced at home. Jim realised this latest missive would withdraw these liberties and impose Jim Crow segregation in Britain.

The ingrained racial discrimination in his home country was a constant source of shame to Jim. He believed all men and women were born equal and should have the same opportunities in life – regardless of the colour of their skin.

He had detested the rigid anti-black laws, for so long an accepted way of life in many US States, since studying Du Bois's *The Souls of Black Folk* at college. That historian's essays on race issues in the Southern US, written at the turn of the twentieth century, resonated as much in American life today as they had forty years before.

And now the powers that be wanted to introduce the same racial caste system to the UK, as if there wasn't enough ingrained prejudice already from the GIs!

Was he any better than his fellow white Americans? Was he doing anything constructive to address the social injustice that he claimed to feel so strongly about? His only stand to date had been to ignore his CO's instruction to get a white driver and appoint private Jerome Stone, a black secondary school teacher from Louisiana, with whom he'd formed a close working relationship in their nine months together. This was nowhere near enough, and he knew it.

Jim understood the need to follow orders in military life, especially in war time. But he thrived on the opportunity to think and act for himself. Heated debates around newspaper policy within the editorial team had been part and parcel of his previous life. *Free speech and justice for all* was the touchstone of the Patriot Ledger's ideals, and Jim strove to introduce these values as a PAO. It was an uphill struggle, as this latest instruction illustrated. Lashing out in anger at the papers on his desk did little to curb his frustration or resolve the problem. Something pragmatic was called for.

He stormed out of his office and headed for the centre of Woolacombe, his heart pounding at this ill-conceived communication. He wanted to gauge the reaction of pub landlords before remonstrating with his CO to get it rescinded, before the ATC had its own 'Bamber Bridge battle' on its hands.

When he walked into the lounge bar of the Jubilee Inn, he was surprised to see half a dozen men and women sitting at tables writing signs on large white card. Jim explained the purpose of his visit to the landlord who pointed to the group nearby with a large grin on his face.

'Here's what we think of the instruction Jim. Hold up your placards everyone.'

White GIs only allowed in with black GIs!
NO colour bar here!
White GIs only allowed in on Mondays!
No blacks? – Then no whites either!

Chapter 15
Cardboard coffins

JIM REPORTED THE LANDLORDS' STANCE TO HIS CO. The Jim Crow segregation instruction to public houses was withdrawn within twenty-four hours. Unrest amongst the troops was the last thing the ATC needed – with the departure for Normandy only weeks away.

Jim's satisfaction was short-lived. The following day's events reaffirmed that racial prejudice was deeply rooted in the US Army in England. Just as it was in civilian life in the States. This reality check came as he was supervising the transfer of dead soldiers from Woolacombe to Plymouth, from where the bodies would be shipped back to the US for military funerals.

Jim and his adjutant watched as the army truck was loaded with coffins, all wrapped in the Stars & Stripes, with a platoon of men ready to march alongside the vehicle out of the village. Everything appeared to be in order – until Jim counted the coffins. There were only ten.

'There's a coffin missing!'

The adjutant shuffled his feet and avoided Jim's stare.

'The eleventh will be added after the send-off once the

truck has left the village. It's ready for the black GIs to load.'

Jim asked for the inventory and scanned down the list to the eleventh name, Private Robert Wallace from Knoxville, Tennessee. He saw the asterisk.

*Black GI – segregated departure, no ceremony or flag required.

Biting his lip to control his anger, he stood within inches of the adjutant's face. 'Inform the CO there's been a delay. The ceremony will commence fifteen minutes late at 1500 hours. Then ask Private Stone to come and fetch me immediately.'

The look on Jim's face left the adjutant in no doubt there was little point in suggesting Jim reconsider. He sprinted off to HQ.

Private Stone pulled up sharply in his jeep and drove Jim to the quartermaster's store to collect a Stars & Stripes flag. They headed to the Black GI's camp where half a dozen friends of Private Wallace were waiting alongside his cardboard coffin. There was no flag. No bugler. No pine casket. They covered the cardboard with the Stars and Stripes, strapped it down and sped back to HQ.

'Tell me how Private Wallace was killed, Jerome, before the CO and I have a showdown.'

Jerome cleared his throat and explained how Private Wallace had been driving white GIs to and from the dunes every day for the past month. Instead of returning to his base in his down time, he would park up on the headland to watch the disembarking soldiers in the demolition teams running up the beach under heavy fire, negotiating barbed wire and booby traps, ready to take out the pill boxes. The last time he was watching he had seen a GI get caught in the wire. He had run across the dunes to drag the injured man to safety. Not knowing anything about the traps, he had stood on a land mine.

'He was a hero, Lieutenant. His bravery saved the GI's life and this is how he's treated. Hiding his body and dumping it on the truck as it leaves.'

Jim knew what he was about to do could result in a court martial and dishonourable discharge. That didn't matter. What mattered was doing what was right. His father had impressed upon him that social justice was worth fighting for, whatever the consequences.

When they pulled up next to the ceremony, Jim's CO was standing on the podium for his recitation and the bugle accompaniment, a platoon of men lined up either side of the road, ready to march. The open truck with the ten coffins was surrounded by military police, their rifles primed.

Jim walked slowly towards the podium, telling Jerome to stay put. He saluted. Before he could say anything, the CO took his arm in a vice-like grip and marched him to a quiet spot under the vast oak tree that had dominated the village for centuries.

'How old are you, Jim?'

'Twenty-seven sir, going on twenty-eight.'

'And you're a liberal, an egalitarian, a man with strong principles.'

'Yes sir, I am.'

'It might surprise you to know Jim, so am I. But I've got fifteen years on you and I know there's a time to stand up and fight, and a time to accept things you vehemently disagree with. That's ok, just as long as we vow to make good these wrongs in the future. Things will change for the better and people like you and I will be instrumental in that change. You're doing a good job for me here Jim, a darn good job. But you're no good to me, your army, or your country if you get yourself locked up and escorted back to New England in disgrace.'

Jim turned around to see all the military police had gone. He watched as Jerome parked the jeep with Private Wallace's coffin adjacent to the truck with the ten coffins. The flag was still in place. The two vehicles would be driven slowly away in tandem.

'Lose today Jim, win big tomorrow. Pick your battles. Play the long game.'

He stuffed a small piece of paper into Jim's top pocket and they walked back to the podium. The bugler played *Taps*, and Jim stood to attention as the CO recited Horace Lorenzo Trim's words, his voice ringing out loud and true above the sound of the distant waves.

'Day is done, gone the sun,
From the lake, from the hills, from the sky;
All is well, safely rest, God is nigh.

Fading light, dims the sight,
And a star gems the sky, gleaming bright.
From afar, drawing nigh, falls the night.

Thanks and praise, for our days,
Neath the sun, neath the stars, neath the sky;
As we go, this we know, God is nigh.'

Two hours later, his office deserted, Jim took the scrap of paper out of his tunic and read the one-liner his CO had scribbled down.

Lady Margaret

He opened the top drawer of his desk and pulled out her note.

'Get me Mayfair 465 please. Yes, Mayfair London.'

The phone was answered by what sounded to Jim like a personal butler, his voice the very essence of upper-class English. The vision of a man dressed all in black, save for a stiff white collar, filled his mind.

'And who shall I say is calling, sir?'

'Lieutenant Jim Ridd.'

'I will see if Lady Margaret is available sir, please hold.'

Jim cleared his throat.

'Jim, how wonderful. I didn't expect to hear from you so soon.'

Lady Margaret's crystal-clear voice resonated down the line, bringing back mixed memories for Jim, some good, some bad.

'Don't tell me you've changed your mind!' Her tone was the usual beguiling mix of flirtation and amusement.

'Hi Maggie, very tempting but it's something way more important. I've got a story for you.'

Chapter 16

Courtship

THE GUARDS UNLOCKED BILLY'S CELL DOOR AT sunrise just three days after his fight with Ritter. He walked briskly out of the glasshouse, exchanging four grey walls for a kaleidoscope sky, a pallet of blues and whites embracing the bright spring Saturday morning.

He stopped, turned his face up to the sun and breathed the fresh air deep into his lungs, savouring his freedom. Why people chose to work indoors had always been a mystery to him. Never more so than at this moment. You can keep your claustrophobic offices and factories, he thought; I'll take the outdoor life.

Billy had his sergeant to thank for his early release. He was needed back in training on Monday. The date for the joint training exercise had been set and, despite his brawl with a British soldier, Billy was to be assistant section leader on one of the four assault landing crafts.

An hour later, he'd showered, eaten a hearty breakfast, and collected supplies from the quartermaster's store. He was on his way to Woolacombe on the back of a motorcycle, courtesy of a GI messenger delivering parcels to HQ.

Susan answered the door at his first knock. After a quick hug, he handed over the 'thank-you' tea and coffee, and they made a plan. She'd arrange for Elsie to meet him outside St. Mary's church in Mortehoe at nine o'clock.

'You look gorgeous!' Billy said as Elsie ran into his arms and stayed there for what seemed like ages, before letting go and smiling her biggest smile. She was wearing a bright green polka dot 'hand-me-down' summer dress of her mother's that Susan had helped shorten and brighten up with new white trim. Its figure-hugging style showed off Elsie's slim body to perfection, emphasising the swell of her breasts and her narrow waist.

Her face was almost back to its pretty self, with a touch of lipstick and her hair tied back with a matching red bow. Billy had never felt prouder or happier as they linked arms and walked through the village towards Elsie's favourite stretch of coastline. They stopped in front of the railway station on the outskirts of the village. Elsie swapped her shoes for a pair of old, well-worn and much-loved walking boots she'd taken out of her small rucksack.

'Not the most glamorous look in town,' she joked, doing a twirl in front of Billy, 'but the path is very steep in places with lots of jagged rocks, and these boots are a must for the five mile stretch we're about to cover.'

Billy put Elsie's half-empty rucksack in his large backpack, and they set off through the undergrowth towards the sea to find the half-hidden path that hugged the coastline. The rough stone and earth path led them towards the lighthouse at Bull Point. It stood proudly on a large outcrop of rock beside the Bristol Channel that separates Devon from Wales.

They set off at a pace Billy's sergeant major would have been proud of. Elsie was obviously very fit, scampering up and down the rugged inclines with ease and giving Billy a running commentary on the local flora and fauna. She pointed out her favourite place for spotting the Atlantic grey seals lazing on the rocks below; and she told him of the weekends she spent helping the farmer at lambing time with the Romney sheep that grazed the exposed headland.

As they approached Bull Point, Elsie pointed to a sheltered spot where they could rest and admire the seascape stretched out for miles in front of them.

'The lighthouse was built sixty-five years ago and is just over sixty feet high. The keeper used to live on site but now has a house in the ...'

Billy put his finger gently to her lips to stop her talking and pulled her towards him. He held her face softly in his large hands, his lips brushing hers, the merest taste of lipstick lingering on his senses as their tongues began the long sensual exploration of each other's mouths. When they eventually parted, Billy saw tears welling up in Elsie's eyes. He hugged her as tightly as he dared, never wanting to let her go, nor the moment to pass.

'What have I done to deserve you, Billy?' Elsie whispered. 'And I'm sorry for rabbiting on. Susan says I talk far too much when I'm nervous.'

Billy pecked her cheek and asked if she was hungry. He took off his jacket for them to sit on and unpacked the food parcel in his backpack for their picnic, courtesy of his friends in the mess. She gasped at the array of fresh food in front of her; more food than she had seen for years. But as they began to devour the spread, ravenous from their morning's exertion, Elsie put down her bread.

'I'm sorry Billy. This just doesn't feel right.'

Seeing the perplexed expression on Billy's face, she explained her world of rationing and coupons; of queuing for hours in all weathers for a few miserable vegetables; of making a tin of spam last over a week, and how flower gardens had become potato patches in the 'Dig for Victory' campaign. She told him about rearing chickens in her back yard and of Susan's trips to buy rabbits off poachers and see what the spivs were touting that week.

'Nobody asks any questions and if you have the money to pay, somebody will try to sell you something on the black-market. Last week it was goat's meat. The newspapers say Germany's plan is to starve us into submission, but the Boche don't know us Billy. We won't give in without one hell of a fight.'

Billy listened intently. How could he have been so brash, so indifferent to the hardship?

'I'm sorry. I just didn't realise how tough everyday life is for you and everyone else. We'll pack away the rest of the food for you to share with your family and friends.'

They cuddled close together looking out at the fleet of fishing boats on their way home with the morning's catch. Elsie pointed out two peregrine falcons scouting for prey, their dark slate grey and white feathers outlined against the vivid blue sky. As the wind got up and storm clouds appeared overhead, Elsie said they'd head back to Mortehoe by the shorter inland route.

'My parents won't get back from Barnstaple until late this evening and we could have some tea.'

Billy joked he could do better than tea, and tapping his pack, said he had some surprises for her. Thirty minutes and a brisk walk later they were sitting at Elsie's kitchen table, her eyes firmly closed as Billy took out her presents – a large block of chocolate, half-a-dozen pairs of black stockings and some cookies as Elsie had learnt to call them. When Elsie opened her eyes, she sat mesmerised by the ensemble of luxuries.

'Susan told me someone special has a 23rd birthday in a few days' time, so this is my treat.'

They sat drinking the coke left over from the picnic and eating chocolate, the sweet taste lingering on Elsie's tongue bringing back memories of life before the war. She knew nothing could persuade her to exchange her world back then for today. War was a truly terrible thing, but without it, she wouldn't have met Billy, wouldn't have begun to fall in love.

'So, Elsie Taylor, if you could choose any birthday present in the world, what would it be?'

The pause was long, the silence deliberate, her mind crystal clear. When she spoke, her voice was hoarse, no more than a whisper, the longing in her eyes plain to see.

'You, Billy. I'd choose you.'

All the emotions of the moment were embodied in those words. As Billy held her close, Elsie knew this might be one of the last times they could be together before he left for France; perhaps never to return. Her heart missed a beat as the words that tumbled out of her mouth scared and surprised her.

'Make love to me, Billy.'

Chapter 17

The Wellington Bomber

'Look lively, Billy. It's a beautiful Sunday morning and we've got a job to do.'

The brothers were off to Mortehoe cemetery to trace their ancestors. Jim had requisitioned a jeep and arrived at Billy's hut to find him still in bed. Ten minutes later the brothers set off for Mortehoe, driving through villages that were now familiar to them, Billy giving his brother a running commentary on the local pubs. As they drove out of the camp up the hill towards Saunton, Jim pulled into a layby overlooking the golf links nestled in the dunes of Braunton Burrows, framed by the sparkling blue of the Taw Estuary at high tide. The once lush green fairways were now obliterated by a blur of grey from row upon row of US tanks lined up in military precision, ready for the next round of training.

Jim wondered how long it would be before the links would resonate again with the sounds of golfers, free and safe in the knowledge that life had, at last, returned to normal. There was nothing he would rather be doing more on a sunny morning than teeing off with his brother. Their last game in Quincy was a distant memory; part of another life they'd taken for granted.

'We will come back, Billy. When this war is over, we'll come back and play Saunton.'

Billy punched his brother gently on the shoulder. 'And I'll beat you once again.'

Jim started the jeep, a broad smile on his face. They sped along the coast road into Croyde Bay, then inland, through the narrow, winding lanes to the village of Georgeham. Ten minutes later, they were driving down the steep hill into Woolacombe, the three-mile expanse of beach in front of them and a thousand-acre sky above.

They passed the Woolacombe Bay Hotel, home to Jim's office, along the Esplanade and up the steep hill to Mortehoe. Jim did a quick detour to show Billy his digs in The Outlook. From the rear garden, high above the village, they looked down on the vast expanse of sand stretching into the distance towards Puttsborough.

Jim felt Billy's hand squeezing his arm. 'That's my office, Jim,' Billy said in a hoarse voice. 'Wet clinging sand, treacherous rocks, angry sea, and freezing wind. That's where I work every time I pull on my combat gear, shit-scared and thinking every day will be my last.'

'And I sit on my backside in a former hotel bedroom, pushing paper around,' Jim said. 'You're the brave one, Billy. I'm just a glorified clerk and would change places with you in a moment if I could.'

The two brothers looked at each other, acknowledging their impotence to change things. This was the first time they'd admitted how they felt since leaving the States. Jim knew Billy hid his feelings well. His strong physique and bravado masked a sensitive young man who desperately wanted to be home with his friends and family.

Billy too could empathise with Jim's frustrations and sense of inadequacy. Jim was the elder brother, used to taking responsibility, whether orchestrating the play on the basketball court, leading debates at his student senate, or guiding his team of reporters at the Patriot Ledger. He knew Jim had never been one for the soft option, and that his brother's non-combat role was eating away at him.

Neither man spoke. They continued to gaze into the distance, lost in their own thoughts.

'Come on,' Jim said, interrupting the silence. 'Let's get some coffee inside you'. He led the way inside and introduced Billy to Mrs May. She welcomed him like a long-lost son, indulged him with some homemade cookies, and chastised him for missing breakfast. As they took their leave, she smiled and told him to behave himself with the local girls.

'No worries on that score Mrs M. I've found the girl of my dreams.'

The sea was as flat as a mill pond today. Billy figured it was saving itself for a big swell when he resumed training on Monday morning. 'Just my luck,' he said to himself.

As they entered Mortehoe, they spotted the signpost for the cemetery, parked the jeep by The Ship Aground public house, and took the narrow footpath west out towards the coast. After half an hour of searching for the family grave, they were on the point of giving up when they met the vicar on his way to morning communion. He suggested they try the burial register in the church.

'With any luck,' he said, 'the grave will also be marked on the cemetery map that forms part of the parish records.'

Five minutes later, Jim and Billy were huddled together in the sacristy, poring over the records of births, christenings and deaths that looked as if they had not been touched for years. They retrieved a hand-drawn map of the graveyard with hundreds of names marked crudely in black ink.

'I can see a Ralph, a Reilly and a Riley but no Ridd.' Jim said. Then Billy let out a cry of surprise and pointed to some feint names in the bottom right-hand corner.

'There, squeezed in between two large plots. Doesn't that say Ridd? It's by a small building at the back of the site.'

The area contained some of the oldest gravestones in the cemetery, heavily weathered and leaning at precarious angles. Jim and Billy trod gingerly around the stones. Right in the middle, they found what they were looking for. Billy went to the hut and brought back an assortment of tools – an old rag, scrubbing brush and an ancient metal watering can full of water. Kneeling down, he washed off the lichen and moss, and scrubbed the stone. When he'd finished, the writing was just about legible.

William John Ridd – Born 1766, Died 1821
Mary Christine Ridd – Born 1770, Died 1825
May they rest in peace at last

'Neither of them lived beyond fifty-five,' said Jim, surprised at how short life was in those days.

Pleased with their endeavours, they returned to the jeep and started down Chapel Hill towards Woolacombe.

Billy was aware of it first and motioned for Jim to pull over.

'That's not a storm coming.' Jim said. 'That's an aircraft in trouble.'

A rumbling noise filled the valley, louder and louder, shattering the Sunday morning calm. A plane was approaching the headland, plumes of black smoke trailing behind as it dropped lower and lower in the sky. Billy jumped out of the jeep, opened the farm gate and Jim sped through. As Billy jumped on, Jim slammed his foot hard down, and the jeep hurtled across the bumpy terrain towards the headland. They could see the plane more clearly now through the smoke. Both engines were on fire and flames engulfed the fuselage. Jim recognised it as a Vickers Wellington, one of the RAF's long-range medium bombers, known affectionately as the Wimpy by its crew.

Billy hung on as best he could as Jim drove towards the rocky headland. Turning around, he saw they were not alone. Half a dozen motley agricultural vehicles were coming up behind them. The sheep that usually grazed in quiet contentment on the hillside scattered far and wide.

As they got closer, Jim shouted to Billy that the pilot was going to try to land on the sloping fields beyond Morte Point.

'He'll never make it,' Billy yelled.

Jim agreed. The hillside was far too steep. The bomber would be torn to shreds by the large outcrops of granite protruding above the turf and heather. He knew the Coastguard would have alerted RAF Chivenor, and prayed that a Coastal Command helicopter would soon appear on the horizon.

But at that moment, whatever rescue was possible would be down to him and Billy and a handful of local farmers. Jim hoped the plane was returning from a mission, having spent its fuel on the depth charges used to destroy enemy submarines. Crashing would be bad enough, but if high explosives were on board, the explosion could kill or severely injure everyone on the headland.

An eerie silence enveloped them, as if the world had stopped still. The menacing noise coming from the distressed plane was suddenly replaced by an almost inaudible hum. The pilot had shut down what was left of both engines, and was attempting to glide as far as he could to find any level ground. No landing gear was visible. All he could hope to do was belly flop onto the unforgiving surface.

The fire engulfing the plane took on a new lease of life. The only thing visible now was a vast fireball careering downwards. Jim turned the jeep sharply right away from the headland, and strained the engine to climb a sharp incline.

The inevitable happened. The aircraft sank lower and crashed nose first into the rocky hillside, destroying the cockpit and sending debris in all directions. Fire engulfed what was left of the main fuselage, but the rear turret had broken away with the rear gunner inside.

Jim leapt out of the jeep and raced towards it, dodging the blazing fragments, aware that any fuel and munitions on board could explode at any moment. He could just make out a man's body inside, twisted sideways from the impact. He pulled at the rescue hatch, red hot metal burnt his hands, fierce heat scorched his face and the smell of blistering flesh invaded his nostrils.

The next moment, Billy was alongside him, the jeep's tyre lever in his hand. They managed to force the hatch open and dragged the unconscious airman away from the wreckage before being blown off their feet as the fuel tanks exploded.

As Jim lay over the airman protecting him from the rain of burning debris, he looked up to see a piece of metal hurtling towards him. Everything went black.

The locals who heard what had happened, thought Jim and Billy must have acted on instinct.

Just been in the right place at the right time.

Not so the farmers on Morte Point. They were adamant. It was the bravest act they'd ever seen. In their eyes, the Ridd brothers were heroes.

Chapter 18
Military Hospital

'HOW LONG HAS HE BEEN UNCONSCIOUS?'
'Forty-eight hours and there's still no sign of him coming round. The longer he's in a coma, the less chance there is he'll ever regain consciousness.'

Jim's CO stood over his bed with the matron in charge of the casualty ward. Jim was in a private room reserved for senior officers. His body resembled an Egyptian mummy, the head completely enclosed with bandages apart from small holes for eyes, nose, and mouth. A brace supported his neck, and bandages covered his burnt hands and sprained left ankle.

Billy knocked tentatively on Jim's door, saluted the colonel and asked for permission to enter. As the matron left she told Billy how pleased she was to see he was ok and told him Lt Ridd was in the very best of hands. Colonel Webb gestured for Billy to sit down and they sat in silence either side of the bed for several minutes, all eyes on Jim.

Billy had just finished a brutal training exercise at Croyde Bay having escaped the airman's rescue with nothing more than a few cuts and bruises. He was still in his army fatigues, soaked from head to foot, his face strained from hours on manoeuvres. He sat, staring at the mummified body in front of him as matron returned to hand him a warm towel. As he dried his face and hair, Colonel Webb spoke in a low whisper, his voice reflecting the solemn mood in the room.

'Jim's physical injuries, whilst serious, aren't what are worrying the medical team.'

The colonel hesitated before continuing, the seriousness of what he had to tell Billy making him choose his words carefully.

'The injury sustained to his head is clearing up well. His hands have second degree burns but the prognosis is good, and he should regain full mobility in his fingers. He'll be on crutches for a few weeks to help reduce the swelling in his ankle. But being unconscious for two days is our primary concern and, whilst he's breathing normally, there's a serious risk of brain damage. There's not been any response to the stimulation the doctors have tried.'

Billy let this news sink in, slumped forward, head in hands, concern etched on his face. He was trying desperately to think of anything that could help his brother. What meant the most to Jim? Two thoughts came to mind. He treasured his weekly letters from Susan and never went to sleep at night without reading a few verses of one of his favourite poems, something Billy had ribbed him about for years. Jim said it was his mind's way of saying goodbye to one day and getting ready for the next. An idea came into Billy's head that had to be worth a try. All he had to do was persuade the colonel!

'Sir, I'd like to suggest something.'

'Speak up, soldier.'

'Jim is a big fan of a poet called E E Cummings. He has one of his books by his bed. It goes everywhere with him and he knows most of the poems by heart. This might sound ridiculous, but I would like to sit and read them to Jim cos it might just help. And, there's one more thing—'

Billy paused, knowing what he was about to say would not go down well with the colonel.

'There's someone else who could read Jim the poems. Someone who shares his love of poetry, and is desperate to help.'

'If there's a fellow officer's voice Jim would recognise just tell me corporal and I'll make it happen.'

Now or never.

'It's not an officer sir. It's Private Jerome Stone.'

Colour drained from the CO's face, his eyes opened wide in disbelief, his hands opening and closing in exasperation.

'God damn-it, what is it with you Ridd brothers? You know black GIs have a separate hospital ward. This room is strictly reserved for white officers and staff. Can you imagine the uproar if I allowed a black private to spend time by Jim's bedside?'

Billy kept quiet. He'd said what he needed to say. Let the colonel remonstrate all he wanted and then he'd try again. Jim regaining consciousness was all that mattered here, not sticking to the wretched despised segregation rules.

The colonel sat back down, his eyes focused solely on Jim lying comatose next to him, working over in his mind the request he'd just rejected out of hand. It would be easy to ignore Billy's suggestion, adhere to the no fraternization rule, maintain military discipline. Easy but not right. Not now, not if he wanted to increase the slim chance of Jim recovering.

'Corporal, your brother is the best PAO I could have asked for. He's won over the local community and helped the war effort far more than he could ever imagine. He has this irrational sense of guilt because he's in a non-combat role, but there are many ways to win a war. We'll win this one by successful assaults on the Normandy beaches. Jim's diligence will have contributed to this success. And when he does wake up, we must never let him forget it.'

Billy took it all in, gratified the CO held his brother in such high esteem. But the CO didn't stop there. He said Jim had proved at Morte Point just how courageous a man he was. Whilst five of the Wimpy crew had perished that day, the rear gunner was recovering well and would return to active service in a few months' time.

'That's another experienced airman back in the air fighting Jerry, something that should make you and Jim extremely proud. As for your request, I'll tell your platoon commander you're excused training tomorrow to be at your brother's bedside. Recite the poetry to him and pray it works! Private Stone *will* be allowed to read to Jim, but can only enter and exit this room from the French window, not through the hospital. That way, only you, me and the medical staff will know anything about it. Understood?'

'Understood, sir, and thank you.'

Billy, showered and replenished, was back at Jim's

bedside within the hour. He recited the poet's words, hoping that they would be the trigger to kick-start his brother's brain back to life.

Twenty-four hours later, Jim was still unconscious, seemingly unaware of anything or anybody. Jerome was on the night shift, his melodic tone bringing the poet's words to life. Many a nurse lingered by the door, listening intently, tears in their eyes.

Jim's favourite poem was to be the final reading of the evening.

It takes courage to grow up and become who you really are; to be nobody but yourself in a world which is doing its best day and night to make you like everybody else. This is the hardest battle which any human being can fight and never stop fighting.

We do not believe in ourselves until someone reveals that deep inside us something is valuable, worth listening to, worthy of our trust, sacred to our touch. Once we believe in ourselves, we can risk curiosity, wonder, spontaneous delight or any experience that reveals the human spirit...

As Jerome was nearing the ending, he heard the faintest of whispers.

I will take the sun in my mouth and leap into the ripe air, alive with closed eyes to dash against the darkness.

Jerome sank back, tears welling in his eyes.

'Welcome back, sir. Welcome back.'

Chapter 19
Lows and highs

MATRON TOOK JIM'S TEMPERATURE AND RE-bandaged his hands. Eight days had elapsed since he'd regained consciousness and he was sitting up in bed, reading Susan's latest letter.

'There's something not right today, Lieutenant. You don't have any visitors! This must be the first time your room's been quiet since you came out of the coma.'

Jim had lost count of the number of locals and ATC staff who'd taken the trouble to pass on their kind regards. They would tap gingerly on the door, tell him to get better soon, and thank him for his bravery. Matron would politely remind them *this young man needs rest if he's to recover quickly* and they'd be on their way, leaving him in peace until the next well-wishers arrived.

Jim's bedside table was covered with hand-made get-well cards, all containing a similar message: *Get back to work soon, we miss you.* Fellow officers had delivered an array of amusing gifts, usually accompanied by a witty note of affection – a pair of US army issue gloves – *Best put these on next time*; a local ordnance survey map – *You were meant to be in Marwood, not Mortehoe!* and a small hand-held fire extinguisher – *Better late than never!*

They brought a smile to Jim's face.

The bandages on his head were gone, and the feeling gradually returned to his hands. Nurse Cameron shaved him every morning, brushed his hair and tidied his bed. This morning she seemed to be taking more trouble than usual.

'You'll do,' she said.

Jim gave her a quizzical look.

'You have a special visitor today and we want you looking your best. You are, after all, representing the US Army! And no, I'm not going to spoil the surprise!'

A few minutes later there was a tap on the door and it opened slowly to reveal a man, a few years older than Jim in a wheelchair pushed by a hospital porter, bandaged head supported by a neck brace similar to the one Jim had discarded the day before. His left arm was in plaster, an RAF officer's cap on his lap, and a broad smile on his face.

'Good morning, Lieutenant. I'm Squadron Leader Harry Mann. I've come to thank you for saving my life.'

When the airman had left, some twenty minutes later, Jim couldn't understand why he felt so deflated. Why wasn't the sheer joy Harry felt at being alive rubbing off on him? The visit, rather than bucking him up seemed to have had the opposite effect. The airman had been so grateful he could fly again, serve his country, beat Jerry, and help win the war.

But all Jim could think about was the five airmen who died on the headland. Could he have done more to save them? Why did he always feel he hadn't done enough?

He wondered if some physical activity would help shake off his blues. The damaged ankle was still swollen and the only way he could get around was with an old set of crutches. He despised those crutches; despised the rough padded tops that scratched away at his armpits. Most of all, he despised being an invalid, unsure when or if he'd ever fully recover.

His visit to the physio did little to boost his morale, and he spent the rest of the day catching up on the backlog of ATC paperwork, relieved that his mind at least was active again.

The assault came out of nowhere. One minute Jim was hobbling towards his room from the cloakroom, the next he was on the concrete floor, crutches kicked from under him, being pulled along by one assailant as the other opened the door to his bedroom.

Jim looked up from his prone position, confusion turning to anger, as he saw two GIs staring down at him, hatred etched on their faces.

'You think you're so fuckin perfect don't you Ridd. So God-damn righteous; a hero who saves Limeys but is too yellow to join us to fight the real war. What is it with you and that n… driver of yours coming to your bedside of an evening? You a queer who fucks coloureds?'

Jim struggled to get up but was pushed down again and kicked hard in the stomach. He lay winded, struggling to breathe.

'Just remember this, *sir*. You say *anything* to *anybody* about tonight and your coloured friend won't be driving you anywhere. If we see you two together again, we'll break his legs. He'll be a cripple for the rest of his life. Think about that *Lieutenant*.'

The soldiers disappeared as quickly as they'd arrived. Jim hauled himself onto his bed and lay still; his body ached and his brain struggled to comprehend what had just happened. The attack had obviously been timed to coincide with lights out; the nurses stood down for the night, no witnesses.

Sleep evaded him and the following morning his mind was made up. The venomous words spat out of the GIs' mouths hurt him far more than the kicks to his stomach. Jim knew hatred fuelled their actions, their minds poisoned by the institutional racism ingrained in US society... and in the US military.

He cursed his feeble efforts to try and make a difference. His arrogance had endangered Jerome's safety, and he owed his comrade too much to let that happen. He penned a note to Jerome.

Just trust me on this. It's for the best and I will explain before you leave for Normandy.

The note to his adjutant could not have been clearer. *Stand Private Stone down and replace him with a white driver.* Jim knew this would hurt his friend deeply. But feelings of betrayal mend. Crippled legs don't.

* * *

On the evening Jim was assaulted, Billy was enjoying some rare R&R with Elsie. Training for the joint exercise had intensified, rumours circulating that departure for Normandy might be imminent.

Billy knew this could be their last time together for a very long time, Susan's empty house providing sanctuary for a few precious hours on their own. Elsie was happy. Who wouldn't be? she thought, as she snuggled close to Billy on Susan's bed as they romanticised a life together on the New England coast.

'Four!' said Billy.

'Yes, two boys and two girls. We'll live in a white clapperboard house with a large flower garden and lawn for the kids to play, and it must have sea views to remind me of Devon. And a dog, I've always wanted a golden labrador and …'

The kiss was long and sensuous, their mouths probing and exploring. As the embrace ended, Elsie knelt on the bed stroking Billy's hair. Hair bleached the colour of golden sand on a sunlit beach. She looked into the bluest eyes she'd ever seen, memorising the tiniest details of his face, tracing the outline with her fingers, kissing the small scar on his forehead. Kissing the face of the man she adored. No, not adored, loved. A love that burnt deep inside her.

If only they could stay like this for ever.

They undressed each other, slowly, seductively, treasuring the anticipation, two bodies made for each other; Billy's finely toned from months of physical exertion; Elsie's petite, shapely, willing, and eager to please. Elsie took Billy's packet of condoms out of his hand and without saying a word, put them on Susan's bedside table.

Their lovemaking was slow, passionate, potent. The erotic sensation aroused Elsie as Billy whispered how much he loved her. They relished the sheer intensity of the moment. As their ardour subsided, they lay exhausted, their bodies spooned in a sensuous embrace.

Elsie was first to break the spell. She turned to face Billy. She kissed his face and moved slowly into him, wanting more, her desire relentless, not knowing when or if she would see him again. They lay as one, tears of joy on Elsie's face. She knew this was the man with whom she wanted to spend the rest of her life.

They loved each other and, as soon as he could return from France, they would announce their engagement, marry at the end of the war and set up home near Quincy. The last thing Billy wanted to do was to ruin the moment, but the dark shadow still hung over them.

'Where's Ritter's regiment now?' Billy asked quietly.

Elsie understood from a neighbour that Ritter was training in South Devon, but she didn't want Billy worrying about her when his priority must be surviving the final days of training.

'I'm not sure, Billy. Don't let's spoil our evening. Susan will be home soon so let's not waste precious time talking about him. I've got a much better idea.'

Billy waited until Elsie dozed off; pulled the bed covers over her, dressed quickly, and slipped quietly down the stairs, two thoughts uppermost in his mind.

When would he see Elsie again? How was he going to track down Ritter?

Chapter 20

The making of a psychopath

'PUGLISSI. WHAT KIND OF FUCKIN NAME IS THAT? Sounds like a Wop. Why do yanks have such stupid names?'

Fred Ritter hovered impatiently outside the US Quartermaster store at the rear of the Red Barn with one of his cronies, Jimmy Knox. Their American contacts were half-an-hour late. Ritter was pissed-off. He didn't like waiting for anybody at the best of times and especially not at 10.45 at night, well past curfew and at risk of being apprehended by the local ARP Warden or – worse – the AMPs on the lookout for GI spivs.

The store was an obvious honeypot. Had tonight's deal not been so lucrative, he'd have told Angelo Puglissi where he could stuff his five thousand Lucky Strike cigarettes.

But this *was* a lucrative deal; the biggest Ritter had set up since embarking on his black-market activities. It had taken weeks to negotiate. If he failed to deliver the consignment of fags by early morning, his customer would go elsewhere and he'd lose one hell of a lot of money. Money he needed for the contraband petrol deal he planned next.

He stubbed out his cigarette end and lit another, careful to shield the light from his match. Where were these American bastards?

'Remind me who else is coming with this Puglissi bloke?'

Knox pulled out the bit of paper from his back pocket.

'Filippo Russo. A nasty piece of work.'

'Yea, well,' Ritter whispered. 'He ain't met me yet. Puglissi and Russo. They sound like a couple of clowns from the circus!'

Ten minutes later with Ritter's temper now on a very short fuse, they heard the low growl of a US jeep and, seconds later, a vehicle pulled slowly into the yard. Two men appeared out of the darkness; their silhouettes framed in the moonlight; one extremely tall; the other very short. They didn't waste time with introductions.

'The deal's off guys,' the short one drawled. 'We got a better offer from the Canadians in Ilfracombe. Better luck next time – if there is a next time. No hard feelings right? Now, we gotta be goin…'

'Not so fast, Angel Face or whatever your name is. No-one welches on Fred Ritter. We had a deal and you're goin to stick to it, yank.'

Ritter went to take the gun from his pocket. Before he'd got the weapon out, there was a flash of steel and Russo had a knife at Jimmy Knox's throat.

'Don't you *ever* threaten a Sicilian, you mother-fucker. Now put that gun away nice and slow or your buddy here is history.'

Ritter's hatred of yanks intensified one hundredfold that night. As the GIs drove off, he turned to Knox, punched him hard in the stomach and threatened to slit his throat if he breathed a word of what had gone down. Losing face for Ritter was almost as bad as losing money. He cursed all the way back to camp and, when safely in his bunk, added the names Puglissi and Russo to the growing list of adversaries he vowed to get even with. As violently as possible.

Violence was second nature to Ritter and had been since he was a youngster. His was the all too familiar story of a dysfunctional family. Beaten with a strap by a father who regularly hit his wife where it didn't show, and abandoned the family home when Ritter was nine. His mother struggled to cope with her meagre earnings as a bar-maid and decided to make use of her only real asset.

Uncles frequently stayed over, many hitting young Fred when his mother wasn't looking. When his mother's liking for alcohol became too much, she offered her only son up for adoption. There weren't any takers. He spent the next four years in and out of foster homes, most stays lasting only a couple of months at a time. Eventually he returned to live with his mother.

Fred fared no better at school. Once the kids learnt he was being fostered, verbal and physical abuse became part of his everyday life. To counter the bullying, Ritter stole sweets and cigarettes from the local shops to hand around. What friendships he did have were short-lived and soon dried-up when he failed to supply the necessary goods.

He became an aggressive loner. School was a waste of time and he left on his fourteenth birthday. The only activity he was any good at was swimming. By the age of twelve, he could hold his breath under water far longer than any of his peers. By the time he was thirteen, he had won the under-fifteen Devon County Swimming Championships – the one and only time he could be bothered to enter.

He did odd jobs after school, and then started doing up bicycles and selling them – but that was too much like hard work. His trading instincts were better suited to the world of wheeler-dealing. He started in a small way, buying stolen goods from local fences and selling them on to the older boys at local youth clubs. Cash pinched from his mother's purse, after she had entertained her latest punter, provided him with the means to move on to bigger and more dangerous deals involving cigarettes and occasionally drugs.

If a deal went wrong or he disliked someone for no apparent reason, his first reaction was to become aggressive. His record of violence led to an ultimatum from the magistrate's court – be sent to Borstal when he turned sixteen or attend some counselling sessions in Barnstaple with a newly-appointed juvenile psychologist. Ritter chose the latter.

The first session did not go well.

'What do you think it is that makes you want to hurt innocent people?'

Ritter looked at the ugly old bat sitting opposite him; contempt written all over his face. She reminded him of some of his foster mothers, pretending to be affectionate but with a heart as cold as steel. Should he punch her or shag her? He decided she wasn't worth the aggro.

'Cos I can.' he replied. And with that, he stood up and walked out. His first counselling session had lasted less than five minutes.

Two more sessions followed at weekly intervals. Ritter did open up for a few minutes at each one, giving monosyllabic answers and mumbling with his hand over his mouth about his absent father and drunken whore of a mother. It was, in his mind, him against the world with no one around to support him and everyone out to get one over on him. His attitude to life was simple.

Hurt the bastards before they hurt you.

The psychologist's report made much of his unstable background, and concluded that Ritter had a complete lack of empathy towards others.

He demonstrates psychopathic tendencies that could endanger others unless his aggression can be brought under control. He appears to have no or little conscience or understanding between right and wrong. Lying is second nature to him. Further criminal activity and promiscuous sexual behaviour are highly likely unless he can be placed in a loving environment with foster parents who do not have any other children and are prepared to commit to his development over the long-term.

Ritter was three months away from his sixteenth birthday. No efforts were made to follow-up on the psychologist's recommendation.

One year on, and labelled a juvenile delinquent, he lived a life of petty crime, stealing anything he could get his hands on and overcoming his adversaries with his favourite weapons, a flick knife and knuckle-duster. The police file on him grew thicker and his appearances in the juvenile court more frequent. Just before his seventeenth birthday, the local magistrate's patience ran out and he was sent to Borstal at Portland in Dorset for twelve months.

Ritter was short for his age but, as his fellow in-mates at Borstal found out, he could look after himself. After a few early skirmishes in which he came out on top, he was left to his own devices. That suited him. He spent most of his time learning motor car mechanics and being taught how to box. He figured both could come in useful on his return to the outside world.

After his year was up, Borstal contacted a local philanthropist who owned one of the first motor garages in North Devon and who looked kindly on young men with troubled backgrounds. Ritter got a job washing cars at Barnstaple Motor & Cycle Works and then became an apprentice mechanic. He kept his nose clean, only doing a few minor deals at weekends.

Engines were too messy for him. He became intrigued by the flash young men selling cars on the garage forecourt, impressed by their smart clothes and air of respectability. It was not long before he'd persuaded the owner to give him a chance, and he swapped his greasy overalls for a smart 'three-piece.' His cocky manner, gift of the gab and eye for a good deal cemented his position as one of the company's leading salesmen within eighteen months of leaving Portland.

Local prostitutes serviced his need for gratuitous sex and violence, but he missed the thrill of breaking the law and getting away with it. Biding his time, he planned a return to a life of crime on a far larger scale than before, confident that an opportunity suited to his talents would present itself before too long.

It did. Hitler invaded Poland.

He was twenty-four when conscription came along. Like several of his mates, he tried hard to avoid being called-up. When his claim for chronic myopia was rejected, he was enlisted in the Devonshire Regiment, known locally as 'The Swedebashers'. Determined to stay far away from any action, he tried to join the catering corps, despite never having picked up a saucepan in his life. His lack of culinary experience was exposed on day one and he was transferred to the infantry as a private. He remained at that rank for the next five years.

This suited Ritter just fine. One soldier amongst many. A chance to become almost invisible to any kind of authority. A chance to build up an illegal trade in black-market goods. A well-practiced conman who befriended British and US Quartermasters and, with his entourage of spivs, created a network along the North Devon Coast, buying and selling everything from tobacco and condoms to fresh meat and petrol coupons. Business was good. If he could stay out of military prison long enough, he reckoned that, by the end of the war, he'd have enough capital to set up in business, procuring and selling stolen goods. A chance to be somebody.

Being turned over by the two Italian Americans had not helped his finances, nor done much for his fragile ego.

Fucking yanks.

'Why *do* you hate yanks so much? Jimmy Knox

asked one Sunday afternoon whilst waiting in the dunes at Braunton Burrows for an assignment of black-market rifles.

'Why do you fuckin think, you stupid bastard? They screwed me on the cigarette deal and put paid to the fuel heist I'd planned. That cost me hundreds. They get paid five times as much as we do, give our women nylons and chocolates, and then fuck them. They show off on the dance floor to Mr fuckin Glenn Millar and splash the cash in *our* pubs. They play all day on their bloody pin-ball machines and brag about how clever their juke boxes are. And they really screwed up at Slapton Sands. I could've been killed!'

Knox egged him on, eager to see Ritter even more riled.

'It's not just the girls that love them,' Knox said. The kids idolise them thanks to all the sweets and gum. The yanks have started a scout troop and set up Saturday morning film shows, and it's like fuckin Pied Piper when they march their band to the seafront and raise that fancy flag of theirs.'

Knox's contribution was not helping Ritter's mood. But all the reasons he'd given Knox for despising the yanks counted for nothing in his mind. His hatred was down to being ridiculed in the pub in front of his mates by that tall blond GI bastard; the same bastard who was now trying to steal his girl. That could never go unpunished.

It wasn't just yanks he despised. The psychologist's report had proved correct. As far as Ritter was concerned, other peoples' lives were cheap. *Number one* was all that mattered, and he had a God-given right to cheat, bully and steal his way through life as long as it worked to his advantage. There was no remorse and no guilt. If he wanted something, he took it.

And when he saw Elsie Taylor for the first time it was a done deal. She was going to be *his girl* whether she liked it or not. As he told his cronies time and time again, *I'll gladly kill anyone who tries to take her off me.*

It was no idle threat.

And Ritter wasn't stupid. He planned his love life with the same meticulous detail he planned his life as a spiv and used false charm to win over Ron and Sheila, Elsie's parents. What was there not to like? A Woolacombe lad, bravely serving King and country and running a successful business in his spare time. He went out of his way to shower the parents with presents, especially tobacco, nylons and scent. He flattered Sheila's cooking and bought Ron copious pints in his local. When the time was right, he asked them if he could court their daughter.

This suited them. They thought it was time Elsie settled down and started a family. 'He might not be Cary Grant,' Sheila said to her daughter after more gifts had arrived. 'But he's attentive, generous to a T and who knows how many young men will be around when this war is finally over?'

Elsie was not fooled. She argued with her parents and could not understand why they couldn't see Ritter for what he was. Then the yanks arrived; Elsie and Susan were invited to a dance at the US base, and Billy Ridd came into her life.

The Saturday evening before his regiment's final exercise at Slapton Sands that coming Monday, Ritter was in the pub plying Ron with pints, telling him he would like to marry his daughter. His prospective father-in-law had had one drink too many…:

'Elsie was whispering with her mother in the kitchen yesterday. I couldn't hear much but there was one word I did catch, *engagement*. Now she might have been speaking about Susan or one of her other friends, but I don't think so from Sheila's reaction. I think Elsie was referring to that yank she's seen a few times.'

Fred picked up Ron's glass, went to the bar for a re-fill and put a fresh pint of cider and a double scotch down in front of him. 'Carry on Ron.'

'Just saying, is all,' slurred Ron. 'You'd better get a move on lad or it could be too late. Before you know it Elsie could be married and off to live in America. That would kill her mother.'

Rage spread across Ritter's face. The muscles around his neck tensed in fury. The image of the yank knocking him down in the pub flashed up before his eyes. He wanted to smash his glass in Billy Ridd's face, blind him, kill him.

He would not let *his* Elsie become a yankee bag. He breathed deeply, counted to ten and stared hard at Ron.

'That ain't goin to happen, Ron. That definitely ain't goin to happen.'

Chapter 21

Plotting revenge

THE PLATOON FROM THE 1ST BATTALION DEVONSHIRE Regiment had arrived back at camp near Barnstaple, relieved their last training session at Slapton Sands was over. The soldiers were wet and exhausted from the beach assaults, wading ashore in full kit with live ammunition raging over their heads. Today's exercises had gone badly. Two of the landing craft had 'turned turtle', drowning three men as the vicious undercurrent sucked them away during disembarkation. Morale was low; the men weary of the continuous grind of preparations for Normandy. They just wanted it over and done with.

The despondent mood in the mess got worse with the announcement ten minutes later. Major Paulton informed them that, at 0900 hours the day after tomorrow, they would be taking part in a final simulation before departing for France. It would be a joint British and American exercise with US infantry assault teams from the ATC joining The Devons to land five crafts on Woolacombe Beach, each craft carrying one officer, twenty-nine men, a Sherman tank, jeep, weapons and ammunition.

'Major White will lead Sword and I will lead Utah. Gold, Juno, and Omaha will be led by the Americans. The Devonshire and ATC assault troops selected, and their respective roles, will be posted on the regiment notice board at 1700 hours tomorrow evening.'

He paused and added:

'This is our chance men to show our US allies how prepared the Devons are. Make me and the regiment proud.'

Private Ritter sneered at the major's words. His mind wasn't on the training, nor even on arranging the next illicit deal. He was figuring out his revenge: how to get rid of Billy Ridd.

Major Paulton's notice was pinned up the following evening at the allotted time. Ritter couldn't give a damn. He lay on his bunk flicking through a copy of yesterday's Daily Mirror. If there was anything worth hearing to his advantage, one of his cronies would tell him soon enough.

Ten minutes later, Jimmy Knox wandered in with the names on the major's list scrawled on a scrap of paper. He let out a big whistle.

'Look who's going to be bossing our mates around tomorrow, Fred. It's your favourite yank, the one who punched you in the pub. And those two wops who cheated us out of the cigarettes are on the same craft.'

Fred cursed at being disturbed, and ripped the paper from Jimmy's hand.

Section Leader (British) – Major Allan Paulton
Assistant Section Leader (US) – Corporal Billy Ridd
He stared at Billy's name and worked his way through

the teams on Utah. Light machine gun; mortar and rocket launch; flame throwers, tank crew – *Corporal Angelo Puglissi* and *Private Filippo Russo (US)*. He didn't recognise any of the names in the demolitions party until he came to the last one; *Private Ted Smithers (British)*.

Ritter leapt off his bunk and strode out to the administration block. He needed to check if the names on the notice matched those scribbled down by Knox. *Word-for-word, Jimmy*, he muttered to himself, his mind in overdrive. He lit one of his black-market Lucky Strikes and set off in search of Ted Smithers. Ten minutes later, he escorted him out of his hut for *a quiet chat*.

Ted had been born in Woolacombe and had enlisted in the Devonshire's at the outbreak of hostilities. He'd seen joining the army as a merciful escape from his humdrum life as an apprentice in his father's plumbing business; his working day spent on hands and knees, handing his father one tool after another. He'd disliked plumbing as much as he'd detested his father. Had war not broken out, he would've packed his bags for London and found a life that hadn't involved toilets and kitchen sinks.

He'd been assigned to explosives training on joining the army and had been sent to the Defence Explosive Ordnance Disposal School in Chatham, Kent, where he'd spent six months with the Royal School of Military Engineering. When amphibious assault training began, he became a member of the Demolitions Party or DPs on assault craft, and was considered a capable DP leader.

Ted didn't smoke and rarely drank alcohol. His one vice was playing poker. The buzz of adrenalin as he played for money, more than made up for his sobriety. His problem was that he wasn't any good. He had one of those faces that betrayed his hand. He lost often and was heavily in debt to the soldier who ran the gambling dens and had a side-line in money lending – Fred Ritter.

Ritter dragged Ted behind the nearest hut and pushed him hard up against it, his face inches from his cohort.

'Right Ted, I'm offering you a way to pay off the three hundred quid you owe me. You're going to let me take your place on that landing craft tomorrow.'

'Oh yeah,' replied Ted. 'And I suppose you're going to be promoted to Major at the same time! Get real, Fred.'

'No, clever dick. All you have to do is have an accident tomorrow morning and not be fit enough to take part. We'll find Major Paulton, tell him at the last moment, leaving it clear for me to take your place.'

Ted's face was a mix of confusion and contempt. Was Ritter barking mad? No, he thought; he's a scheming bastard who'll stop at nothing to get what he wants.

'Why would *you* want to be on that craft? You hate training exercises almost as much as you hate Yanks.'

'Let's just say it suits my purpose. I need to get even with some GIs, and tomorrow's exercise might give me the opportunity to do just that. Three birds with one stone! It's a win-win for you, old son. By the time you're fit again, the war might well be over. But if you *ever* breathe a word of this to anyone, it'll be your fuckin neck that's broken, not your arm.'

Ritter put his plan into action. He knew it was a long shot but he wasn't going to miss the chance to get revenge on the three yanks who were top of his hate-list, however long the odds .

He was accustomed to being out after curfew. What self-respecting spiv wasn't? He knew the back lanes and little-used footpaths like the back of his hand, using them frequently for his dead-of-night black-market activities.

With blackened face and hands, a short coil of rope over one shoulder and a three-foot wooden plank in one hand, he scrambled around the large outcrop of rocks that dominated the western edge of Woolacombe Bay. Clear moonlight guided him to where the assault craft were moored for tomorrow's exercise, Sword, Gold, Juno, Omaha, painted on the side. He found Utah last and hid the plank under a tarpaulin in the stern. His rifle butt would probably be sufficient but there was no harm in having a back-up. So far so good; now he had to get wet.

He'd first discovered the old fisherman's stake as a young boy swimming and snorkelling in the sea around the rocks. The beach and sea had provided refuge from his abusive father and had become his second home.

'I really should've gone in the Navy,' he said to himself.

He made his way out to the farthest outcrop of rock and, taking a big breath, slipped under the water; his hands guiding him deeper and deeper along the rockscape until finding the stake, he tied the rope securely around its base

Thirty minutes later, the adrenalin still pumping through his body and pleased with his night's work, Ritter lay curled up on his bunk going over the second part of his plan. As sleep caught up with him, he pictured the body of a fair-haired GI, trussed up deep on the ocean bed.

Chapter 22

The joint exercise

'CONDITIONS ARE APPALLING AND WILL NOT improve during the morning. They are likely to get worse as the day goes on. There's a black east wind that brings with it low temperatures, high seas and lethal undercurrents; rare for this time of year, but not unheard of.'

Jim did not like what he was hearing. It was three weeks since he'd been discharged from hospital. Lt Frye, the monitoring officer for the joint exercise, was making his 6.30 telephone call to the Coast Guard.

It was Lt Frye's job to ensure the final preparations were in place for the 0900 start. He'd thought they were, but it seemed the weather hadn't got the memo.

'The risk to life in these conditions is extremely high. We strongly recommend your exercise today be aborted.'

Both men believed the only course of action was to accept the Coast Guard's recommendation, and to pray the weather improved in the next twenty-four hours. Jim knew Billy had been selected as an assistant section leader on one of the five crafts. His life and the lives of the hundred plus soldiers taking part would be in jeopardy if the exercise went ahead as planned.

How the hell were they going to persuade the CO to postpone the exercise, with one hundred and sixty thousand troops due to leave for Normandy in the next few days?

Colonel Webb remained stony faced as Lt Frye explained the situation.

'We don't have any option but to abort, Colonel. The Coast Guard knows these waters far better than we do. They've made it abundantly clear we would be putting all the men's lives at risk. Hopefully the weather will have improved by tomorrow morning.'

The CO said nothing, grabbed his coat, instructed his orderly to make sure his driver was ready and told Jim and Lt Frye to accompany him. The three men rushed down the stairs. A few minutes later, they were being driven across the beach at breakneck speed.

The colonel pointed up to the dunes behind them and asked Lt Frye what he could see.

'The viewing platform for the ATC and selected media, sir.'

'And what do you see fifty yards west of that platform, Lieutenant?'

Lt Frye saw a much smaller platform set back barely visible in the dunes. The platform would have a panoramic view of the beach where the assault craft were due to land. The colonel didn't wait for an answer, his frustration obvious.

'Two men will be standing on that platform just before

the exercise gets underway. One of them, the shorter of the two, will be wearing his usual Homburg Hat, greatcoat, and smoking a large cigar. The other, all five feet nine of him, will be in his specially-tailored general's uniform, giving a running commentary in his Texas drawl.'

He told them forcefully that the exercise could *not* be delayed. It must proceed as planned despite the atrocious conditions.

'This could be a dummy run for the weather the men have to contend with in Normandy, so let's just hope God is on our side today. Now, I have two important people to meet and greet, and you both have final preparations. Dismissed and start praying.'

Two hours later, Jim and Lt Frye were on the viewing platform amongst a cluster of US and British military personnel and media observers watching intently for the five assault craft to round the bay. Far from abating, the weather had taken a turn for the worse. Rain lashed down; the temperature had plummeted and storm clouds hurtled above a turbulent sea as waves crashed on the shore, relentless and unforgiving.

A feeling of dread came over Jim, sucking the air out of his lungs as images of Billy at the mercy of the sea flickered in front of him. His gut told him nothing good would come of today. Lt Frye leaned into him and shouted, the wind picking up his words and launching them into an angry sky.

'This is suicide, Jim. They don't stand a chance.'

Jim felt helpless. Fear emanated off him like a bad odour. White knuckles gripped the cold metal bar of the handrail, wanting to cry out a warning; wanting to be in Billy's place; wanting to turn back the clock; be safe back home with his kid brother. He so despised being a spectator, detached from the danger; stuck on the sidelines. Impotent.

Loud shouts brought him back to the here and now as the landing crafts came into view. The small armada rounded the bay like a flock of geese in perfect V formation; the craft labouring their way through the heavy waves, heading towards the shore and the most perilous stage of this mini-theatre of war – the safe disembarkation of men, tanks, and equipment.

Jim allowed himself a small sigh of relief, willing for everyone to survive as the craft prepared for the onslaught of artillery fire that would soon erupt from high up in the dunes. Live ammunition, courtesy of Eisenhower, aimed to land just over the soldiers' heads into the sea beyond.

All the landing craft were pitching badly, defying the storm that raged around them as they approached the shore, vast waves breaking over the sides, soaking everybody and everything. Jim was only too well aware how difficult navigating the correct course would be with the vicious undercurrents and poor visibility. But everything seemed to be going to plan.

And then it wasn't.

One of the craft was heading for the large outcrop of granite rocks to the north of the beach. Unless it changed course soon it would hit the rocks head-on. It turned parallel to the shore and the inevitable happened. The waves lifted the craft into the air as if it were a toy and flipped it onto its side some forty yards from the shore.

As cries of alarm rang out from the platform, Jim and Lt Frye scrambled down the dunes and sprinted towards the shore. Jim looked around desperately for any sign of Billy, praying his brother was in one of the four craft safely disembarking in the middle of the bay.

He was comforted by the sight of crew members from the upturned craft swimming and scrambling towards the beach.

'It's the two soldiers inside the tank who are at most danger,' shouted Lt Frye. 'We *must* get to them first.'

Jim froze.

Had Billy made it?

He couldn't see him on the beach, nor amongst the soldiers wading dejectedly towards the shore. Surely he was ok? Jim was so torn. He must check Billy was safe …

Lt Frye shouted at him again. 'Come on Jim. It'll take two of us to open the tank's hatch. We've got to get those men out before they drown.'

Duty first screamed inside Jim's head. Decision made. As he made his way towards the capsized craft, he tried to convince himself Billy had reached the dunes and was enjoying a well-earned cup of coffee.

That's got to be the case, it's just got to be!

The two men clawed their way through the heavy surf until the sea was deep enough to swim, the icy water slicing them like a thousand cuts. As they closed in on the vast grey tank, two soldiers appeared by their side. All four men were determined to rescue the soldiers trapped inside.

With the tide receding, the turret was visible inches below the surface, but it took several agonizing minutes to rotate and open the cover. Jim crawled inside the black hole, hauled the men out one at a time for the rescue party to carry their sodden bodies to shore.

Jim scrambled wearily back to dry land and collapsed, shivering with hypothermia and praying his efforts had not been in vain.

Several long minutes later the medics stopped trying to resuscitate the bodies. Both men were dead, drowned in the most horrific of circumstances. Jim vomited and turned away from the desperate scene, all hope lost. Semi-conscious, he was carried to the waiting ambulance, vaguely aware of someone talking nearby.

A soldier's missing. It's a GI from the capsized craft.

Chapter 23
The aftermath

L<small>T</small> F<small>RYE</small> <small>DISCHARGED</small> <small>HIMSELF</small> <small>FROM</small> <small>HOSPITAL</small> later the same evening, shocked by the tragic events he'd witnessed and determined to make it clear who was responsible.

Assault Training Centre Woolacombe North Devon
Joint Training Exercise – 2 June 1944
Evaluation Report – Prepared by Lt Barry Frye
For the attention of Colonel PW Webb – Commanding Officer
Status – Private & Confidential
The joint training exercise on 2 June 1944 consisting of assault crews from the US and Great Britain demonstrated the difficulty of assault landings when, as witnessed today, the sea is extremely rough and there are gale force winds.

An investigation must be undertaken to determine why one landing craft, Utah, went offline and did not follow the designated course towards shore and the sandy beach. Utah headed towards the rocks on the western side of the bay and capsized when turning to avoid them,

Despite valiant rescue attempts, the two soldiers in the Utah tank, Corporal Puglissi and Private Russo drowned, and one soldier, assistant section leader Corporal Ridd is missing, presumed drowned. His body has not yet been recovered despite Coast Guard and helicopter surveillance.

The Utah crew were slow to emerge from the sea after the capsize and a significant number could have drowned in the cold conditions. Many panicked and got into difficulties because their lifebelts were worn incorrectly. Several men thrown into the sea at the time Utah capsized were flipped onto their backs by the weight of their combat packs, pulling their heads under water and nearly drowning them.

As monitoring officer, it is my duty to put on record the Coast Guard's unequivocal advice to not proceed with today's exercise. They warned how treacherous the sea would be with the prevailing black east wind. This advice was ignored by the ATC CO, Colonel Webb.

The training exercise should have been postponed until weather conditions improved.

Lt B Frye. 2200 hours, 2 June 1944

Lt Frye was in no doubt the penultimate paragraph would be redacted. He slipped a carbon copy into his jacket pocket, put the master in an envelope and made his way to the CO's office to leave with his adjutant.

Colonel Webb and Major Paulton stood beside Jim's

hospital bed, relieved to see him sitting up and looking better. The major introduced himself and told Jim how much he appreciated his efforts to try and save the tank crew's lives. He thanked him again for his bravery that morning and took a step back for Jim's CO to speak. Despair filled the air; the pained expression on the colonel's face witness to the distressing news he was about to impart.

'Jim, a GI from the capsized craft is missing. An RAF Chivenor helicopter is searching for him but the Coast Guard has advised me it's highly unlikely anyone would survive for long in the cold sea.'

The colonel paused, his voice quivering, struggling to find the right words, knowing full well nothing he could say would soften the blow.

'Jim, I'm so sorry. Your brother Billy is the missing soldier. Trust me; we will keep looking until we find him.'

Jim didn't say anything. He just stared at his CO, not comprehending what he'd heard, his face a mixture of horror and confusion.

'There must be some mistake, Colonel. Billy's as strong as an ox. There's no way he wouldn't make it to shore, no way.'

'There's no mistake, Jim. I wish to God there was.'

Jim collapsed back on the bed.

He knew Billy wasn't a strong swimmer, but the capsized craft hadn't been far off shore and he'd seen lots of men wading through the water towards the beach. Billy was as fit as any of them and tougher than most.

How could this happen to Billy? Why didn't I make finding him my priority?

The two men by his bedside kept quiet as Jim tried to make sense of what he'd been told. His bewilderment turned to anger as he remembered the Coast Guard's advice and Lt Frye's words on the viewing platform a few hours earlier ...*suicide, they don't stand a chance.*

Rage welled up inside him and he turned to his CO, vitriolic words spewing out of his mouth.

'You know damn well the exercise should not have gone ahead today. Men's lives were on the line, and for what? A PR stunt to demonstrate the Yanks and Brits could work well together? Tell me, Colonel, was it worth sacrificing my brother for? Well, was it?'

Colonel Webb turned to Major Paulson and asked him to leave. However much he empathised with Jim's anger he had a job to do. They all had a job to do. War was hideous. And D-Day hadn't even started yet.

'Listen to me, Lieutenant. If Billy *has* drowned, he will have died fighting the cause for justice and liberty. We will keep looking but if he *is* lost, it's your duty to keep quiet. You, more than anyone, understand why we need to broadcast a positive message. Boosting the morale of one hundred and sixty thousand troops departing for France is what's important now. Is that understood?'

Jim glared at his CO; nodded and turned away in shame. Guilt overwhelmed him.

At 1100 hours the following morning the RAF surveillance helicopter and Coast Guard abandoned their search for Billy's body.

Colonel Webb followed Eisenhower's orders and instructed the media and his troops to keep quiet about the fatalities. Churchill did the same. Secrecy was imperative for the war effort.

No landing craft capsized.

The exercise was heralded a complete success.

Lt Frye's report never saw the light of day. It became one of thousands of files transported back to the US.

On his release from hospital, it suited Colonel Webb for Jim be transported to a US military convalescent home in the depths of Wiltshire so that he could recover from his ordeal and mourn the loss of his brother, far away from Woolacombe.

Chapter 24

Unanswered questions

TIME PASSED SLOWLY FOR JIM IN THE REST HOME. He kept to himself and, whilst not being rude to his fellow inmates, made it perfectly clear from day one he preferred his own company. His head, more often than not, buried in the well-thumbed copy of *Tulips and Chimneys*, the poems Billy and Jerome had read to him in hospital as he lay in the coma. How long ago that seemed. A world away from where he was now, his brother missing, presumed drowned, Jerome in Normandy, hopefully surviving one day at a time.

The doctors and nurses tended to Jim's every need and were pleased with his physical progress. It was his mental state that concerned them. They'd been told he'd recently lost his younger brother in combat but knew nothing of the circumstances. They wouldn't learn anything from Jim. He'd keep the promise he'd made to his CO, but that didn't stop him dwelling on Billy's disappearance every waking hour. He'd given up any hope of his brother being alive, but prayed his body would be found to put his mind at rest and enable the family to bury him at home in Quincy.

Grieving had not got any easier. He often sat, slumped on a chair in his bedroom, head in hands; tears trickling down a gaunt face; images of Billy's smile taunting him, reminding him of his loss as he relived what had happened on the beach; over and over again. The taste of sand in his mouth; the smell of the sea in his nostrils; the piercing wind blowing right through him.

I'm sorry Billy, I'm so sorry.

For the first time since being apart from Susan, he struggled to write letters home. So many unanswered questions were spinning around in his head. Billy had been involved in hundreds of similar exercises during the past ten months and had come through them all unscathed, bar the occasional bruise or torn muscle. What could have gone so wrong on this one? And why, after such an extensive air and sea search, had Billy's body not been recovered?

He should have made sure Billy was safe before trying to rescue the tank crew. His efforts had been senseless. They had both drowned. He'd failed them and failed his brother. Why had he wasted precious time? Time he should have spent searching for Billy. Time he could never have back.

He knew why. Flawless Jim Ridd had the biggest flaw of all. He always had to be seen to do the right thing; to be exemplary; to feed his excessive need for approval; to do his duty above all else. Even before his family.

It wasn't bravery that made him rescue the airman from the burning Wellington bomber. It was his need for validation. The need was like a drug. It gave a purpose to his life. It made him feel alive. The GIs who'd beaten him up in hospital were right. Mr Fucking Perfect. Except Mr

Perfect didn't have the guts to stand up to his CO when ordered to keep quiet about the capsize.

The torment was relentless and Jim knew it was making him ill. Depression began to envelop him like a sodden blanket wrapped around his mind twenty-four-seven. On the day before his departure for London, he finally managed to write a letter to Susan. He explained how troubled he had been and resolved to try and move on for her and Amy's sake. The never-ending soul-searching had to stop. He would seek reparation in the future.

I owe you, Billy. I will return one day. I promise you that.

* * *

On the 6th of June 1944 convoys of ships passed through Woolacombe Bay on their way to Normandy. Hundreds of aircraft passed overhead, the three white line invasion markings on their wings.

The D-Day invasion had begun.

The coastal settlements of North Devon were like ghost towns; the camps disassembled; every one of the ten-thousand combat GIs transported across the channel to fight for their lives on the French beaches.

One moment the troops were everywhere. The next, as if someone had flicked a switch, they were gone. There was an eerie silence on the beaches and hinterland. The hundreds of tanks parked in neat rows on Saunton Golf Course had disappeared; the only reminder of their presence the large indentations, like giant footprints, in the hallowed turf.

The locals, who had at first despised the presence of the noisy tanks and jeeps on their roads, stood around, as if lost for words without the continual hum of military activity. The shops and pubs were empty; the constant twang of GI accents never to be heard again. Life gradually returned to normal in this hitherto sleepy community. As normal, that is, as life could be in 1944 wartime Britain.

The Devonshire Regiment followed-on twenty-four hours later in the second wave, leaving Private Fred Ritter just enough time to complete one last piece of unfinished business in Woolacombe. Personal business.

Elsie was oblivious to the transition from wartime military hub. She had locked herself in her bedroom grieving for Billy. She wanted to kill herself and would have tried, had it not been for the tiny new life she felt sure was growing inside her.

Part Two

Thirty-two Years Later

Chapter 1

From Watergate to Woolacombe

THE SEAT IN FRONT OF HER WAS RECLINED AS FAR back as it could go, forcing her knees up to her chest. Not the most relaxing way to spend an eight-hour Pan Am flight across the Atlantic to Heathrow. Goodness knows how she'd have survived had she not been a slim five six.

Next time, Amy Ridd said to herself, if there was a next time, she'd fly business and to hell with the cost. She shifted again in her seat, trying to get as comfortable as possible and reflected on how 1976 was not turning out as she had expected.

Six months earlier she'd been planning her wedding, imagining her father walking her down the aisle to marry the man of her dreams. It was now four weeks since her father's death from early-onset Alzheimer's, and three months since she'd kicked out the man she had expected to spend the rest of her life with. He'd been cheating on her during his all-to-frequent overnight business trips to New York. How could she have been so naïve?

Then, to cap it all, her editor at the Boston Globe wanted to move her from investigative reporter to an office-bound editorial role. She'd told him where he could stick his boring job and walked away with head held high, pride intact, but with no idea whatsoever where her future lay.

Not that she really cared. She desperately needed a change of scenery and the letter her father had given her, the day before he'd passed away, presented Amy with the perfect opportunity to get the hell out of Boston and escape to a foreign land. And she couldn't think of a better way to spend the wedding cash.

As she took her father's letter out of the slim attaché case, the odour from the envelope transported her back to the hospital where he'd died and the vivid memories she had of their last time together. How she'd hated the smell of that hospital ward. It permeated every pore of her body, stuck to her clothes; a constant reminder of misery and heartache.

Her father's bed, one of six on the ward, had been furthest from the door. He'd liked the corner position, giving him a panoramic view of his fellow patients, an uninterrupted window on the tiny space that was now his world. It had afforded him a little privacy; one step removed from the seemingly endless hubbub that went hand-in-hand with hospital life.

He had always been a private person. Here in the corner, he could cocoon himself in his books, a barrier to the inane conversation that drifted around him, attempting to pierce his armour and invade his thoughts. That was, of course, in his early hospital days when he knew who he was, where he was and why he was there.

Those days had long since disappeared. His once lucid mind had become more confused, irrational and most of all, agitated. Few things had registered on his consciousness. Nothing or nobody had made sense to him anymore, especially the young woman visitor, who, as regular as clockwork, had sat with him every evening for one hundred and eighty days.

Amy recalled her father's actions the evening before he died. Actions so bizarre and so frightening that, for one awful moment, she had thought that this must be the end, his final goodbye. But no. His vice-like grip on her hand had not been the actions of a man about to leave this world. They'd been of a man whose mind, for one brief moment, had the clarity and purpose missing for the past few months.

He had pulled her close, desperate for her to understand the urgency of his message; a message destined to change her life forever. He pushed the crumpled envelope into her hand and whispered he'd written the letter six months earlier and that it was now time. Time for her to read it in the peace and quiet of his study. Time for him to say goodbye.

She'd done as he'd asked. A plea from one heart, fading fast, to another beating like a drum. The adrenalin had surged through her body; the eyes that had scanned the words too frightened to focus too clearly in case the message they contained brought further disquiet and disruption to her life. Which of course it had.

She knew no amount of re-reading would change her father's words or why she was on this flight.

My darling Amy

Your Mum and I talked frequently, during our happy years together before she died, about me making a trip to England. This letter explains why.

I've carried a burden of guilt around for thirty years since your Uncle Billy's mysterious disappearance in the sea in June 1944, and constantly reproached myself for not returning to North Devon as soon as the war ended to find out more about what happened.

Selfishly, when the hostilities were over, all I wanted to do was come home to Quincy, to be with my darling wife and baby daughter. I pushed Billy's disappearance to the back of my mind, always promising myself I would go 'next year.' Except next year never came. I found lots of excuses – pursuing my writing career, supporting my family, your mother's illness, and subsequent demise. But, truth be told, it was cowardice, pure and simple. I was afraid that I'd find out I could have saved Billy's life, just as he saved mine many years before.

Billy took part in a joint training exercise on 2nd June between British and US troops and his craft capsized. Had I looked for him straight away instead of acting the hero trying to rescue a tank crew, he might have survived. As it was, both men in the tank were dead when I pulled them out. Family should have come first and I let him down, with tragic results.

Billy apparently drowned in the sea that day, but his body was never recovered. There were thirty men on the capsized craft. Two drowned inside the tank but Billy was the only member of the assault team to be lost. That fact has never made any sense to me. Whilst he was not the best of swimmers, he was fit and strong. Why was his body never recovered?

He'd participated in hundreds of similar training exercises during the ten months he spent in Devon. The one and only time the US Army had combined with the Brits, Billy's craft strayed off course, capsized and he was reported missing, presumed drowned.

I've prayed there might be a straightforward answer. That his death was just one of those freak accidents that happen in wartime. Your mother said many times this was some kind of guilt trip for me. That I should focus on the future, not the past. She was probably right, and I have spent too long reproaching myself for something that might have a simple answer.

Go in my place, Amy. Find out the truth and put the matter to rest once and for all. You're an investigative journalist and will make a far better job of it than I would have done.

Take your golf clubs and find a good-looking Limey to play Saunton. I promised Billy when we arrived in Devon, we would return one day and, for old time's sake, treat ourselves to a game and a drink or three at the Red Barn in Woolacombe.

Travel safely. Accomplish what I should have.

Your loving father

Jim

2nd January 1976
The Salt Box
Quincy Massachusetts

Tears welled up in Amy's eyes. It was as if all the grief she'd felt these past few weeks had been compartmentalised from her everyday life. Not anymore. The letter was her catharsis. It gave new purpose to her life. It held out a challenge. A challenge that perhaps subconsciously she'd been looking for all her life.

She knew little of what her father had been through in World War Two and even less of her late Uncle Billy. She wiped the tears from her eyes, put the envelope back in her case and told herself to get a grip. She was up for this, even if she had to investigate the coldest of cold cases that had happened thirty-two years ago. A fool's errand? Perhaps not, she thought.

Amy pulled out the aide-memoire she'd prepared to help with the 'cotton wool' jet-lag brain she'd read about. She had heeded all the advice; declined the in-flight food and alcohol and sipped gallons of water, stretching her legs as best she could on frequent trips to the restroom.

Nancy, an old college friend who'd forsaken Boston for Battersea, had trolled through Yellow Pages and forwarded Amy the names of several private investigation agencies in and around Barnstaple. One of them stood out. Amy, knowing how important local knowledge and contacts would be to the investigation, planned to call them as soon as she landed.

She scanned copies of the letters she'd written to the US

Ambassador in London explaining her mission, pleading him to assist with her investigation and prayed for a positive response soon.

Satisfied that she was as prepared as she was going to be, Amy put the papers away, closed her eyes and tried once more to get some shut-eye. But sleep continued to elude her; her mind working overtime; her imagination running riot with the challenge that lay ahead,

She resigned herself to watching the in-flight movie, *All the President's Men*, and wondered if her investigative skills could match those of Redford and Hoffman. Was a 1972 political scandal easier to solve than a three-decade old Second World War mystery?

From Watergate to Woolacombe. She couldn't wait!

Chapter 2

Nick Webber Private Investigator

THE PROPRIETOR OF THE WEBBER PRIVATE
Investigation (PI) Agency sat in his office tucked
away behind the clubhouse at Saunton Golf Club. The
office was an old storeroom that had lain empty for years
until it had taken on a new lease of life six months earlier.
It contained all the necessary fundamentals for Nick
Webber to operate as a PI – a telephone, desk with in and
out trays (both empty), a bright orange Anglepoise lamp,
note pad, his favourite fountain pen, and a desk diary.
Telephone directories for Barnstaple and the surrounding
area and several client folders were stacked neatly on the
corner of the well-worn desk and in pride of place sat, at
considerable recent expense, a new, but hardly used, fax
machine.

A pristine black-and-white leather golf bag with a full
set of Ping irons and woods stood in the corner, untouched
for three years. Nick Webber was monogrammed on the
bag in white lettering and above it, the 1973 Ryder Cup
emblem. A framed photograph of the 1973 Great Britain &
Ireland Ryder Cup team hung over the bag with the non-

playing captain Bernard Hunt in the middle of the front row beaming at the camera.

The team photograph, with several familiar faces on view: Barnes, Jacklin, Coles, O'Conner, Oosterhuis, and Huggett, had been taken at Muirfield, the day before the first day's play. One face, Nick Webber's, was missing, lost to the record books for ever. Nick had been an early selection for the twelve-man team and had been expected to play in at least one of the singles matches and in both a four-ball and foursomes match. That was not to be, and his late replacement didn't feature in any of the matches over the three days of the tournament which the US won 19-13.

Nick had been allowed to keep the bag, and remembered fondly the support from his not-to-be teammates who, to a man, visited him in hospital a few days after their departure from Muirfield. He often stared at the photograph as he sat at his desk waiting for the telephone to ring or the fax machine to kick into life.

Saunton members who popped their heads around the door to chat wondered why he tortured himself seeing that photo every day and told him as much. *Take it down and move on with your life,* was said in a good-humoured way by the visitors who looked upon Nick as fondly as they would their own son.

He had risen to become one of the UK's top players at the age of twenty-seven, having made his mark on the European Tour three years prior to his much-anticipated Ryder Cup debut. His career was typical of many successful players of his era; starting life as an assistant professional at his local club, Saunton, and becoming club pro three years later before his talent and commitment led to success on some of the best tracks Europe had to offer.

Life had never been better for the young man for whom the golf swing was the most natural thing in the world and who had all the hallmarks of a future grand-slam champion. Everything had changed in an instant. One minute, Nick was being compared to a promising young Spaniard named Ballesteros. The next, he was flat on his back on an Exeter hospital bed with surgeons fighting to save his leg.

He'd been on his way to join his Ryder Cup colleagues in Edinburgh; had parked his car at Exeter Airport and was walking across to the terminal building. A young boy right in front of him was trailing behind a group of adults who were strolling quickly towards departures. The boy stopped to look skyward as an aeroplane flew overhead and then, realising he was being left behind, sprinted to catch up.

An airport bus turned the sharp corner just as the boy, totally oblivious to the oncoming vehicle, ran straight across the road in front of it. With no thought for the consequences, Nick managed to push the boy out of harm's way, but the bus collided with Nick's right leg before screeching to a halt. Half an hour later, he was being examined by a consultant orthopaedic surgeon at the Royal Devon & Exeter. The prognosis was his right leg would need to be amputated just below the knee.

Rumours circulated that the surgeon had fought so hard to save Nick's leg because he was a keen golfer who knew of Nick's reputation and of the circumstances that led to him being on his operating table that afternoon. Others said he was just doing his job. Fact and fiction became entwined in national and local headlines for weeks. One minute, the Devonian golf star was on his way to potential Ryder Cup glory; the next, a hero with a shattered right leg.

Nick had three operations over the next six months and was then transferred to the Alexandra Hospital in Barnstaple. Nine months since the accident, he was allowed home, but returned daily to undergo a brutal physiotherapy regime. When the medics informed him there was nothing more they could do, Nick was resigned to walking with the aid of a stick. His right knee struggled to support his weight, let alone the rigours of professional golf. He'd been stripped, in one agonising moment, of his boyhood dreams, his livelihood and a stellar career.

Pain and frustration frequently got the better of him. Black moods enveloped his senses. Wallowing in self-pity, he would lock himself away for days on end, ignoring family and friends. The surgeons had saved Nick's leg, but no one had given any thought to the state of his mind. He needed help, but pride had got the better of him and he sought assuagement in solitude, desperate to find something worthwhile to do with his life.

Endless conversations with his father had followed. Peter Webber played off a three handicap, and had retired early as a chief-constable with the intention of caddying for Nick occasionally on tour to give his usual caddy a break. Yet another dream shattered on the tarmac of Exeter Airport. Whilst Nick recovered, Peter had used his thirty years' experience in the force advising local private investigators, most of whom he considered lazy and unprofessional. Far better, he thought, to set up his own agency, albeit working part-time. He and Nick hatched a plan.

They'd set up the Webber PI Agency, Peter providing advice behind the scenes, leaving Nick to run the day-to-day business, making use of his intuition and strong analytical skills. Nick had hoped his new life would put an end to the morosity. But his new career to date had been a disappointment. Proving a husband's infidelity and finding a long-lost relative for a family reunion fell a long way short of his aspirations.

The wall clock above his desk struck five. He was resigned to yet another day with no new enquiries, let alone clients. Then the phone rang for only the third time that day. What sounded like a young American woman asked if Nick could meet her to discuss a family mystery from the distant past. A mystery that had brought her halfway across the world and was, she said, 'colder than a New-England day in January.'

A smile etched on his face; the first in a very long time. *Roll on tomorrow.*

Chapter 3

A meeting of minds

L EAVING HIS COTTAGE IN CROYDE, NICK DROVE
inland towards Mortehoe. There was little point in
hurrying on the country lanes. The school holidays were
in full swing; the area thronged with visitors (or grockles
as the locals called them) and he had to stop frequently to
give way to on-coming traffic.

As he drove down the hill into Woolacombe, the vista
of the Atlantic surf crashing against Morte Point made him
catch his breath. He was, like many others born and bred
in these parts, fiercely proud of the tapestry that shaped
their lives.

He passed the melting pot of hotels, guest houses and
caravan sites that had fused together to create the resort
– popular since Victorian times when factory workers
had swapped their Midland cities for industrial fortnight
holidays by the seaside; a far cry from the well-heeled
Bristol merchants who first ventured here by train to build
their grand Edwardian houses overlooking the ocean.

He pulled into a layby halfway up the steep hill out of
Woolacombe, and sat looking out to sea, thinking about

his impending meeting. He had fifteen minutes before his rendezvous with the client who'd called him out of the blue.

Could this be the opportunity he'd been waiting for? An opportunity that challenged his investigative skills and helped build his reputation as a PI. He'd grown weary of being treated like an ex-golf pro who didn't know what else to do with his life.

More animated than he'd felt in a very long time, he entered the quintessential Devon village of Mortehoe, nestling snugly in the valley, sheltered from the prevailing winds and modest in comparison to its extravert neighbour. The parish church of St Mary stood large on his left, fronted by a war memorial commemorating the soldiers who'd perished in two World Wars. The church anchored the square of old fishermen's cottages, three pubs and a cluster of shops.

He parked next to the museum and headed towards the cemetery between the church and The Ship Aground pub, still quiet at this time of day save for the drayman's lorry unloading its kegs of ales and ciders. High hedges on either side of the path screened his view of the tombstone that, to his shame, he'd not visited for a year. Memories came flooding back as he placed the white roses, his Mum's favourite, on the Webber family grave and closed his eyes, visualising his mother in happier times before cancer had ravaged her body.

With his old nine iron for support, he walked the fifty yards down the uneven gravel path to the dry-stone wall that protected the graveyard from the worst of the Atlantic winds and the sheep grazing hungrily on the exposed headland. Tripping on a stone, he cursed out loud, the jolt of pain, like an electric shock in his kneecap, making him nauseous. He took some deep breaths and leant on the wall for support, waiting for the throbbing to subside, forcing himself to focus on the panorama.

No wonder the locals had, for centuries, chosen this resting place to bury their loved ones. Grunta Beach lay immediately below, named, so the legend went, after a ship carrying live pigs ran aground. And in the distance, the headland of Westward Ho! home to England's oldest golf course. Recollections flooded back of the times he'd steered his ball skilfully between the undulating dunes and the sheep that grazed peacefully on the rugged links.

But that was then, and this was now.

Different challenges beckoned, but Nick had the same gritty resolve to succeed at whatever came his way. He checked his watch and sensed the merest trace of eau de cologne wafting behind him.

'That's a spectacular view.'

Nick recognised the accent from the telephone conversation the day before.

'I'm pleased you're on time.'

'I don't do late,' Nick said pleasantly as he held out his hand.

'Nick Webber, Miss Ridd. It's good to meet you.'

Nick saw a beguiling face; warm smile and eyes as seductive as they were engaging. Her slim figure and the fair hair blowing across her face gave her an air of fragility. There was nothing fragile about her handshake.

'Please call me Amy.'

If she was conscious of him staring, she hid it well. Her first impression of Nick was one of sadness. His manner, reflecting perhaps a life he had loved so much torn apart by one reckless act of bravery. But there was a fierce determination on his face as if he had something to prove.

That works for me, she thought.

She glanced at the golf club propped against the wall and Nick told her he didn't go anywhere without it. 'It supports what's left of my right knee. Let's find somewhere more sheltered to talk.'

He led the way to a wooden bench outside the groundsman's hut. As they approached, she placed her hand gently on his arm.

'If you look closely, you'll be able to make out the Ridd family names on that gravestone.'

He knelt down beside her and peered at the weathered slab of grey stone no more than four feet high resting at a forty-five-degree angle.

'This is believed to be one of the first gravestones here,' Amy said. 'The Ridd family lived in Mortehoe from the sixteenth century. My grandfather told me several generations of the family have been buried in this plot.'

Wiping some stray leaves off the bench, they sat quietly for a moment, looking out on the ocean, sunlight sparkling on the white horses of incoming waves. Nick was loath to disturb the poignancy of the moment. He waited for what seemed an age when, still looking out to sea, Amy spoke with an urgency that shook off any illusion that this attractive American was at ease with life.

'I'm looking for someone to help me investigate my

uncle's death on Woolacombe beach thirty-two years ago; someone with the courage to take on the military establishment and, if necessary, be prepared to upset the locals. So, Nick Webber, why might that someone be you? All I know is that you're an ex-golf pro with a busted right knee and a nine iron for a best friend, who goes around saving young boys' lives.'

Nick had anticipated her question.

'There are five reputable PI agencies in the area,' replied Nick. 'I'm sure they would all like to work with you. Some of them may even have lower day rates. But I'm local, am respected in these parts and have several quality associates to assist me. One of them is my father, an ex-chief constable with excellent contacts and over twenty years' investigative experience.'

'And you Nick, how determined would *you* be?'

Nick paused. Face resolute, words carefully crafted, first-tee nerves banished.

'Imagine being seven shots down on the final day of a golf tournament with the odds stacked against you and winning with the final putt on the 18th. Imagine being told for months on end you'd spend the rest of your life in a wheelchair and proving everyone wrong.'

Nick allowed himself a tentative smile. 'And imagine a real stickler for detail or a dog with a bone! Come on, let's get out of this wind.'

They adjourned to the shelter of the lounge bar at the Ship Aground. The bar empty, save for a couple of local farmers enjoying their first pint of the day with their ploughman's lunch. Nick collected their drinks. After a couple of pleasantries about the old-fashioned décor, it was his turn to ask the questions.

'Tell me more about the conundrum that brings a Bostonian thousands of miles across the Atlantic.'

He pulled out his notebook, pen at the ready.

* * *

'What makes you think I'm from Boston?'

'I played a number of courses around Boston and lodged with a family whose ancestors came from Devon. We've kept in touch, and your accent sounds very similar.'

'You're close! I grew up in Quincy, ten miles south of Boston. My great-great grandfather emigrated from Mortehoe in the middle of the eighteenth century and developed a fleet of fishing boats. He swapped Ilfracombe for Boston, and herring for tuna.'

Amy told Nick that he'd drowned, along with several of his crew, trying to catch one of the whales that appeared in the deep waters beyond the harbour. This prompted her great grandfather to turn from fishing in boats to building them, and he'd founded the local shipyard in 1883. She explained that her grandfather William Ridd was a keen golfer and, bemoaning the opportunities to play locally, joined forces with local businessmen to create the Woolaston Golf Club.

'My father and Uncle Billy had played there regularly before the outbreak of the Second World War. Golf is in my blood and I've played the game since I was old enough to walk. I'd love to tell you we're having this conversation because of your glowing reputation as a private investigator. We're not! But if your investigative skills are anything like as good as your golf, we might rub along together just fine.'

Nick ordered some sandwiches as Amy explained that her parents had recently died, and that having split up from her partner, she had no reason to stay in Quincy. With her father's letter burning a hole in her pocket and her career as a journalist on hold, she had decided there would never be a better time to honour her father's wishes and discover what had happened to her uncle.

'You see Nick, whilst my uncle did die in the war, he was not, like so many of his compatriots, killed on the Normandy beaches. He died in Woolacombe Bay on a training exercise and his body was never recovered. Read the letter that my father gave me just before he died while I powder my nose. It describes the mystery that haunted him.'

Nick read the letter slowly and then read it through again; engrossed and intrigued. He looked up to see Amy had returned and was sitting still looking out of the window. She took in little of the village landscape; all she could see was the look of desperation on her father's face as he'd stuffed that envelope into her hand.

Snap out of it!

She reminded herself there was a job to do, wiped her eyes, put on a brave smile and turned to Nick.

'Do you think I'm on a wild-goose chase?'

Nick gathered his thoughts. He wanted to help her; to assure her that everything would be alright.

'From what I've read, it feels like there's a subliminal

message in your father's letter. It's as if he believed the circumstances of your uncle's death were not as straightforward as they appeared. I think we should start by compiling as many facts as we can about Billy's life when he was stationed here.'

And thinking he should lighten the mood a little, he added,

'I may not be that good-looking Limey your father referred to, but when we *have* solved this mystery, I'd be delighted to play that round of golf your father suggested.'

Amy grinned and stifled a yawn; her weary expression belying the fierce determination she felt inside.

'I'm sorry Nick, the jet lag's kicking in. That's enough discussion for one day. I'm still tired from my Boston flight. Comfort and Pam Am aren't synonymous, and the drive from London on your quaint country roads took much longer than I'd anticipated.'

They agreed to meet again at ten the next morning. Amy was staying at the Woolacombe Bay Hotel and he suggested they find a quiet spot in the lounge. They walked down the hill to her hire car. It was somewhat conspicuous amongst the Morris Minors, Escorts, and tradesmen's vans. Nick thought it made his Mini Cooper appear somewhat dowdy. She noticed his keen appraisal and smiled properly for the first time since they'd met just two hours before.

'It's a Renault Caravelle, the same car I drive back home. Not easy to find but well worth the effort. If you get to know me better, Nick, you'll find I'm a creature of habit who likes her cars; always convertibles and always red!'

She wound down the window and told him she'd see

him in the morning, when hopefully she'd feel more like herself.

'Thanks for listening; it's been good to share. We could have the makings of a successful team. And yes … I have brought my clubs!'

She drove off to the sanctuary of her hotel. Nick stood, letter in hand, pondering how best to prepare.

He had no intention of letting Ms Amy Ridd down.

Chapter 4
Tanks on the course

NICK PICKED UP THE MESSAGES ON HIS ANSWER phone and spent the next couple of hours on mundane tasks relating to a current case. He'd cleared his desk by three o'clock and was able to focus on what he'd logged as the Billy Ridd case. He left a message for his father suggesting they meet up tonight for a pint in his dad's local, asking him to rack his brains for anyone who might remember the GIs back in 1943/44.

Filing his papers into an old briefcase purloined from his father, he remembered a black-and-white photograph that hung in the golf club secretary's office. He walked round there. Bill, the club secretary was sorting out score cards from the monthly medal competition. Nick stood quietly in front of his desk, eyes focused on the photograph. Bill smiled up at him.

'Nick, good to see you in my humble abode. You're not after your old job back, I suppose?'

'Not yet, Bill, but I do have a favour to ask. I'd like to borrow that photograph behind you and hear what you can tell me about it.'

Bill turned and looked at the faded black-and-white image. It was as if he was looking at it properly for the first time and was not sure what to make of it. He took it from the wall and handed it to Nick.

'All I can tell you is that it was taken around 1943 when the yanks took over the golf course and made a right mess of it with their tanks. We didn't get the course back until 1951, and it took years before the links were up to their old standard.'

He suggested Nick speak to Tom White, the Club's Life President. Major Tom was in his late seventies and had been around the Saunton links for nigh on sixty years. His game might not be what it was, but his mind was still as sharp as ever.

That evening, Nick spent a couple of hours updating his father. Peter Webber had come prepared and revelled in his son's pleasure at long last having an investigative challenge. He had a number of acquaintances who'd farmed locally during the war, and Nick left with several names to follow-up.

'Pace and judgement, Nick,' was his father's favourite mantra, relayed too frequently for Nick's liking.

'As always, Dad,' and he promised to be back in touch soon. His father offered to visit Barnstaple library archive to review the North Devon Journal for 1943/4 on the off chance he could find anything relevant.

Nick woke early the next morning to find the sun streaming through his bedroom window. It was one of those mystical summer mornings when he felt lucky to live in such a beautiful part of the world with its mile upon mile of coastal paths flirting with the cliff edge, and the green and purple tableau of heather that adorned the headland; accompanied, more often than not, by contented sheep on its lush turf.

He dressed quickly and, as was his custom, walked into the village to breakfast with the local surfers who frequented the cafés nestled along the main street. Before his accident and when not away on tour, Nick would have run the five miles around Baggy Point before setting off for Saunton, to breakfast in the clubhouse and begin his day-long practice.

These days, he satisfied himself with as long a walk as he could manage, his nine iron helping to take the strain. Fed, watered and energised by the sheer enthusiasm for life that embodied the surfing community, he headed for his rendezvous with Amy.

Climbing the steps of the grandest hotel in Woolacombe, he was reminded of the important role the Edwardian establishment had in the war. Was it mere coincidence that Amy had chosen to stay here? It was three minutes to ten when Nick made his way towards the residents' lounge only to be apprehended by a diminutive man dressed in a black morning coat.

'Good morning Mr Webber, I'm the hotel manager. Ms Ridd asked me to hand you this note personally. May I suggest you read it in the lounge where your coffee is waiting?'

'How did you know who I was?'

'Ms Ridd gave me a description of you, saying that you would appear promptly at 10 o'clock and to look out for a golf club impersonating a walking stick.'

He led Nick across the hall to a lounge overlooking the

hotel gardens and sea beyond. A table in the corner had been set for coffee. Once Nick had sat down, the manager was at pains to let him know if there was anything he needed he only had to ask. Amy had obviously made a good impression. It was perhaps unusual to have a young American woman staying at the hotel. Nick poured his coffee and opened the envelope.

Dear Nick

    Sorry not to be here to meet you as arranged.

    I've been in contact with the American Embassy in London for several weeks asking for a meeting to discuss the events surrounding Uncle Billy's death. My requests had been met with a stony silence, until yesterday when a telegram arrived saying that if I could get to London by 2pm today, someone would meet me and discuss my numerous requests for information.

    I'm on the early train from Barnstaple to Exeter and from there to Paddington and Grosvenor Square and hope to return sometime tomorrow, but will try and telephone your office to give you an update and rearrange our meeting.

    This note also confirms my intention to retain your agency to work with me on this investigation. We can finalise terms and discuss progress when we next meet.

    Wish me luck in the big city!

    Yours

        Amy Ridd

Nick read the note a couple of times. He knew it was important to make some progress whilst Amy was in London, and decided Major Tom should be his first port of call. He wanted to hear first-hand what, if anything, the major remembered about the thousands of American GIs stationed nearby in World War Two. Whilst the major was known to be a mine of local information, Nick doubted he would know anything to help unravel the mystery behind Billy Ridd's disappearance.

He couldn't have been more wrong.

Chapter 5
The American Embassy

A MY'S JOURNEY TO LONDON WAS EXCRUCIATINGLY slow. Her train from Barnstaple to Exeter felt like something out of an Agatha Christie novel, and stopped every few minutes at stations in the middle of nowhere. At last it pulled into Exeter St David's eighty-five minutes later. Amy had to sprint to catch the Cornish Riviera Express to Paddington. She just made it, collapsed on her seat, and prayed her carriage would remain empty for the scheduled three-hours. She needed some quiet time to read through her notes, and knew that a short doze before arriving in London would help stave off the jet lag likely to kick-in by mid-afternoon.

Her luck held until the train pulled into Bristol Temple Meads, where her carriage filled up quickly with an assortment of passengers, most of whom were intent on discussing in very loud voices, everything from the weather to local politics. Amy put away her folder and did her best to nap.

On arriving at Paddington, she found a café on the concourse and ate a bland cheese sandwich. Her coffee was equally disappointing, and she suddenly felt homesick for Quincy. She asked herself what on earth was she doing here, and then felt guilty as she pictured her father's face the last time they were together. Clutching her overnight bag, she strode out of the station and waited patiently in line for a black cab. She didn't have long to wait.

'Twenty-Four Grosvenor Square please. The London Chancery Building.'

'The American Embassy it is Miss. Fastest or tourist route?'

'Fastest please. I need to get there as soon as I can.'

Amy took the opportunity to freshen her makeup, paying particular attention to her mascara. She knew that her eyes were one of her best features and was well aware from experience with male bureaucrats in the States that she'd need all her feminine charm today. Twenty minutes later, she was waiting anxiously in the embassy's foyer.

The young female receptionist had been expecting her and had offered a coffee which Amy politely declined. She sat quietly rehearsing the questions she needed answers to, determined not to be dismissed as some misinformed young woman stuck thirty years in the past.

A tall fair-haired man in a tailored suit that wouldn't have looked out of place on Savile Row, walked confidently towards her, a thin blue folder in his hand and engaging smile on his face. He looked to be in his late thirties and had the manner of someone totally at ease with his position. He held out his hand.

'Ms Ridd, a real pleasure to meet you. My name's Adam Inglis, and I'll be looking after you today.'

He led Amy through a maze of corridors with doors on either side until they arrived at an office just large enough for a desk and two chairs. He opened the folder and looked intently at Amy.

'First of all, may I wish you a warm welcome to the Embassy and, on behalf of the Ambassador, thank you for the letters you have written to him over the past few weeks. This is obviously a matter you feel strongly about and you're clearly a very determined young woman. Rest assured that I and my colleagues will do all we can to assist you. Are you in England for long?'

Amy ignored his slightly condescending tone, well used to being patronised as a female journalist.

'I'm here, Adam, for as long as it takes. My ancestors are from North Devon and, as you know from my letters, I'm here to find out everything I can about my father's and uncle's time there during wartime Britain.'

She relayed what she knew about her uncle apparently drowning in the sea just yards off the beach at Woolacombe, and commented how strange it was his body had never been found. She told him, in no uncertain terms, that she didn't intend returning to the States until she'd resolved the mystery surrounding his disappearance.

'I asked if the Ambassador could find any documents relating to the incident that took place in Woolacombe Bay on 2 June 1944. I'm hoping you have some positive news for me and my visit hasn't been in vain.'

Adam looked at the papers in front of him.

'Amy, the Ambassador instructed me, as the person overseeing our World War Two archive, to undertake a thorough search of everything we have on the Assault Training Centre. I've also liaised closely with related agencies and am confident that the information we have collated is as comprehensive as possible.'

He informed her that he'd pored over hundreds of pages and was extremely confident nothing had been missed that would throw any light on the incident her letters referred to. He stressed that nothing of any substance had come to light and the conclusion remained that, despite her uncle's body never having been found, he drowned when his landing craft capsized. There was no evidence, whatsoever, to suggest anything other than that this had been a tragic accident, just as it was for the two GIs in the tank. The fact that this was a joint exercise with the British was immaterial.

'I've found no evidence of any malpractice, and I hope this will help put your mind at rest and allow you to move on with your life.'

Amy looked straight at the man sitting across the desk from her. Pulse racing; breathing irregular. She'd rehearsed this moment of rejection many times in the past few weeks. It's what she had anticipated.

She leant forward, revealing the merest hint of cleavage, and smiled.

'Thank you, Adam. It's good to know you have been so thorough, and I do appreciate your efforts. Perhaps, before I leave, I can ask you one or two quick questions, just for my own peace of mind?'

'Of course, Amy, ask away. But before you do, if you don't have any plans for dinner this evening, it would be my pleasure to take you to a favourite restaurant of mine. No shop talk allowed!'

Amy smiled inwardly to herself. She'd noticed the white ring of skin on Adam's wedding finger where his band should be. Married and taken it off for our meeting? Recently divorced?

She wasn't interested in a liaison, romantic or otherwise, but she was adept at putting men at their ease. The more time she spent with Adam, the more he might open up about the only thing that mattered – finding out what happened to her uncle.

'Dinner sounds good thank you. But I'll need to sort out a hotel for tonight.'

Adam's face lit up.

'We have guest rooms here in the Embassy, Amy. Just give me a minute to call housekeeping.'

As he excused himself, Amy deftly turned Adam's folder around and carefully opened the cover to reveal several typed pages with the heading *Lt Jim Ridd and Corporal Billy Ridd 1943/44*. Just as she was about to start reading, the door opened.

'That's all settled, Amy. You have a guest room on the top floor and should be very comfortable. You can rest easy knowing that Embassy staff, me included, sleep on the floor below.'

The glint in his eye was obvious. She stifled a grin, managing to keep her poker face on. She had her father to thank for teaching her to play the game at a young age. Amy was no prude, nor was she anyone's easy lay.

'And I've booked a table for six-thirty at La Corniche,

a cosy French restaurant just around the corner. Now, you had one or two questions for me?'

Amy took her notebook out of her bag, her pen poised.

'How many landing craft were involved in the training exercise, and was Uncle Billy's the only one to capsize?'

Adam was not the first and wouldn't be the last to underestimate Amy Ridd. He'd been taken in by her pretty face and feminine charm, but this was not a lady to be put off easily. He opened his folder and scanning through the first page, appeared to be reading verbatim from the notes in front of him.

'Five craft were involved. The section leader on your uncle's craft was Major Allan Paulton, a Brit, and your uncle was the assistant section leader. Each craft carried a tank, miscellaneous armoury and equipment to be unloaded on the beach in preparation for battle.'

He told Amy Billy's craft had become detached from the others and had headed for a large outcrop of rocks when the craft had veered too quickly to avoid a collision and ended up parallel to the beach. It capsized in the rough surf. The other craft moored safely near the beach and carried on with the exercise as planned.'

'And the names of Uncle Billy's crew?'

'Unfortunately, those names wouldn't be any use to you,' said Adam defensively. 'Three men died in the training accident, your uncle and the two tank crew. All the other GIs named on the craft that day were killed on the June 6 assault of Omaha Beach.'

Amy took a deep breath. She'd known digging up the past was not going to be easy.

'I'm so sorry to hear that, Adam. My generation has no real understanding of the sacrifices made so that we could enjoy the freedom and liberty we do today.'

A sombre mood had descended on the room. Amy was tempted to call it a day and be grateful for the information she had gleaned. But she knew that this was going to be her one and only chance and decided to push on with her next question.

'And what about the names of the British troops on the craft? Did you obtain these from the other agencies you referred to earlier?'

Amy could see Adam's patience was wearing thin. He seemed to be weighing up whether to terminate the interview there and then, or to continue to answer her questions in return for the dinner date. He picked up some papers in the folder and shuffled them about as if playing for time. Coughing slightly, he put on his *I really do want to help you* face.

'Neither we nor the British Ministry of Defence appear to have any information on the British soldiers with Major Paulton. The MOD may well consider it classified, and I can only suggest you appeal personally to them.'

Adam stressed that digging around for information on what was an embarrassing day for both countries would not do much to enhance current US-Anglo relations, even though the incident had occurred a long time ago. Amy considered for a moment. Rather than challenge this point of view, she decided to change tack and move on. She had most of the evening to follow up loose ends, despite what Adam had said about not talking shop.

'What was the weather like on the day?'

Amy quickly added that this was her final question and was going to add 'for now', but decided that she'd have a better chance of sweet-talking him later after he'd had a few drinks.

Adam had anticipated this question. Without opening the folder, his response was word perfect.

'I'm sure you appreciate that I'm going out on a limb here and our conversation has to be completely off the record.'

Music to the ears of a journalist.

Amy leaned forward again. She knew she was being a tease, but desperate times call for desperate measures – as her father was prone to say when he'd used unconventional means to put a story to bed.

'There's no official report concerning the weather,' said Adam, 'but note the word *official*. We did find a report prepared by a Lieutenant Frye who appears to have been responsible for coordinating the US's participation in the exercise. It would seem that Lt Frye contacted the local Coast Guard early that morning to check on the strength of the prevailing wind and general weather conditions.'

Adam told Amy that, from the note he'd found in the archives, the Coast Guard had warned Lt Frye there would be abnormal conditions that morning with what they called a black east wind. The wind brought with it high seas and lethal undercurrents. The Coast Guard's explicit advice had been to abort the exercise.

'It's not clear who decided to ignore this advice but what *is* clear from Lt Frye's report is that the appalling conditions were extremely hazardous for amphibious craft attempting to disembark men and machines. It's not surprising your uncle drowned in such treacherous conditions. What is surprising is that there were not more fatalities.'

A few minutes later, the meeting over, Adam showed Amy to her room and suggested they meet in the foyer at six-fifteen. As it was a lovely evening, they might walk to the restaurant so that he could show her the sights on the way.

Amy collapsed on the bed, pleased with her day's work. There were a number of leads she and Nick could follow up. She called his office and left a message saying she'd be back in Woolacombe tomorrow evening, suggesting they meet the following morning.

As for Adam Inglis, she was just getting started!

Chapter 6
Amy digs deep

AMY LAY ON THE BED BEFORE DRESSING FOR dinner. She felt strangely at home. The décor was simple enough; a small Stars & Stripes flag on the desk and a photograph of Gerald Ford above. Amy's politics were deeply rooted in Democratic principles and she hoped that, were she to return in November, Jimmy Carter would be smiling down at her. Still, it was comforting to feel that she was in a tiny part of the US, despite being thousands of miles from Norfolk County.

Freshly showered, she sat in front of the mirror to apply a little make-up. She knew Adam had found her attractive in her day gear and it would not hurt to put on a hint of lipstick, especially as the bright red contrasted well with her pale skin and fair hair. Satisfied with the *less is more principle* she picked up the one item of her wardrobe she cherished above everything else.

Memories of Susan, her mother, came flooding back and she sat on the bed hugging the little black dress to her face. Her mom's favourite saying, *cause you just don't know,* resonating clearly and said every time she had helped Amy pack for an overnight trip.

They would end up in fits of laughter, playing out scenarios of meeting tall dark strangers or needing to impress stuffy East-Coast newspaper editors over dinner. Her mother was adamant there was one article of clothing ever-present in her luggage and that was an LBD. Susan's advice had stuck, and Amy never travelled without one.

How she missed her mother. She missed the warmth radiating from her face; missed her wicked sense of humour, her giggle and the smile that captivated everyone she met. Susan Ridd was her own person. She'd been a talented artist with a gallery on Quincy harbour, splitting her time between selling hers and other local artists' work and lecturing history of art at the local college. This pretty petite woman was also a fiercely proud wife to Jim and mother to Amy. She did everything in her power to make sure their lives ran as smoothly as hers seemed to do.

Jim and Susan Ridd were soulmates. Her untimely death from breast cancer had completely devastated her husband, and Amy was convinced it was Susan's premature demise that had brought on her father's illness and, with it, the rapid mental and physical decline of Alzheimer's.

He often whispered to Amy during his early days in hospital that he wanted nothing more than to be with his beloved wife once again, surrounded by her sun-filled seascape paintings and his beloved books.

Amy wiped the tears from her eyes and chided herself for letting her emotions get the better of her. With clutch bag in hand, complete with her tiny notebook, pen, and lipstick, she did a twirl in the mirror and almost toppled over on the patent black high-heel shoes she only ever wore with her LBD.

Pleased with what she saw, she closed her bedroom door and made her way down to the reception. She was early. With no sign of Adam, she had a quiet word with the receptionist who, from her response, obviously enjoyed gossiping about Embassy staff – Adam in particular. The information Amy gleamed proved most useful later that evening. She sat demurely in the foyer as Adam came to greet her. Her appearance was having the desired effect.

The evening went very much to plan as far as Amy was concerned. She had to admit that, for the most part, Adam acted like the perfect gentleman and was an entertaining host. During the short walk to the restaurant, he pointed out local landmarks and was obviously very much at home in this part of London.

The restaurant was tiny. Amy's first impressions were that it had all the characteristics of a lovers' hideaway where illicit encounters could be enjoyed in the intimate atmosphere. Adam was obviously well known to the discrete staff – Amy wondered, as they were guided to *your favourite table, sir* how many unsuspecting young women had been enticed here over the two years he'd been in post.

The menu was as extensive as the restaurant was small, and it had been a long time since Amy had been treated to such fine French cuisine. Adam was keen to show off his knowledge of wine and he selected a Chablis, followed by a Bordeaux, or Claret as Adam called it, finishing with a delicate Sauterne.

As the evening progressed, Adam got more and more tipsy. He didn't notice, when the Sommelier appeared to top up their glasses, Amy giving a surreptitious shake of her head whilst at the same time encouraging him to fill Adam's. He played along happily throughout the evening, pouring the tiniest amount into her glass, whilst always replenishing Adam's to good order.

Once again, she said a silent *thank you* to her dad. Not only had he taught her to play a mean game of poker, but he'd also explained how to appear to be drinking along merrily with everyone else whilst taking tiny sips. Emptying his glass into an adjacent flowerpot when his dinner companion excused him or herself to go to the cloakroom was a favourite ruse. If it could work in her father's time, working with the US Embassy in Moscow, having to endure four-hour dinners with interminable vodka toasts, it could work for his daughter in a dimly lit Mayfair restaurant.

Throughout the evening Amy had purposely kept the conversation away from her uncle's death. As coffee was served, however, she decided it was time for business.

'Adam, I know we weren't going to talk shop, but please do tell me any personal anecdotes about my father and uncle you might've picked up whilst doing your research.'

Adam gazed at her intently; the emotion in his voice when he responded taking Amy completely by surprise.

'Amy, I gotta tell you, your dad was a real hero. Despite not being in a combat role during the war, he proved himself to be one of the bravest men I've ever read about.'

Adam recounted how he had saved a British airman's

life by rescuing him from a Wellington Bomber that had crashed and was about to explode, and how her father had ended up severely burnt and in a coma for days.

'And, as you know, he risked his life trying to save the two members of the tank crew who drowned in horrible circumstances on the day your uncle disappeared.'

Warming to the idea of getting closer to Amy by using what he knew about her father, Adam told her that her dad obviously had liberal views as a young man.

'He was an egalitarian, ahead of his time in his disgust at the way the US Army treated Black GIs during the war.'

'Mind you,' he said. 'I'm not saying he was a saint and I read an interesting report about his relationship with a Lady Margaret, a British journalist. There's nothing to say this was anything but professional but they appear to have gotten to know each other rather well in a very short space of time.'

Amy excused herself at this point and made for the cloakroom. Sitting ungraciously in her locked cubicle, she scribbled some notes with the firm intention of following up on this Lady Margaret first thing in the morning. When she returned Adam had, in her absence, ordered them both a cognac and as he took a large swig, she pretended to take a sip and then asked very casually, whether Adam had found any personal information about her Uncle Billy.

'Ah now,' said Adam, revelling in the chance to reaffirm just how robust his investigations had been on Amy's behalf. 'Corporal Ridd was a different character altogether. He featured in several Military Police reports and was something of a hot-head who seemed to have enjoyed drinking copious amounts of cider and ending up, on one occasion, in the glasshouse.'

Adam described one report where he had come to blows with some local British soldiers, knocking one soldier out in what was reported to be a completely unprovoked attack.

'There appeared to be considerable animosity between Corporal Ridd and some of the British troops based nearby. I think, from what I've read, your father spent considerable time trying to keep his younger brother out of trouble!'

Amy was somewhat distracted on the short walk back to the Embassy. She had allowed Adam to take her arm but did so in a detached kind of way, her mind not on the here and now but playing over again the news she'd just heard about Uncle Billy's scrapes during his time in Devon. Perhaps this Lady Margaret character would be able to elucidate? If, of course, she could track her down.

The climb up the stairs to the floor where Adam had his room was a slow one. He'd obviously had a lot to drink, and Amy anticipated his amorous intentions, bracing herself for the rejection she suspected he might not take kindly to. She politely declined his offer of a nightcap in his room but knew he would insist on walking her to hers. As they stopped outside her door, she quickly put her key in the door and prayed he would not try to force his way in.

'Thank you, Adam. You've been a wonderful host and I'm so grateful for your time today. I'll be sure to write to the Ambassador commending your work and will let him know how very helpful you've been.'

Adam bent forward to kiss her, but Amy ducked under his advancing face and, holding him firmly at arm's length, whispered, 'I'm sure you can't wait for your wife and daughter to arrive this weekend. You must miss them terribly.'

Her words had the desired effect. Adam stepped back, appearing to sober up in an instant. She thanked him again and deftly opened her door, locking it from the inside and saying how much she looked forward to seeing him at breakfast.

After a few moments, she heard him walk back down the corridor and sighed with relief, ever grateful to the Embassy receptionist for the gossip on Adam's family she had passed on earlier that evening.

Chapter 7
Lady Margaret

A MY WASN'T SURE WHETHER IT WAS THE JETLAG OR not wanting to bump into Adam that saw her close the Embassy front door and head down the street a few minutes past six the following morning. She'd woken at five and lain in bed looking at her notes, trying to make some sense of what Adam had told her about her father's and uncle's time in Devon.

There were several leads to follow up. The most intriguing being his reference to a Lady Margaret. Was this some kind of nickname her father had given her, or was she actually titled? And if so, could Amy track her down?

She stopped at the first café she came to for a caffeine-fix. As it kicked in, she pondered more on the female journalist her father had befriended three decades earlier. She looked in her bag to check she'd got her press card and decided to call in a favour from an ex-Globe colleague Alastair Cox, now working for Reuters in London. Her cab driver told her they were heading towards Threadneedle Street in the heart of the City.

As she approached the imposing Royal Exchange

building, she wondered if this was going to be a mistake and if her time would have been better spent trying to see somebody at the MOD. But her journalist instincts told her that to turn up there without an appointment and no contact name to ask for would have been complete folly. Especially when she told them she wanted information about an incident that occurred on a North Devon beach in 1944.

Trusting her judgement, she headed through the grand foyer to a large reception desk where she was directed to the lifts and the fifth floor. When the door opened, the Reuters reception was directly in front of her, and she was greeted by a young girl who looked to Amy as if she should still be at school. 'Probably a new intern,' she said to herself. She could not help but be impressed by the efficient way her request to see Alastair was handled.

After producing her press accreditation, thankfully still valid, she was escorted to another reception area and asked to wait. Two minutes later, as she scanned the magazines, a pot of steaming hot coffee arrived with some delicious shortbread cookies – or biscuits, as Amy was learning to call them.

As she finished her coffee, a tousled young man with a broad smile on his freckled face walked towards her with hand outstretched in welcome. It turned out Alastair was on leave back home in Boston and Matthew was his enthusiastic assistant, obviously relishing having some responsibility in his boss's absence. He led Amy to a small meeting room. She explained her predicament and asked Matthew if he could help. He excused himself and returned promptly with a folder and a tome of a book bound in red cloth with bright gilt lettering.

The folder contained a current register of NUJ members and they looked carefully under L for Lady and M for Margaret but couldn't identify anyone whose entry sounded remotely close.

'If she *is* a member of the aristocracy,' said Amy, 'I can't quite see her being a union member and if she is a similar age to my father, she'd be into her sixties and probably retired.'

They turned their attention to the 1976 edition of Who's Who. Looking under L, Matthew found the entry for Lady Margaret Randall-Harris-Adair. Her date of birth put her at 66 years of age and her profile referred to a long and industrious career as a journalist and advocate for equal rights. Several of her publications were dated 1943/44 and one, in particular stood out: '*Jim Crow segregation for Black GIs is Abhorrent.*'

'That clinches it,' Amy said. 'This has to be our Lady Margaret and there are addresses in Mayfair and somewhere called Castle Combe.'

Amy wrote down the London address and phone number. Matthew ran off to photocopy Lady Margaret's entry, saying she could use the phone in the room and to dial nine for an outside line. She stood by the phone for at least a minute thinking about what she was going to say, keenly aware that this mysterious aristocrat might well have some answers to the questions whirling around in her head.

She couldn't remember her father ever talking about

her, but nor had he said anything about risking his life rescuing an airman from a World-War-Two bomber. In fact, despite her father being an open-book kind of guy, she realised he'd buried his wartime memories deep in his subconscious and left them there. No doubt, she thought, a common trait for war veterans on both sides of the Atlantic.

Amy took a deep breath and dialled. The call was answered after what seemed an interminable delay. The voice on the other end sounded so out of breath that she imagined a wizened old butler.

Whoever he was, his hearing was poor. Amy had to shout. She thought her message had finally been understood when he told her to wait for a minute or two whilst he presumably spoke to Lady Margaret – or her maid?

Five minutes later, and with Amy despairing that he would ever return, the butler told her that her Ladyship was about to leave for the country, but that she could spare Amy a few moments of her time if she could be in Mayfair in the next thirty minutes. Amy rushed out of the room with a satisfied smile on her face. Matthew was walking towards her with the profile. She gave him a hug; told him she would tell Alastair how lucky he was to have him, and ran to the lifts to find another black cab for her journey to Audley Square.

The Square seemed to Amy a wonderful place to live; imposing mid eighteenth-century buildings surrounded by a garden, enclosed on all sides by mature trees creating the best of both worlds – a luxurious home in the heart of London with its own green oasis. Amy knocked gingerly on the impressive door of No 48 and waited… and waited.

When no one came, she realised that if the person she had spoken to was the deaf butler, he probably hadn't heard her tentative knock. She knocked again more firmly this time. At last, the door opened slowly to reveal a stooped and extremely old man in a well-worn black suit, stiff white collar and black tie which Amy assumed was standard attire for butlers to the aristocracy.

He ushered her in and asked her to wait. Amy was surrounded by seven antique brown leather suitcases monogrammed in gold with the initials MRHA. Lady Margaret didn't travel lightly.

As the minutes passed and with no sign of Lady Margaret or the butler, Amy was beginning to think he'd forgotten all about her. She was about to cough loudly when the butler reappeared and led her to a door at the end of the hallway. He knocked, opened it slowly, and shuffled away. Amy stood motionless – not sure whether to enter the grand drawing room or wait to be invited by the extremely elegant woman sitting on a purple velvet chaise longue. Slim with light-grey hair cut short, reminiscent of the supermodel Twiggy in the mid-60's, Lady Margaret turned towards Amy.

'Come in, girl, don't stand there gawping. Sit down beside me so that I can have a good look at you.'

Amy sat as close to her as she thought appropriate and Lady Margaret, to Amy's surprise, proceeded to touch her face, tracing the outline with her fingers. It was only then that Amy realised that she must be blind or, at best, extremely myopic.

'You've got your father's fine features and if your eyes

are any match for his, you certainly won't fall short in the looks department. Now, tell me how your father is and what brings you to London.'

Having regained her composure, Amy told her of her father's recent demise and why she was in England on his behalf investigating something that had troubled him deeply for many years. Lady Margaret was a good listener but, knowing time was limited, or probably because she was used to being the centre of attention, put her finger to her lips and stopped Amy in mid-flow.

'I'm so sorry to hear about your father. Jim was a good man. He was brave, kind and damn good at the PAO role they dumped on him. That's how we met. And just to put the record straight, despite my attempting to seduce him on more than one occasion, he was having none of it.'

She explained to Amy that she wasn't used to being rejected, but it hadn't taken her long to realise that his friendship was more important than a quick fling between the sheets. She said Jim taught her a lot about social justice and risked his army career by giving her the heads-up about the appalling discrimination black GIs endured when serving their country in wartime.

'That gave me the impetus to focus on human rights issues for the next twenty years before my sight started failing and glaucoma took its ghastly hold. Now, if you look on the bookshelf by the piano, you'll see a black-and-white photo of your father and mother with you as a toddler.'

Amy walked across to a shelf adorned with photos, all finely mounted in slim silver frames. She found the Ridd family photo and turned it over to read the inscription on the back: *To Lady M, a dear friend and ally, from Jim, Susan, and Amy. Quincy 1946.*

'You must have been about three years old when that photograph was taken. It was typical of your father to want to share his family with me.'

She said that they sadly lost touch soon after, but that he was often in her thoughts. The photo brought back very pleasant memories of their work together.

'I can see the photograph clearly in my head. So I want you to have it as a memento to remember me by.'

Amy's protestations were quickly rejected, and she sat back down, took hold of one of Lady M's hands and told her of her escapades with Adam Inglis the previous evening.

'Oh, darling, you should have slept with him,' Lady Margaret scolded her. 'I obtained most of my best stories from pillow talk.'

Their discussion took on a more serious note when Amy explained what Adam had said about Uncle Billy, saying she was just not sure how best to proceed, especially with not having any contacts at the MOD, let alone finding out more about pub fights with British soldiers. At that moment, the butler knocked to inform Lady Margaret that her car was loaded, and ready to leave for Wiltshire.

'I will be five minutes, Hargreaves – no more, no less.'

As the door closed, she told Amy that Hargreaves had been with her forty years and she didn't have the heart to let him go. He apparently lived very comfortably in the servants' quarters in the basement and would have been the person Amy's father had spoken to on the telephone thirty-three years earlier.

She told Amy to leave the MOD to her. Having 'entertained' some of the top brass over the years, she should be able to discover what happened on the day her uncle disappeared. She would also call in some favours to see if she could obtain a list of the British soldiers on Uncle Billy's craft.

'That would give you and your private investigator something to work on. As for your uncle's punch-ups, something is ringing bells. I vaguely remember warning your father about a mendacious individual Billy needed to be wary of.'

She said her assistant Stephanie acted as her eyes these days. When she got back from the country next week, she'd tell her where to find the war diaries.

'This is quite like old times. Who knows, we may even visit you in Woolacombe? I've fond memories of the hotel and especially playing the grand piano with all those gorgeous young men lusting after me. Trust me to pick your father for a tryst!'

Amy walked Lady Margaret to the door and helped her down the front steps, watching as the chauffeur guided her into the back seat of the Bentley. She wound down the window and as if by a sixth sense looked straight at where Amy stood, clutching the treasured photo frame to her breast.

'Don't forget to have some fun, Amy. Life's too short to dwell on the past for too long. Next time we meet, I want to hear about your latest love affair. And by the way, the

Diorella perfume you're wearing suits you. It epitomises your free spirit.'

As the Bentley glided away, Amy realised she'd just said au revoir to a remarkable woman.

Chapter 8
Major Tom

AT THE SAME MOMENT, NICK WAS PLANNING TO meet Major Tom White at his home in Braunton. He'd called earlier that morning and spoken to Annie, Tom's housekeeper. She'd told him that there was no way Tom was going to be indoors on a bright sunny day like today. As it was a Thursday, he'd be playing his weekly foursomes at Westward Ho! with three old friends.

Nick was tempted to drive around the headland to meet Tom at the club. On Annie's advice, he decided it would be better to let him come home, have his afternoon nap and eat the light supper she'd prepared for him. She'd leave a message for Tom to say Nick would drop in about six o'clock.

He and Amy had agreed that, when talking to the locals, Nick would explain he was helping a journalist research the impact of American troops in England in WW2 for a series of articles she was writing.

As the clock of St Brannocks Parish Church struck six, Nick knocked on Tom's door. It was an artisan cottage, hidden away in the oldest part of the village, steeped in farming and salmon fishing. He had with him the black-and-white photograph of the US tanks on Saunton, his notebook and a couple of bottles of Guinness, Tom's favourite tipple according to the club's bar steward.

The door opened to reveal sparkling eyes, a welcoming smile and affection radiating from a well-worn face that reflected every one of Tom's seventy-nine years. Looking wistfully at the nine-iron he was used to seeing in Nick's right hand, he placed it by the front door and knew now was not the time to lecture him about playing again.

'Come in, Nick. Make yourself at home and I'll get the glasses.'

Nick did the honours and handed a glass to Tom who sipped his drink as if it were nectar from the gods.

'Cheers Tom, and thanks for sparing the time to see me.'

'Time's not in short supply when you get to my age, Nick, and what could be better than talking about golf and the old days over a drink of stout. Now what can I help you with?'

'First things first. How was your game at Westward Ho!?'

Tom waxed lyrical for several minutes describing his round of golf with the enthusiasm of a novice. Tom and his partner had won on the 18th with Tom holing a six-footer to win the match and share in the spoils of a hearty lunch paid for by the losing pair.

To Tom, golf was much more than a sport. For half-a-century, it had been a way of life that brought him companionship, exercise and mental focus.

'It keeps me young, and where else would anyone want to be on a beautiful day like today? Now, enough of my rambling. Tell me what has brought you to my humble abode this evening.'

Nick passed the photograph to him, explained he was assisting Amy Ridd, an American client who was keen to learn more about the area in the war years. Tom stared at the photo for what seemed an age without saying anything. It appeared to be the catalyst for a myriad of memories, some good, some not so good. He took a long swig of his drink, put the glass gently on the table and looked at Nick, the hint of tears in his eyes telling their own story.

'This photograph takes me back to a time that was like nothing I will ever experience again in my lifetime, and one I will certainly never forget.'

Tom explained his wife Joan had died of TB in 1939 at the age of thirty-seven, just a few months before war broke out. They'd not been blessed with children and he was a lonely, angry, and frustrated middle-aged man of forty-two.

'Angry,' he said 'because our good Lord saw fit to take the only woman I'd ever loved. And frustrated because I was a farmer and one year over the conscription age. Despite serving in the Great War, and being awarded the Victoria Cross, all I was allowed to do was join the Home Guard.'

He told Tom he'd done his bit in what was called *the last line of defence* against the invasion everyone thought was inevitable. But that was no consolation, he said, for not being allowed to sign up. He had resented having to wet nurse a load of old men, expected to fight with a motley collection of weapons.

'Because of my experience in 1914-18, I was appointed Company Commander for the Braunton Area with the rank of major, reporting to the Battalion Commander in Barnstaple until we were disbanded in 1945. Major Tom stuck!'

Tom stopped talking as if in a trance. Nick let him reflect for a few moments, sipping quietly on his drink, and then brought Tom back to the here and now.

'Braunton must have been a very different place to live when the American troops arrived?'

'It certainly was, Nick. I only hope my memory is good enough to provide you and your American with some useful information. If not, I kept a diary during the war which you might find helpful. But let's start with the photograph.'

Tom explained how the club had housed the large number of American tanks used in the training exercises on the dunes and beaches. Both courses were occupied by American military. No golf was played from 1942 until green staff and German prisoners-of-war made them fit for purpose almost a decade later.

'You'll appreciate playing golf was not uppermost in our minds at that time, and we locals were proud of Saunton's role in helping our American allies prepare for the D-Day landings.'

He said there were many stories told about the course during the latter years of the war. There was even a rumour that an American GI was murdered by some locals and buried under a bunker on the West Course.

'All stuff and nonsense I expect!'

Tom walked gingerly to a mahogany bookcase that looked as old as its owner. He unlocked a cupboard and pulled out several black leather-bound books. He found the one he was looking for and wiped the dust off the book with his sleeve.

'I've not looked at this for over twenty-five years, nor have I shared its contents with anyone before now.'

Tom told Nick the diary would provide a good insight into what lives were like for the locals during the war and handed it over – with one condition.

'These memories are personal to me and me alone Nick. If your client does want to use any of the material, she must come and talk to me first. Some things should remain where they belong – in the past.'

Nick agreed, and promised to bring Amy with him next time.

'Make sure you do, lad. It will be good to talk to an American again. I think my last time was a couple of days before D-Day in June '44.'

Tom opened his front door, shook Nick firmly by the hand and sent him on his way, diary in hand, both men oblivious to the shady-looking character watching intently from across the street.

Chapter 9
Tom's Diary

THE DRIVER OF THE SILVER JAGUAR KEPT A STEADY distance behind the mini cooper, well used to tailing cars on the winding coast road to Saunton. He'd had many years of practice in a former life. Being patient had gone with the territory; waiting for the right deal; waiting for the right time for retribution. All part and parcel of the night job. Things were somewhat different now. He was a respectable businessman, a prominent figure in the local community with numerous lackeys on his books; paid to do his dirty work; paid to keep their eyes out for the next opportunity... or threat.

Biding his time brought back memories of his life as a spiv. He smiled as he remembered wheeler-dealing in anything he could lay his hands on back then – nylons, condoms or fags from those bastard yanks. Now look at him; Mr Big in his made-to-measure suits; running legit businesses with plenty of cash to splash around on his lady friends and the occasional prostitute when a bit of rough sex took his fancy. Posh house, posh car, posh holidays in Benidorm with his latest floosie.

'Boy done good.' he said to himself. There was no way he was going to let some amateur detective or smart-arse American bitch take everything away from him.

Nick climbed the hill towards Saunton Sands Hotel, unaware of the car tailing him. He turned sharp left into the golf club car park. There were still plenty of cars around as golfers savoured the delights of the nineteenth hole. He entered his office, Tom's diary in hand and emerged a couple of minutes later with the Ridd case file and diary safe in his briefcase, and headed for home.

Jaguar *FRT 1* pulled out of the car park five minutes later. He'd seen all he needed to see. He had another deal to close and a new woman to take to bed. Job done, for now.

At eight that evening, Nick made himself a sandwich and coffee and sat down at his dining table with Tom's diary. His plan was to scan through it for an hour or so and then have some down time.

He was still at the table four hours later.

Tom had recorded his thoughts in a series of jottings, his entries a mixture of humour and pathos. They painted a picture in Nick's head of the challenges the local population faced in wartime Britain, and would certainly help Amy conceptualise her father's and uncle's time in North Devon. But there was nothing yet that offered any clues as to what might have happened to Billy. He read on.

3rd September 1939 – We are at War.
I heard the announcement on the BBC. Neville Chamberlain's glum voice announcing a state of war existed between us and Germany.

10th September saw the arrival of the London Yeomanry to defend the North Devon coastline against invasion. A territorial unit made up of bank clerks and office workers, they appear keen enough, but heaven help us if this is who we have to rely on to save us from the Hun.

Nick checked his watch and realised he'd been immersed in Tom's jottings for hours. He made himself another coffee and spotted a headline, underlined twice in black ink by Tom. It screamed out at him from the bottom of the page.

25th September – They're here! The Yanks have arrived! And a bloody noisy lot they are too!

2nd October – The rumours we'd heard over the past few weeks have turned out to be true. Thousands of GIs are setting up camps from Braunton to Mortehoe; they're here to train on our beaches for the assault on Normandy.

9th October – Twenty-five square miles of coastline between Woolacombe and Appledore have been acquired to train for the D-day landings. They've brought masses of equipment – amphibious landing craft, jeeps, tanks, trucks and one hell of a lot of armaments.

15th October – An Assault Training Centre has been

established and the Home Guard has been asked to support them on exercises using our local knowledge. At last, something useful for me to do!

22nd October – They've commandeered the Bungalow Café in Woolacombe; turned it into a Red Cross Centre and renamed it The Red Barn. Is nothing sacred?

29th October – Several GIs were killed in training today. They're now using live ammunition. Thank you Eisenhower; I'm sure the dead soldiers' families think the world of you.

4th November – Tensions have been high today as local families were kicked out of their houses to accommodate GI officers. Animosity is growing and I worry where it might lead.

12th November – What's wrong with these Yanks? They wanted to introduce a colour bar but am proud to say our landlords weren't having any of it and threatened to ban the white GIs in favour of the black soldiers who are, by and large, more polite and considerate to the locals.

Nick scanned the next few months' entries but nothing much grabbed his attention until he came to the spring of '44.

30th March – More hostility this week with pub

fights between the GIs and our soldiers jealous of the yanks courting local lasses. I wonder just how many GI brides will be leaving for the US when the war is over. And GI babies!

19th April – It's not all bad news between the Brits and the yanks. Heard today about the bravery of an American officer who saved the life of a British airman when his Wimpy bomber crashed on Morte Point. Witnesses said it was the bravest thing they'd ever seen. Just hope both the airman and the GI make it.

Nick drank the cold dregs of his coffee as he flicked through several more pages of the diary. He was just about to head for bed, when Tom's notes returned to further tension between the GIs and British troops.

27th April – the Home Guard was called out yesterday evening after a ruckus at the Jubilee pub. I arrived with several men to see AMPs (nasty buggers!) piling into the pub and bringing out several GIs and bundling them into an open truck. They asked us to check on the British soldiers involved in the brawl. One of them looked at me as he slinked off into the night, his tail between his legs.

Bob Taylor, the landlord, told me the Brits were to blame. One soldier in particular went out of his way to cause trouble with the GIs but had met his match with a tall fair-haired American Bob knew as Billy.

Nick thought there must have been hundreds, if not thousands of GIs called Billy stationed locally. But it was a start. He couldn't stop now. His persistence was rewarded when he found what he'd been hoping for.

1st June – There's to be a final exercise tomorrow between British and GIs troops to land amphibious craft on Woolacombe Beach. My battalion is to be stationed up in the dunes to observe and assist should any of the landing craft get into difficulties.

2nd June – What a disastrous day! The mistake was to carry out the exercise in such appalling weather. I heard the Coast Guard Coxswain had strongly advised aborting the exercise. The 'powers that be' supposedly knew better!

One of the landing craft got into difficulty and capsized near the rocks. We helped exhausted soldiers to the safety of dry land, but two GIs drowned in their overturned tank and another is missing, presumed drowned. His body has not yet been recovered.

One Tommy staggered out of the sea a long time after the exercise was over, but he seemed ok. His face seemed vaguely familiar.

Nick didn't get much sleep that night.

Chapter 10
The American Road

THE NEXT MORNING, AMY AND NICK SAT AT A TABLE in the residents' lounge of Amy's hotel, both totally engrossed in the papers spread out in front of them – Amy's nose in Tom's diary and Nick absorbed in Amy's notes from her meetings in London with Adam Inglis and Lady M.

Amy, captivated by Tom's words, would have gladly sat there all day. The diary was a treasure-trove of invaluable information. And, intriguingly for Amy, the entries Tom had made were building a picture of what her father's life had been like in Woolacombe all those years ago.

Nick's excitement grew as he pieced together Amy's threads with the notes he'd made the previous evening – the fight in the pub *(surely this must be Uncle Billy?)*, Lt Frye's report *(was he still alive?)*, could they track down Uncle Billy's Section Leader Major Paulson, *(would Lady M come up trumps with the MOD?)*, Major Tom's recollection of the lone British soldier staggering out of the sea *(was it significant Tom felt he recognised him from somewhere?)*

So much to work on, thought Nick. But where to start?

'Amy, we should ...'

He stopped mid-sentence. Amy looked across at him with tear-filled eyes. He hardly recognised the self-assured young woman he'd met just days before.

'I'm sorry Nick. I've just read Tom's entry about the GI saving an RAF officer after his plane crashed on a local headland. Adam Inglis told me my father risked his life to rescue an airman on Morte Point. Reading it in black and white has made me realise how much I miss him and mom. I guess I'm just a bit homesick.'

Nick pondered a moment.

'Didn't you tell me you've brought your hiking boots? Go and put them on and I'll take you to a tiny part of the USA very close to here. And some fresh air will do us both good.'

Amy gave him a quizzical look but, pleased and intrigued that Nick had taken control, she headed for her room. She returned ten minutes later, looking more like her old self and with the hint of a smile on her face. Nick offered to drive so that she could sit and enjoy the view. He was not just being gallant. He relished the opportunity of sitting behind the wheel of her sleek convertible with the roof down.

As they passed through the local villages, Nick pointed out the landmarks and places of interest that related to the Americans' time here in 1943/44. But as they climbed the hill out of Croyde village, he saw an old grey Ford Transit van in his rear mirror that he'd noticed as they'd left Woolacombe. It appeared to be keeping a constant distance behind him. If he didn't know better, he'd think they were being followed. He pulled sharply into a layby so that Amy could see the vast expanse of Saunton Sands with a hint of the golf courses behind.

As Nick explained the important role the beaches had played in Billy's life, the grey van passed them, heading towards Braunton. Scolding himself for letting his imagination get the better of him, he moved on, passing the imposing white structure of Saunton Sands Hotel. Amy was beginning to look and sound like her old self again. A mile further on he stopped the car and pointed to the large housing estate on their left.

'That was open fields in the 1940s and is most probably where Billy lived. The camp resembled a self-contained village with Nissan Huts housing ten-thousand men at any one time. It had shops, recreation halls and anything else the soldiers might need, all built apparently by the hard labour of black GIs.'

'You have been doing your homework!' said Amy, her mood lightening the more engrossed she became in Nick's narrative. As he turned back onto the main road, the grey van was behind them once again. Sounding calmer than he felt, he asked Amy to get out her notepad.

'Don't look behind but I've a nasty feeling we're being followed. I'll call out the registration for you to write down. It may be something or nothing, but it won't do any harm to get it checked out by my contact in the local police.'

Amy was stoical but relieved when Nick turned off the main road into a small car park. The van went speeding past. Doing his best to avoid the potholes, he parked the Caravelle in front of a large, weathered notice board that had seen better days.

'Welcome to the American Road,' he said, pointing to the stone track beyond an iron gate with a sign telling them that only military vehicles could access the dunes.

'This used to be an old ferry track that weaved its way to the sea. When your countrymen arrived, they widened and straightened it to transport all the assault vehicles from their camp to the beach. Let's see what the notice board can tell us about Braunton Burrows.'

In different circumstances, Amy would have been interested in learning about the thirty-foot high dunes and the myriad of bridleways that crisscrossed the rugged landscape. But not this morning. She was too engrossed in a faded black-and-white photograph of US soldiers. They were loading an assault vehicle onto a concrete structure, built in the dunes, to replicate the amphibious landing craft. Amy was scrutinising their faces.

'I know it's stupid of me to think Billy could be one of them and not great odds with nine GIs out of ten-thousand, but what really hits home is how young they are.'

She thought they looked as if they'd just left high school. She supposed photos like this were taken to inform the folks back home what the GIs were doing in this faraway land. Nick left Amy to her thoughts, locked the car and picked up his nine iron for the ramble towards the estuary at Crow Point.

'We obviously learnt a thing or two from the Romans,' joked Amy as they set off along the dead straight road. Every few hundred yards on their right there were large stiles enabling access to the dunes themselves, many with signs reminding walkers of *no fires, camping, litter or naturist activities.*

'The mind boggles,' laughed Amy, as she imagined naked men and women dancing around their open fire.

'We have a few naturist beaches near Quincy but I suspect our summers are somewhat warmer than here!'

As they got closer to the estuary, Nick suggested a detour into the dunes. They climbed a stile and scrambled across the rough terrain towards a well-worn grass path that took them towards the water's edge. His knee was beginning to ache and Amy, noticing his limp becoming more pronounced, suggested they stop to take in the view.

Nick pointed out the village of Instow at the junction of the Taw and Torridge rivers and, beyond that, the old fishing port of Appledore and the Royal North Devon Golf course in the distance.

'The Club was founded in 1864 and designed by the Scottish golf architect Old Tom Morris. It was home to a local player JH Taylor and he dominated the game for thirty years, winning five Open Championships including the US Open in 1913!'

As Amy smiled at the thought of how much her father would have enjoyed the golfing banter with Nick, the calm of the dunes was suddenly shattered. A loud crack rang out and a bullet embedded itself in a fence post, not more than five feet from where they stood. Nick instinctively pulled Amy down and rolled on top of her to shield her body. They lay motionless, not daring to move, waiting expectantly for the next shot.

After several minutes, Nick whispered to Amy that he was going to throw his nine iron towards the fence post to see if their pursuer shot again. He lobbed the club into the air, fully expecting another bullet to fracture the silence. Nothing happened. Amy was curled up in a small ball, her body shaking and a look of complete bewilderment on her face. Nick took his sweat top from his shoulders and wrapped it around her.

'I'm guessing that was a message from our friends in the transit van,' he whispered. 'If I'm right, the shot was a warning to frighten us off and they're probably long gone by now.'

'And if you're wrong? We're sitting ducks here in the middle of nowhere and a good mile from the car. Someone isn't happy with us asking questions and you know what that means.'

'It means we're on to something.' Nick replied. 'It means somebody may have been hiding the truth behind Billy's disappearance for over thirty years. And that somebody doesn't want us to find out what it is!'

'I owe you,' said Amy.

'Owe me for what?' asked Nick.

'You didn't hesitate to shield me. I didn't realise your day rates included bodyguard duties!'

'All part of the service. Let's hope for both our sakes, it doesn't happen again.'

It took an agonising thirty minutes to reach the car park. Crouching as low as they could, Nick led Amy on a meandering route using the high dunes for cover and avoiding exposed footpaths. His knee hurt like hell. After a particularly undulating stretch, he let out a cry, cursed loudly, threw down his nine iron and collapsed to the ground rubbing his knee.

'My knee will be the size of a football by the end of the day. It just makes me so angry.'

Amy knelt beside him. 'Stop beating yourself up. There's nothing wrong with giving vent to your feelings. It's much better than bottling them up, and I should know. My dad was a past master at that. Having a good rant is fine by me.'

A couple of minutes later, Amy helped Nick to his feet and they made their way back to her car. It was the only one in the car park and there was no sign of the transit van. As they got closer, it was obvious something was wrong. The car looked very lopsided. The nearside front and back tyres had been slashed and were completely flat and there was an ugly scratch running the whole length of the bodywork.

'No quick getaway then,' said Nick.

He saw the piece of paper tucked under the wiper blade, the note looking as if it had been torn from a school exercise book. Holding it by his fingertips, he let Amy read the scribbled words.

Piss off home yank
There aint nothin for you here
We had enough of your kind during the war
We won't miss next time

Chapter 11
Breaking and entering

A S THEY SAT IN A TAXI ON THEIR WAY TO HIS OFFICE, Nick suggested that perhaps Amy should put her safety above everything else, get on a plane back to Boston and leave him to unravel the mystery behind Billy's disappearance.

Amy gave it short shrift!

'I'm not leaving you to have all the fun. And besides, we're just beginning to make progress.'

Their visit to the police station in Braunton had not been a productive one. They'd debated the merits of telling the police everything but decided not to say anything about the shooting or the note.

A young police constable had told them the grey van had been stolen from outside a pub in Ilfracombe, probably by joy riders. He had been perplexed about the vandalism to Amy's car, telling them malicious damage was unusual around these parts. He asked them if they could think of anyone who might have a grudge against them. They had shaken their heads.

As their taxi approached the clubhouse, a police car was parked outside Nick's office with its lights flashing. Bill, the club secretary came striding towards them, a troubled look on his face.

'You'd better come and take a look.'

Nick's office door was hanging off and the lock looked as if a crowbar had been used to smash it. His usually pristine office had been ransacked, filing cabinets upended, papers strewn all over the floor. His desk was on its side, the telephone pulled off the wall and his fax machine smashed to pieces. The only things not damaged were his Ryder Cup bag and the team photo above it.

'That's ironic,' said Nick. 'The only items of real value to me haven't been touched.'

The police constable told Nick they'd taken a statement from Bill and would start checking for fingerprints. Not that he was hopeful of finding any.

'They didn't take your petty cash box, so it looks as if they were searching for something specific. Any idea what that could be?'

Nick and Amy looked at one another. They knew what that something was.

'Probably some incriminating paperwork relating to one of the cases I'm working on,' said Nick. 'I'm going to borrow the pool car to take Amy back to her hotel and will be back soon to clear up this mess.'

* * *

When Amy opened the door to her room, she let out a small cry of alarm. The room had been ransacked, suitcases thrown open and clothing strewn all over the floor. Her underwear had been laid out on the bed, bras and panties slashed to pieces in what looked like a frenzied attack on her most intimate of possessions.

Nausea rose in her throat at the feeling of being violated. Shock gave way to anger; anger turned to panic. She raced to the bedside cabinet and opened the drawer and slumped to the floor, the pieces of jewellery she treasured more than anything in the world clutched to her breast.

'My mom gave me these. Every ring and necklace has its own story and each has its own place in my heart; a reminder of how much she taught me, loved me. This has now gotten very personal, Nick. We're dealing with one sick bastard.'

Nick went off in search of the hotel manager and they returned a couple of minutes later together with a diminutive figure who Amy assumed was a chamber maid. Her name tag said Denise and from the state of her face, it was obvious she'd been crying.

The manager was incandescent with rage. He told them he hadn't experienced anything like this in his thirty-year career. He wanted to call the police, but Nick suggested they should hear what Denise had to say first. She was obviously petrified of the manager and looked as if she was going to be physically sick. Amy gave her a glass of water and guided her to one of the sofas.

'Take your time and tell us in your own words what happened.'

'I was in the corridor and had just finished cleaning the bedroom next to this one when a man in a dark suit came up the stairs, fumbling in his pocket. He told me he'd forgotten his key and asked me to open this door, saying he needed some urgent papers for his meeting and would only be a moment.'

Denise told them he looked just like the kind of business guests who stayed at the hotel and that she opened the door with her master key and carried on cleaning her next room. It was only when she'd overheard the conversation in reception about someone disturbing things in a bedroom that she came forward.

'I am so sorry Miss, so very sorry.'

'You will be Ms Shaw,' said the manager. 'You can go and pack up your locker. Your time in this establishment, all six weeks of it, has come to an end.'

Denise burst out crying and headed for the door. Amy got up, caught hold of her and gave her a hug.

'That's not going to happen,' she said and beckoned the manager to join her in the corridor, leaving a desolate Denise in the room with Nick. She knew he'd get as accurate a description of the intruder as Denise could give in her distressed state.

'Firstly, Mr Johnson, you are not going to get rid of Denise. If you do, I'll write an article for one of your national newspapers castigating this hotel and the appalling way the management treats its staff. Secondly, you're going to instigate a staff training programme to ensure they understand room security and have clear procedures to follow, should anything like this ever happen again.'

Amy told the beleaguered manager that he should apologise to Denise for losing his temper and thank her for being brave enough to admit her mistake.

'Most people wouldn't have come forward as she did. Instead of reprimanding her, you should be acknowledging her honesty. I hope we understand each other?'

'Of course, Miss Ridd, you're quite right. I will see to it straightaway.'

As she went back into the room, Nick smiled at Amy and gave a little clap.

'I suppose you heard all that?' asked Amy.

'Every word. Now, let's go and check you know where.'

The duty manager guided them down a winding corridor to the bowels of the hotel and opened the vast door to the hotel safe. He handed them a deposit box which Amy opened with the small key she kept on her necklace. Having satisfied themselves that the contents were in order, they made their way back out to the pool car.

As Nick got in, Amy voiced what they were both thinking. 'Whoever we're up against suspects we have Tom's diary and is obviously concerned there's something incriminating in it.'

'That's one of the points we need to put to Tom just as soon as we can,' Nick replied. 'By the way, Denise told me she's something of an artist. She's going to draw the intruder's face tonight and bring the sketch to your room first thing tomorrow morning. Let's meet up this evening and I'll treat you to supper at the local hostelry your father suggested in his letter.'

* * *

Amy's face gave it away. When Nick entered the hotel

lobby a few hours later, he knew something significant had happened. She ushered him to a quiet corner.

'This fax was delivered to my room a few minutes ago.'

Dear Amy

> *I'm dictating this note to Stephanie.*

> *I called in some favours with the MOD hierarchy (it's amazing how effective a few subtle reminders of their misspent youth can be!). Despite much protestation that what I was asking for would be buried deep in the archives, my favourite Vice Chief of the Defence Staff came up trumps!*

> *He can't guarantee the names of the British troops didn't change as the date of the joint exercise drew closer but couldn't find any reason why they would. The darling man even got his minions to find out whether the individuals were still alive and their whereabouts. Very sadly, the majority of them died on the Normandy beaches. He did add a footnote to say there may be some gaps, but it would be inadvisable for the MOD to be seen to dig any deeper. In other words, 'don't ask me for anything else!'*

British Soldiers in Billy's Landing Craft – 2nd June 1944:

Major Allan Paulton – Section Leader – In a care home in Exeter

24 members of the Devonshire Regiment – Killed in the D-Day Landings

Private Ted Smithers – Believed to be living near Ilfracombe, North Devon

Corporal John Akers – Killed in Normandy five weeks after D-Day

Corporal Jack Acon – Killed in Normandy seven weeks after D-Day

Major Peter White – Section Leader of Sword landing-craft – Living in France, whereabouts unknown

I've not forgotten about trying to unearth the name of the troublemaker I warned your father about. Stephanie is going to spend tomorrow going through my Devon notebooks and I will telephone you if we strike gold.

> *Yours affectionately*
> *Lady M*

PS Make sure you have some fun!

Nick read the fax again, his excitement palpable. They had names to follow up. They were closing in.

Chapter 12
The Red Barn

THE PUB WAS CENTRE STAGE IN WOOLACOMBE, JUST as it had been in 1943. Located next to the Esplanade, close to the beach car park and village shops, its large bright red roof acted like a beacon to locals and tourists alike. The establishment prided itself on opening every day of the year except Christmas Day, whether it was serving one customer or one hundred. It did not, unlike many of the other venues in the village, retreat into winter hibernation.

A variety of colourful surf boards hung over what was reputed to be the longest bar in North Devon, with large black and white photographs of surfers plying their trade in Woolacombe's surf, with their ancient VW camper vans parked nearby. It had no airs and graces, no pretence at being anything but big and brash. It served old-fashioned grub and pints a plenty, all accompanied by a jukebox playing Surfin' USA and other Beach-Boy favourites.

Amy's eyes took in the dark interior with its wooden benches and stained linoleum flooring. Posh it was not, and she'd certainly not seen anything like it back home. She warmed to its lack of pretentiousness.

'Your father mentioned this place in his letter,' said Nick. 'It was a favourite with the GIs, and Billy probably spent many hours here. According to Tom's diary, it was a GI who dubbed it the Red Barn; the name stuck and the business has grown into the thriving one it is today.'

Nick guided Amy through the maze of tables and chairs and found the quietest corner he could, away from the music and the crowds at the bar. He left her gazing at all the memorabilia and returned a couple of minutes later with their drinks.

'You sure know how to show a girl a good time, Nick!'

The wall clock chimed seven as they looked through the menu: bangers and mash, shepherd's pie, and similar hearty meals to feed the surfing community. They were waiting for someone called Martin to join them. Nick had described him as his eyes and ears in the local community; a trusted friend who had the uncanny knack of finding out things that eluded everyone else.

'He's a valuable colleague who's worked with me since day one and is a mine of local information. But he's one of the shyest men I've ever met. Take my word for it, appearances *can* be deceptive.'

They turned to see a tall, extremely thin middle-aged man coming through the front door, trailing a dog of indeterminate breed on a length of old string. The man's long salt and pepper hair was tied back in a ponytail below his shoulders by a bright red ribbon, and he wore a faded blue denim top and jeans that looked as old as he was. His ruddy face bore all the craggy signs of someone who spent most of his time outdoors in the sun and wind.

Amy likened him to the Californian hippies she'd come across on the trip to the west coast she had taken with her best friend after leaving college. Distant memories came to mind of open fires on the beach, too much wine, and inept singers with guitars in hand not doing justice to Dylan's *Blowing in the Wind.*

It was on a Santa Barbara beach that she'd had her one and only flirtation with marijuana. Her heart missed a beat as she remembered making love for the first time amongst the white sandy coves, below a sky totally devoid of ambient light, full to overflowing with stars so bright you wanted to reach up and touch them.

She was brought back to reality as Martin tied his mongrel to their table leg beckoning for him to sit. The dog complied, apparently happy to rest and enjoy the smell of food wafting from the nearby kitchen.

'A pint of Taunton will do it,' Martin said to Nick in his broad North Devon accent with its relaxed cadence and lengthened vowels. An accent, so Amy had read, best described as an amalgam of Anglo Saxon, old French, and vintage cider.

As Nick left the two of them together and headed for the bar, Martin sat down and without saying a word, slowly looked Amy up and down. This, she sensed, was not an appraisal of her appearance but more akin to an introvert weighing up the situation before venturing a greeting. His actions had none of the sexual overtones she was used to from male colleagues who seemed to think her shapely figure gave them the right to make sexual innuendos on a daily basis.

'You're not from these parts then,' Martin said, relieved he'd managed to say anything at all to the attractive young woman sitting opposite him. He was relatively at ease with people he knew but meeting a person for the first time was always something of an ordeal.

'No, I'm not. But my great-great grandfather was born and brought up in Mortehoe before emigrating to the States. So, I can make claim to having North Devon roots and I'm very proud of my heritage. My name's Amy, Amy Ridd.'

Martin seemed to take an age to mull over this information. As Nick returned with his drink, he whispered softly 'welcome home, then, miss.'

'Now that you two have met, let's order some supper and we can get down to business. Your usual, Martin?' Nick asked. And, as if by explanation to Amy, who was struggling to find anything on the menu that was remotely healthy, he volunteered that Martin would have sausages and mash with onion gravy as he did every time they ate here.

'Nothing wrong with sticking to what you know,' said Martin quietly, 'and Jumble will share it with me.'

He told Amy he'd found the dog a year ago almost starved to death, tethered to a barn door at a local farm he walked past regularly. He'd found out who the farmer was, reported him to the RSPCA and took the dog to a friendly vet who fought hard to save him, having informed Martin he was a real jumble of breeds.

'That's how he got his name and I think there's a good dose of Labrador in him the way he loves his food.'

As they ate, Nick brought Martin up to speed – the warning shot on the dunes, the damage to Amy's Caravelle, the note that left little to the imagination and the two break-ins. He explained Amy was in North Devon to find out more about her father's and uncle's time here during the war, and to discover what they could about her uncle's disappearance in the sea, just days before the departure for Normandy.

Martin listened intently. He didn't interrupt or ask questions, and just seemed to soak up all the information. They finished their food and sat in silence for a few moments, the jukebox now playing softly in the background, barely audible above the babble of conversations taking place around them. Nick replenished their drinks and the three of them talked through several scenarios and agreed who was going to do what.

Martin knew many of the locals in this part of the world. It was agreed he would put the word out that Nick was offering a £100 reward for information about damage to the red Caravelle. He was confident this would arouse interest amongst the local riff-raff and generate some leads. He'd also trace Bob Taylor, the Jubilee Inn's landlord at the time of the fight in December 1943 and talk to ex-colleagues at Ilfracombe Coast Guard to find out who the coxswain was when the joint exercise took place. The name Ted Smithers rang a bell with him, and he volunteered to track him down.

Nick and Amy would concentrate on Major Paulton and pay a visit to Major Tom to jog his memory on the soldier he saw coming out of the sea. They agreed to reconvene when, hopefully, Lady M had sent through the name of the troublemaker. As they were about to leave, Martin got up the courage to ask Amy how much she knew about her father's time in the area in 1943. She told him that, from a couple of letters her mother had shown her, he was something to do with public affairs, was not in a combat role and was based at the Woolacombe Bay Hotel.

'And I now know he and Uncle Billy helped save an airman's life on Morte Point and that dad suffered serious injuries as a result of the rescue.'

Martin gave Amy a potted history of the growth of Woolacombe as a resort from the Second World War to the present day. Nick gave him a puzzled look, intrigued as to where all the information had come from. Martin shrugged his shoulders.

'I read history at Bristol University and did my postgrad thesis on the growth of North Devon as a tourist destination after the arrival of the railway in 1874. For a few years, I lectured in tourism at Bristol Poly, but I missed the sea and surf too much and returned home.'

He nodded to Nick as if to say, *enough said*, finished his pint, said his goodnights, and walked off quickly into the night, Jumble by his side.

'Well?' asked Nick. 'What do you think?'

'I liked him. He's an interesting character and there's a quiet confidence about him once you get below his shyness. How did you guys meet?'

For a moment Nick didn't respond, giving his whole attention to the beer mat he was fiddling with on the table in front of him. He'd only known Amy for a few days. She was an important client. His most important client to date. He wasn't sure how much to let on.

Finally, he looked up at her. 'We met at a local group counselling session. There were six of us, all of whom had suffered a recent loss of one kind or another. Martin's relationship with the woman he loved deeply had come to a sad and tragic end. I'd just kissed goodbye to my career as a touring pro and was still coming to terms with the fact that I'd never walk without the aid of a stick, or nine-iron as it turns out. We became kindred spirits, looking for something that might give our lives some purpose again.'

He told Amy Martin didn't know one end of a golf club from the other, so the subject, thank goodness, never came up in conversation. It made, he said, a refreshing change from everyone telling him how sad they were his burgeoning golf career was over.

'I told Martin about the PI agency I was setting up with my father and he said that sounded like the ideal way to get his mind active again. He started off doing research and, I guess, as a throwback to his academic life, excelled at it. He took on more responsibility with each new assignment and I can't imagine now not having him alongside me.'

Amy smiled. 'Thanks for sharing. It means a lot. And call it a woman's intuition if you like, but I have a feeling Martin will prove to be a real asset in this case.'

She wasn't wrong.

Chapter 13

Martin investigates

M ARTIN LIVED IN A STONE-FACED 1920S TERRACED
cottage in Mortehoe he'd inherited from his parents,
both long dead. Since returning from Bristol, he had lived
there with just Jumble for company.

He was known to the locals as Martin, no surname
necessary. They had no idea he was a Doctor of Philosophy
and he'd stopped using his academic title as soon as he'd
given up lecturing. Gossiping neighbours would say he
never had visitors and that he didn't appear to have any
close friends or family. He was considered a loner which
suited Martin just fine. It meant he could get on with the
odd jobs he did for various people, Nick included, in his
own time and in his own way.

There were times, however, when he reflected on what
life would have been like if Christine hadn't been taken
from him. Joy not sadness; companionship not loneliness;
someone to hug; someone who felt as passionate about
Devon as he did.

They'd lived together in Bristol for five years when
she was knocked off her bike and killed by a hit-and-run

driver. The driver was never identified, never brought to justice. Martin had vowed, there and then, that he'd never drive a car again. He found it impossible to live in a city that served as a constant reminder of the tragedy that had brought the happy life he had shared to such a devastating end.

Tears these days were few and far between. When they came, they came in a torrent of emotion that left him, once more, feeling bereaved and very much alone. He had, half-heartedly, tried a few years later to find someone to share his life with, but his efforts had ended badly and he'd resolved to accept his lot. He couldn't bear to be hurt so badly again.

A creature of habit, he left the house every morning at seven to walk Jumble several miles around Morte Point headland. Returning home through the village, he picked up the Guardian from the post office before cooking his usual breakfast of poached eggs on toast. As is customary with people who walked their dogs at the same time each day, he'd built up a large number of acquaintances from this daily routine. Despite his reticence to engage in idle chit-chat, he would usually drop a little gem of local gossip into the conversation, especially when he was working on a case for Nick.

The morning after the meeting in the Red Barn, he mentioned to everyone he met on his walk, the unfortunate incident with the Caravelle, the sizeable reward and how disconcerting it was that a young American visitor to these parts should be treated so badly.

A little after nine o'clock, Martin walked out of the

village with his old leather satchel over one shoulder, the only reminder of his former life, to catch the 9.10 bus to Ilfracombe, Jumble as ever by his side. His destination was the Coast Guard station where he'd arranged to meet the current coxswain over a coffee and to pore over the station's records.

1978 would mark the station's one hundred and fifty years in service. He must have been reminded of this fact ten times by the proud coxswain who opened a safe and placed the station's records carefully on a table in front of him. Martin desperately wanted to be left alone to plough his way through the large bundle in peace but, good-natured as he was and grateful for access to the many years of history in front of him, he acknowledged this milestone and congratulated the numerous crew who popped their heads around the door to say hello.

As a former volunteer crew member, he was highly respected by the search and rescue community and still seen as very much one of the family. During his ten years on the lifeboat, Martin had been awarded a commendation for rescuing a man from the sea in treacherous conditions. Not something the local crew or the community were likely to forget.

It took him some time to find the records for the war years, and he could find only one reference in the log to the ill-fated day of the joint exercise. There was a paragraph by Cecil Sharp, the coxswain at the time formally recording his advice to both the US and British military that the exercise should be postponed due to the unusually strong winds and heavy swell. The note continued that this advice was ignored; one landing craft capsized; two men drowned in a tank and despite days of searching, one GI was missing, presumed drowned, his body never recovered.

The report concluded with the coxswain praising his men in their valiant attempts to find the missing soldier and commended two US officers for their bravery in trying to rescue the soldiers in the tank.

Lieutenants Ridd and Frye showed remarkable courage in the face of appalling conditions, risking their own lives to try and save their comrades. We are humbled by their bravery.

Martin wrote down the commendation word for word. After checking there was nothing further on the incident in the days and weeks that followed, he carefully packed the files away and returned them to the safe. He felt sure Cecil Sharp was recently deceased. His suspicions were confirmed when the coxswain told him Cecil had passed away six months earlier.

His next stop was to the oldest pub in Ilfracombe, the George & Dragon tavern beside the harbour. Neither Martin's budget nor his constitution allowed for lunchtime drinking. Had the barman not known who he was, his request for a glass of tap water might well have resulted in a frosty reception. As it was, Martin was able to carry his drink around the pub talking in his unassuming way to anyone he knew.

He relayed the message about the reward to over twenty locals, urging them to pass the information on to anybody who might be interested and was confident the prospect of earning £100 would grab people's attention. He was just about to leave when he spotted a former lifeboat crew member sitting on the wall overlooking the harbour. He recounted his message and casually mentioned the name Ted Smithers, explaining that he couldn't remember why the name sounded familiar to him.

'You're losing the plot Martin,' laughed his former colleague. 'Smithers Plumbing was around these parts for years. Ted took over from his father about ten years after the war, but failed to make a go of it.'

He told Martin most people said Ted's heart was just not in it the way his father's had been. They reckoned he struggled too much, having the use of only one good arm. He thought the business had gone bust a decade ago and that Ted spent most of his time drowning his sorrows in his local.

'A dark character if ever there was one. His wife left him and I think he rents a shabby bedsit in Lee Bay, living off his meagre pension and scrounging a drink off anyone foolish enough to buy him one.'

Martin did not need to ask the name of the local. There had, to his knowledge, only ever been one pub in Lee and he knew The Grampus well. He set off with Jumble by his side for the three-mile walk along a stretch of what, three years earlier, had been designated the South West Coastal Path.

With an estimated hour of strenuous walking in front of him, he had plenty of time to spare before the pub opened its doors for the evening trade. He decided to find a phone box and call the Jubilee Inn in Woolacombe.

He knew the likelihood of tracing the wartime landlord

Bob Taylor with a phone call was remote – but it was worth the five pence he would need. What followed was one of the most bizarre conversations he'd experienced in a long time.

He got the Jubilee's number from directory enquiries. With pen and paper ready, he called the pub. After what seemed an eternity, his call was answered by someone obviously not best pleased to be disturbed.

'Don't you know the pub is closed until six-thirty and you've disturbed the only chance I get for a quick nap. What the hell do you want ringing at this time of day?'

Martin was ruing his decision to make the call, but very quietly asked if he could speak to a Bob Taylor.

'It's Bob Taylor speaking. What's so important you have to interrupt a man's kip?'

Amazed that he had made contact with just one call, Martin told him he was investigating an incident in Bob's pub in 1944 and could he call in tomorrow to talk to him.

'Are you taking the piss mate? I must've been a few months old and in my pram. Who are you anyway?'

Just then all Martin could hear was raucous laughter on the other end of the line as the realisation dawned.

'Sorry pal, my mistake. The Bob Taylor you want is my father. He was here from the early '40s until he retired in the late '60s when I took over. Best give him a call on 01859 777654.'

'That's not a local area code,' quizzed Martin.

'You're not wrong there. Dad moved to the Isle of Harris in the Outer Hebrides. Reckons their beaches are the best in the British Isles; even better than ours and a damn sight quieter! I'll let him know you'll be wanting to speak to him. What name shall I give?'

'Please tell him Nick Webber, private investigator, will call to see if he remembers an incident in his pub in the spring of 1944.'

'Will do. And best call him just before six pm. He's seventy-six, but still helps out in his local pub most evenings.'

Martin headed out of town to link up with the path to Lee Bay. He entered the village soon after six. With a good half hour to spare before opening time, he walked down to the bay itself and sat on one of the benches overlooking the sea.

He knew the village was one of those marmite places. You either loved it, as no doubt its four hundred residents and many summer visitors did, or you considered it a rugged and inhospitable stretch of coast, located deep in the Fuchsia Valley, devoid of sunlight for much of the day, with a rocky bay and mud coloured sand.

Martin had no strong feelings either way. But he did regret the way the social fabric of the village was changing as shops closed, one after another, and guest houses were converted to self-catering cottages. The Lee Bay Hotel was still open, but he wondered how long it would survive. He walked back the way he'd come, arrived at the centuries old Grampus pub, and stooped to enter the low doorway, hoping the detour from his route home would prove worthwhile.

'Long time no see, Martin. You been avoiding us?' asked the barman.

'Not at all, Bill, been a bit busy is all. Can you make me and Jumble up a couple of sandwiches to eat on the walk back, and I'll have a pint of my usual please? Quiet in here tonight.'

'It will fill up soon enough, once Coronation Street's finished. One of our regulars is in.' He nodded towards a gaunt old man sitting at the very back of the pub nursing what was left of his pint.

'I'm thinking of entering him for the Guinness World Records. He's a cert to win for taking the longest time to drink a pint of ale.'

Martin asked if this was Ted Smithers. When he got the nod, he asked Bill to pour a pint of Ted's usual and walked with Jumble to the adjacent table. He could see Ted's left arm had wasted away and was hanging limply by his side. He took a sip of his pint and when Ted looked up, slid the other jar across the table towards him.

'Bill said you might appreciate this, and I don't like drinking alone. Cheers.'

Ted eyed him suspiciously for a moment, his eyes straining to see if he knew this ponytailed man sitting near him. He didn't recognise Martin but was not about to say no to another drink. He finished the meagre amount remaining, picked up the fresh pint and gulped down a long swig, gripping the jar with his right hand as if his life depended on it. Martin could not help but notice how long Ted's fingernails were.

'Ta, very hospitable of you.'

Martin bided his time as Ted asked about Jumble and where Martin lived and then proceeded to bemoan the state of just about everything he could think of – from the local council to the noisy grockles and a country going bankrupt with Callaghan in charge.

'You'd think it was us that lost the bloody war, not the Germans,' said Ted in an embittered manner that gave Martin the opening he was hoping for.

'Were you injured serving King and country?' asked Martin, gesturing towards Ted's atrophied left arm.

Ted looked sheepishly at Martin and said his arm was injured preparing for D-Day and the bloody irony was that it happened here in Devon, not on a Normandy beach.

'I was invalided out after that and never saw action in France. It's been buggered ever since, but do you think I got any compensation from the sodding government? No, not a fuckin penny.'

Martin was tempted to dig a bit deeper about the injury, but Ted looked as if he wished he hadn't shouted his mouth off about his arm. Suddenly, after downing half of his precious pint, he stood up, mumbled his goodbyes, and walked quickly out of the pub.

'Blimey Martin,' Bill said, coming over with his sandwiches. 'I don't know what you said but I've never seen Ted not finish his pint, nor move so quickly.'

Martin shook his head as if to say he had no idea what made Ted flee. He told Bill about the young American woman, the damaged car and the reward. Bill offered to put a notice up in the pub and Martin gave him one of Nick's business cards.

He stepped out into the warm night air, his mind awash with questions about Ted's hasty exit.

Chapter 14
Major Paulton

'GIVE ME ONE GOOD REASON WHY I SHOULD SPEAK to you young man! I can only discuss our residents with relatives and certainly won't divulge anything to a complete stranger over the telephone.'

Nick's usual persuasive telephone manner was not cutting it with the matron of Major Paulton's care home. He decided to change tack and introduce Amy into the conversation.

'Matron, my client has flown halfway across the world to see Major Paulton. She's from Boston USA and her father's dying wish was for his daughter to meet the major and other former comrades who he'd trained with in Devon for the D-Day landings in 1944.'

The line went quiet for a moment and Nick thought he'd been cut off. Matron's tone, when she did speak, was far removed from her previous officious manner.

'I was ten when my father left for Normandy. He appeared so big and strong to me, I thought he was invincible, and I waited and waited for him to come home so we could be a family again. I couldn't understand why he hadn't returned until my mother finally told me that he was killed on Juno beach with hundreds of other soldiers in what they'd called the first wave.'

Nick offered his condolences and was ready to leave it at that. But then matron did a volte-face and gave him the information he needed, saying how much she was looking forward to meeting Ms Ridd. He caught up with Amy as she was having breakfast in the hotel restaurant.

'According to the matron, residents' visitors have to be a family member or have approval from the family. It just so happens that today is the day Tony Paulton, the major's son, comes to see his father, regular as clockwork at twelve noon prompt, half an hour before the major has his lunch.'

Nick explained matron had hinted that if they were to 'bump into' Tony in the car park, he might be willing to let them meet the major. She'd also told Nick that he drove a blue Range Rover and always parked as close as he could to the main entrance.

No vans tailed them this time on their sixty-mile journey to Exeter. The time passed quickly. Nick regaled Amy with locker room tales of his time on tour and she, in return, recounted some of the more lurid stories she'd had to cover as an investigative journalist.

'Aren't you missing the buzz of newspaper life?' Nick asked as they approached the city outskirts.

'Not one bit,' laughed Amy. 'Although my time in the UK has been a bit dull so far! An American diplomat has tried to seduce me, I've met the amazing Lady M, been shot at in the dunes, my rental car's been vandalised, and my hotel room has been ransacked by a perv who has a thing for ladies underwear! It beats being a journalist any day!'

Amy opened her notebook and began to read the notes she'd prepared for the meeting with Tony Paulton. Nick took the hint and concentrated on navigating them around the city centre towards their destination. He found the care home, tucked away behind the Royal North Devon & Exeter Hospital, and parked close to reception.

A blue Range Rover pulled in a few spaces away at three minutes to noon. Tony Paulton, as predicted, had arrived dead on time. As they approached the car, Nick couldn't help smiling as the driver opened the large tailgate to retrieve a small package. Next to it, lay a set of golf clubs in a leather Callaway bag with a large green and purple bag tag on it.

Tony Paulton's demeanour was that of a man who takes life seriously. He could have been ex-military and had the air of an accountant or bank manager. The plan was for Amy to initiate the conversation, hoping her American accent would arouse his curiosity long enough for her to tell her story. Door-stepping a stranger in a car park was not the ideal way to introduce herself, but Amy was adept at situations like this.

'Good day, Mr Paulton. May I have a quick word with you about your father? I believe my uncle served with him in the Second World War.'

A bemused expression greeted her words; its owner mystified as to how this young American woman knew his name. Before he could remonstrate, Amy carried on talking as quickly as she could.

'I know this is most unusual, but I'd really appreciate it if you could just give me a couple of minutes to explain.'

'Young lady, I'm not accustomed to being ambushed by someone I don't know and, if you're using some cock-and-bull story to try and sell me something, I can assure you, you've picked the wrong man.'

'Excuse me, sir,' said Nick. 'Isn't that the Exeter Golf Club tie you're wearing?'

'It is, but if you think you can soft soap ...'

Tony Paulton stopped in mid-sentence; mouth open.

He looked closely at Nick's face and then down at the nine iron by his side.

'I know you. You're the golf pro who saved that young boy's life at Exeter Airport.'

'Nick Webber, sir. It's a pleasure to meet you. This is my client, Ms Amy Ridd from New England. Perhaps we could buy you a cup of tea inside before you meet your father and explain the reason for our visit?'

Tony Paulton's whole persona changed in an instant when he realised he was in the company of a Ryder Cup team member and local hero. He ushered Nick and Amy inside and insisted on buying them refreshments at the small café in the foyer. They listened as Tony explained he was club captain this year and proceeded to quiz Nick on his golfing career since the accident. Nick played along for as long as was necessary and promised to speak at the captain's annual charity dinner in a few months' time.

'As we don't want to take up more of your time Tony, perhaps Ms Ridd could explain her dilemma?'

Amy condensed the salient points into as short an

explanation as she could. Tony listened attentively. When Amy had finished, he said he understood how his father might be able to help with their investigation, but warned against getting their hopes up.

'His condition has deteriorated significantly in recent months since being diagnosed with Alzheimer's. Some days, he even fails to recognise me, let alone remember something that happened over thirty years ago.'

He agreed it was a worth a try, and would tell his father he had some special guests today. He advised them matron was a stickler for punctuality, and lunch would be served in fifteen minutes.

'And one thing I *can* tell you is that dad won't miss his lunch for anybody! Come on, I'll introduce you.'

Major Paulton stared at his visitors through pale watery eyes with a faraway 'little boy lost' look. His head appeared too large for his emaciated body, especially the ears which appeared to have outgrown everything else. He reminded Amy so much of her father in the weeks before he died. And yet, behind the frailty there was no denying his bearing; the upright posture that belied his age reminding them he *was* a retired army officer.

He shook their hands. Amy explained about her uncle, Corporal Billy Ridd. Speaking slowly and clearly, she took him through the day of the joint exercise and the capsized craft, in the hope that one tiny detail might spark something in the major's memory. She reached the part about the tank and her uncle's missing body, but his face remained impassive.

There was no indication that he had any idea what she

had been talking about. She finished by saying the Coast Guard and RAF helicopter had failed to find any trace of Billy's body and, despite the brave attempts to rescue the tank crew by her father and a Lt Frye, the soldiers had drowned.

She stopped talking and looked at the major's face for any sign of recognition. There was none. Tony shook his head as if to say at least we tried. Amy and Nick rose to leave, shook the major's paper-thin hand, and mouthed their thank yous to Tony. They were just opening the bedroom door when the major suddenly became very agitated and shouted at them.

'He broke his arm you see. He broke his bloody arm!'

'Who broke his arm Dad?' asked Tony as Amy and Nick sat back down.

'Private Smithers, of course. Who else would I be talking about?'

Amy lent forward and gently took hold of the major's hand again and asked him to tell them more about the broken arm.

'It happened half an hour before we were due to assemble on the landing craft. Some stupid accident Smithers told me and the private with him backed him up. I had no choice but to stand Smithers down and take the other soldier in his place.'

The major looked straight at Amy and told her it was lucky the replacement soldier had all his gear with him, so they were able to arrive at the rendezvous on time. Tony looked on in amazement at how lucid his father had become. The old man fell silent and everyone assumed that was that, but his mind was now very clearly focused on the day's events.

'We set off with the other landing craft and headed around the bay to disembark on Woolacombe beach. But we started going off course and I sent Assistant Section Leader Ridd back to investigate. As he did, we were headed straight for a large outcrop of rocks.'

The major was quiet again for a few seconds as if he were trying to picture in his head what happened next. He continued in a low whisper.

'The craft was being pulled off course by the current. Capsize was inevitable. Soldiers did their best to survive the chaos, trying to swim or scramble ashore through the rough waves, many pulled under the water by the weight of their backpacks.'

He stopped speaking and the weeping began; a sudden outpouring of grief as unexpected as it was inconsolable. Tears flowed down the major's gaunt face and wrinkled hands grabbed at his son's lapels, pulling his face towards him; his agony clear; his voice, when he did speak again, punctuated by the sobbing, tormented by the guilt.

'I never saw Corporal Ridd again. The nightmare etched on my memory is of him being lost at sea whilst under my command. Remorse enveloped my world that day. I was the section leader. If anyone was to drown, it should have been me.'

The room was silent; its occupants reflecting on the major's words, trying to make sense of the story. Just as Amy thought it fit to intervene, a loud clang rang out to disturb the moment. The major stood up as if to attention, his mind back in the here and now. He took his son's hand. 'It's lunch time; it's lunch time; we mustn't be late.'

They walked the major to the dining hall, and watched as Tony sat him down and put a napkin around his neck. Knowing he had nothing to lose, Nick sat down next to the major and whilst he knew the spell had been broken, and more in desperation than anything else, quietly asked the major the name of the soldier who'd replaced Smithers on the landing craft.

'He wouldn't have been my first-choice laddie, I can tell you that. In fact, if truth be told, he probably would have been my last.'

The major's lunch arrived, and his attention was solely focused on consuming his meat and two veg and rice pudding for sweet. Tony told them that he'd followed his father to Sandhurst and the Devonshire Regiment. After a ten-year military career and frustrated by the MOD's inept procurement of equipment, he had joined an insurance broker and was now the senior partner.

'I stopped using my military rank when I resigned my commission. There was already a major in the family. Dad's the real soldier.'

The major normally had his nap after lunch. When Tony tried to re-engage his father and talk about Corporal Ridd, the major looked at his son with a look of complete bewilderment on his face.

They left the old man to the sanctuary of his room and walked to the reception where Tony introduced them to matron who gave Amy a big hug.

They said their goodbyes and thanked Tony for his help

and Nick handed over a business card. Tony promised he would return the next day and the day after that to prompt his father to open up again about that fateful day.

One thought alone occupied their minds as they drove away.

Who the hell took Ted Smithers' place on the landing craft?

Chapter 15
Flash Harry

MARTIN HAD SUGGESTED NICK AND AMY WALKED around the headland with him to clear their heads and take in the crisp morning air. They were sitting on a bench overlooking Morte Point with Jumble on the ground in front of his master, desperate to chase the Longwool sheep grazing nearby.

The landscape boasted its usual riot of colour for this time of year as the sun drifted in and out of the sparse clouds overhead. The heather was still in flower covering the hills in a pallet of purples, greys, and greens; the tranquillity of the morning broken only by the sound of the breaking waves below.

But the rugged beauty of the vista was lost on Amy. She was still absorbed by the note Martin had given her. The coxswain's tribute had brought tears to her eyes. She planned to have the note framed as a permanent memento of her father; a father she was discovering more about in these past few weeks than she had in the last thirty years.

Martin recounted his meeting with Ted Smithers, trying to make sense of his abrupt departure from the pub.

'It was as if he was frightened of saying the wrong thing and shooting his mouth off with some drink inside him. He certainly clammed up when I broached the subject of his arm. And whoever did that crippled him for life.'

'We need to track down Smithers and find out who took his place on the craft,' said Nick. 'When we know who that soldier was, we'll be a step closer.'

Amy showed them Denise's sketch of the businessman-cum-thief. A pug face with narrow squinty eyes and thin nose looked back at them; the face of a man trying too hard to hide his age with jet-black dyed hair or a toupee.

Amy felt that Denise had talent and should be headed to art school, not learning how to make hospital corners on hotel beds.

'Perhaps the mysterious soldier and our businessman are one and the same?' she mused. 'Let's find out.'

The church clock in Lee struck twelve as they entered the village down the steep hill to the bay. Martin gestured for Nick to pull over so that he could have a word with the postman delivering mail on the other side of the road. The friendly greeting showed that they knew one another. Martin was soon back, job done.

'We served on the lifeboat together,' Martin said by way of explanation.

Martin told Nick to carry on a few hundred yards and turn sharp left. Ted Smither's bedsit should be on the right. Nick parked the car out of sight of Ted's place and they walked the short distance to number 62a.

Martin was the first to spot the bottom half of a decrepit terraced cottage that had seen better days. Nick knocked and waited. He tried again and, with no response, peered through the grubby front window to see if there was any sign of life. An upstairs window opened and an elderly woman with hair in curlers and a cigarette hanging from the side of her mouth looked down at them.

'Ted's long gone, me luvver; you're too late!'

The last thing Nick wanted was a conversation in full view of the neighbours and he asked if she could spare them a few moments. Several minutes and many rasping coughs later, the woman appeared from a side door and ushered them inside.

'He took off suddenly without a word; owes me two month's rent and left this place in one hell of a mess. I'll have to clean this lot up before I can find a new tenant. He's very popular all of a sudden, what do you want him for anyway?'

Nick explained Martin and Ted had got talking in the pub about the war years and they wanted to ask him about the injury to his arm as it could be connected to a case they were investigating.

Doris, *my friends call me Dottie* went quiet as if thinking back thirty years.

'Ted was never the same man after the incident with his arm. I don't mean the physical problems it caused him; he suffered mentally as well. All the life had been squeezed out of him and he became afraid of his own shadow, living in constant fear of someone or something. But he'd never tell me who or what.'

Dottie explained that Ted had liked to play poker especially when he was in the army. She'd always thought he had run up sizeable debts, and whoever he'd owed money to, had taken their revenge.

'He must have packed up and left in the middle of the night. Yesterday this flash geezer turned up with some cock-and-bull story. He told me Ted had rushed off to see his brother on the south coast who was critically ill, and Ted had asked him to settle the rent.'

She said he'd peeled off a hundred quid to see her right and told her to keep shtum about the cash.

'It was all bollocks of course, but I wasn't going to say nothin' as he had this menacing look about him. And money's money when all's said and done.'

'How'd you know he was lying?' asked Amy.

'Well dearie, I'm not just Ted's landlady. We're twins and I think I'd know if we had another sibling.'

'Where do you think Ted might be now?' Nick asked.

'Your guess is as good as mine. He's probably got as far away from here as he could without needing a passport.'

Amy took out Denise's sketch and passed it to Dottie. 'Do you recognise this face?'

'That's him; a good likeness as well. Ugly bugger, isn't he? Never seen him around these parts before and I don't particularly want to see him again.'

They thanked Dottie. As they walked back to Nick's car, she shouted after them.

'If you come across Flash Harry, tell him he should spend some of his cash on a better toupee. His belongs in the pantomime.'

Nick pulled in at the phone box at the bottom of the hill. He had an overdue call to make.

Bob Taylor Snr was every bit as lucid as his son had alluded to, and said he remembered the pub brawl as if it were yesterday.

'It was obvious the local soldiers were out to make trouble for the GIs that night, and for Billy in particular. I warned him things could turn nasty and that he and his pals should drink up and get out quick. He wasn't having any of it and did what any self-respecting man would do in the circumstances. He let the ringleader make the first move and outmanoeuvred the bastard. He made him look stupid and left him spread-eagled on the floor.'

'Can you recall Billy's rank and surname and who the ringleader was?'

'Billy was a corporal and I think it was something like Rudd or Ridge. The local soldier, unfortunately for us, remained in the area after the war. He's one of life's least savoury characters. I've heard he abused his wife and has been had up for fraud, corruption and God knows what else.

'Fred Ritter's his name. And good luck chasing him down; you'll need it!'

* * *

'My money's on Ritter being Dottie's Flash Harry,' said Amy as she and Nick sat at the hotel bar enjoying a pre-dinner drink.

'And what if he's the soldier who took Smithers's place on Billy's craft that Major Paulton referred to? We need to check with Major Tom to find out if the ringleader in the pub brawl and the half-drowned soldier he saw the day Billy disappeared are one and the same.'

Amy smiled. 'It's a long shot but I've an idea how we can prompt Tom's memory without putting words in his head. I'm going to put Denise's artistic talents to good use again.'

As they went into dinner, a message came over the hotel PA asking Amy to take a telephone call. The guest telephone box next to reception was an elaborate affair of wood panelling and latticed windows with enough room inside for two people. Amy picked up the phone.

'Amy darling, its Lady Margaret. How are you getting on in the wilds of North Devon?'

The two women chatted as if they'd known each other for years. As the discussion became more serious, Amy beckoned Nick to listen in.

'Stephanie has found the names of two troublemakers in my notebooks. Have you pen and paper?'

Amy replied that she was ready and that Nick, her private investigator, was listening in.

'Well, make sure you get your money's worth from him! These two characters were apparently as thick as thieves in the war years and spent their time baiting GIs, accusing them of stealing their women. Private Jimmy Knox and …'

Amy interrupted, 'Private Fred Ritter.'

'Spot on. But tread carefully. Ritter was a particularly nasty type who beat up a local girl for befriending a GI. That GI was most probably your Uncle Billy.'

Amy updated Lady M on Ritter and promised to speak again soon.

'Make sure you do, darling, and by the way, I've asked Stephanie to put a small parcel in the post for you; something you might find useful. Keep it in your handbag.'

'That sounds intriguing,' said Nick.

'Not really,' replied Amy. 'She's probably sending a lipstick she suggested I try!'

As they walked back to the restaurant, there was another announcement over the PA, requesting Nick to take a call. It was Amy's turn to listen in.

There was a woman's voice on the line. She sounded desperate, her words so incoherent, Nick wondered if she might be drunk. She'd heard about the reward; had information about Amy's car and wanted to meet Nick and *his American friend* the next day. She was insistent they told no one about the rendezvous and to come alone.

She refused to give her name but said she'd been in Woolacombe in 1943 at the time the GIs were there. She whispered that she had to warn them about *a Mr big shot, a lying devious bastard*. The line suddenly went dead, the caller most probably interrupted.

'She wants us to meet at a small outcrop on Croyde Beach called Cock Rock at eleven tomorrow morning. Probably a timewaster, trying to get her hands on the reward money, but you never know. It seems a strange place to meet, but at least we won't be overheard.'

Nick asked the hotel receptionist for the tide charts. Low tide the next morning was at eleven o'clock.

Chapter 16
The meeting at Cock Rock

NICK AND AMY SCRAMBLED DOWN ONTO THE beach at Croyde Bay accompanied by a deep blue sky and the occasional white cloud nudged along by a gentle south-westerly. The few surfers who'd turned up in the hope of some half-decent waves sat disappointed in the cafés dotted along the main street, their owners eager to exploit the mid-morning trade of hot chocolate and perennial full English. The tourist season was almost over. In a few more weeks the visitors would have departed, allowing the locals to recuperate from the frenetic activity of the summer.

As they walked across the sand, they could see a petite middle-aged woman standing in the middle of the bay, staring out to sea as if mesmerised by the waves and the intricate patterns left behind in the wet sand. She heard their approaching footsteps and turned; red puffy eyes looked out from a face that had been very pretty once but had aged beyond its years; a face that embodied heartache and sadness.

Before they could introduce themselves, the woman pointed to the slab of rock almost hidden in the sand. 'This was a much revered-landmark in 1943. It had been a ten-foot-high rock with sheer sides which the Americans blew up because it interfered with their training for the D-Day landings.'

She spoke softly with a distinct North Devon accent that Nick had grown up with. It reminded him of his mother, born and bred in Croyde, and for whom this bay was a second home.

She told them that this had annoyed many of the local men who had taken umbrage at anything associated with the GIs – the constant barrage of noise from the exercises being carried out on the beaches, to the mud on the roads from their tanks and armoured vehicles.

'The pubs were full of GIs at weekends. They made sure the locals didn't go short of cigarettes or miss out on free rounds of mild-and-bitter or sherry for the women. Despite this generosity, the American soldiers' boisterous behaviour annoyed many of the small-minded local men. Men who, for one spurious reason or another, had not signed up to fight Jerry.'

The woman stopped talking and took out a piece of paper from her handbag.

'Local bigots chose to ignore how the GIs had lit up their austere lives at a time when war was inching ever closer to our shores.'

She told them most of the young soldiers had no idea why they'd been ordered to risk their lives fighting on a continent thousands of miles from home.

'They were just kids really. Training for an invasion that would see many of them killed on the sodden beaches of Normandy. Or in a sea, coloured red from the blood of their comrades.'

She hesitated with just the faintest hint of a smile on her face, as if reflecting on something personal; opened the piece of paper and handed it to Amy. It was brown and brittle to the touch. The typed words feint. Amy could just make them out. An invitation from the ATC to join the GIs at a Glenn Miller concert. Her heart missed a beat when she read the signature at the bottom.

Lt Jim Ridd, PAO 1943

'Why shouldn't the GIs have let off steam? Got drunk on Taunton cider? Flirted and had some fun whilst they could? The local girls, me included, loved the attention, the nylons and most of all, the dancing. This incensed British soldiers stationed nearby. Especially the ones born and bred around these parts. They detested the GIs' presence. Jealousy was rife; fights commonplace.

'You should know,' she said, looking directly at Amy and putting her treasured memento back in her bag, 'your countrymen were especially kind to the local children. They set up a scout troop, organised parties, handed out sweets. They were courteous to their elders and great fun to be around at a time when smiles and laughter were few and far between.'

She paused to draw breath, her audience spellbound by the commentary, conscious of the tears in her eyes and the pained expression on her face.

'The GIs were, for the most part, brave, beautiful men. Our lives were richer for the short time they graced us with their presence.'

She stopped talking just as suddenly as she had begun, as if she'd completed her tour guide script and was waiting for questions.

Perhaps it was a woman's intuition. Perhaps it was the raw emotion in the woman's voice or the faraway look in her eyes, remembering a time gone by when she had been truly happy. Amy took a step forward, looped her arm through Elsie's and walked her away towards the shoreline. Two women together, sharing the sensitivity of the moment. Their shoes flirting with the waves, oblivious to everything and everybody.

It was a good ten minutes before they turned and walked purposely back towards the rock. They stopped some thirty yards away. Amy gave the woman a gentle hug and, after holding both her hands in hers, they parted like two old friends who hadn't seen each other for years, for whom separation was premature, even painful.

Amy watched as the woman walked quickly towards the footpath that led to the nearby car park. She waited until the small figure had turned the corner and was out of sight.

'Her name's Elsie. She told me she knew Uncle Billy well and was checking whether she could trust us. She has no interest in a reward but does know who instigated the damage to my car. She'll join us in an hour's time after her AA meeting to tell us her story. You presumably know where Putsborough Café is?'

Nick did. They drove inland towards Georgeham and then headed west to the coast on some of the narrowest lanes Amy had ever seen. During their short journey, Nick recounted memories of the long hot summers he'd spent growing up with his friends on Putsborough Sands.

'It was a rite of passage for my generation,' he said. 'Playing in the rock pools as a toddler, learning to swim and body board as a youngster and then, as teenagers, surfing, open fires on the beach, the illicit taste of local cider or hesitant puff on a cigarette and that first stolen kiss and more in the dunes.'

'Way too much information,' laughed Amy.

Chapter 17
Elsie's story

THEY LEFT THE CAR AT THE TOP OF PUTSBOROUGH Beach and headed down the steep grass bank towards the wooden shack that served as a café. Perched on an outcrop of rock at the top of the bay, it rewarded its customers with stunning views out to sea, the outline of Lundy just visible on the horizon.

Clambering down the rocks to the water's edge, Amy skimmed a pebble across the calm sea. She looked up to the large, grassed shelf above the rocks where a few random tents were pitched in haphazard fashion, looking out on the Atlantic Ocean.

'That must be one of the most picturesque camp sites in the world. I'm tempted to vacate my hotel, buy a tent and go native.'

'You might want to think about that!' Nick pointed out that the shower and toilet block were a good hundred yards away and that many a tent had been blown onto the beach below by the infamous North Devon wind.

They walked back the way they'd come towards the café. Elsie had arrived early and acknowledged them with a tentative wave and suggested they sit on the nearby rocks away from prying eyes and ears. She was clearly petrified of someone or something.

For some moments they sat in silence, Elsie playing with the spoon in her coffee, seemingly trying to come to a decision. Suddenly she looked at Amy and took a deep breath.

'Sixty thousand British women left these shores after the war to marry their GI sweethearts. I should have been one of them. Amy, if your Uncle Billy had not been lost at sea, I would have been your aunty.'

Amy gasped; her hands went instinctively to her face; mouth open; eyes wide.

'Oh my god!' she cried.

Elsie took hold of Amy's hands and held them tightly. 'Your Uncle Billy and I were in love. We had planned to marry as soon as the war was over and live in Quincy. I was the happiest a girl could be.' She paused, catching her breath. 'Fred Ritter had other ideas.'

'I don't understand,' said Amy. 'Where does *he* fit in?'

'Billy and I met at a dance in the spring of '44. We courted then became lovers. Fred found out. He'd convinced himself and everyone he met I was *his* girl and that we were soon to be married. It was all lies; a figment of his distorted imagination.'

Elsie told them she and Billy had made love just days before his unit was to depart for Normandy and that she'd persuaded him not to use any protection.

'I knew it would be the last time I saw him before he left. If Billy *was* killed, there was the tiniest chance I could have his baby.'

She said she'd heard two days later that Billy had drowned in a training exercise, but she wouldn't believe it. Especially when she found out he was the only soldier lost overboard.

'Like a woman possessed, I spent days wandering around the rocks where his craft had capsized; willing him to appear out of the sea. There was no body. No closure. I locked myself in my bedroom. I didn't eat a thing, mourning the man I loved so much; the man who'd made me so deliriously happy.'

Tears streamed down Elsie's tormented face; her body shaking; breathing laboured; eyes red. Nick wrapped his jumper around her shoulders as Amy cuddled her close. Small acts of kindness alien to a woman who'd suffered so much distress.

'Fred turned up at our front door. He'd convinced my parents he could help me see sense and slipped my dad a pound note to take him and mum off to the pub. Dad shouted up to me that I should consider myself lucky this brave British soldier still cared for me. They were, like many people around here, taken in by his smooth words. I refused to let Fred into my room, but he forced his way past me.'

She told them that Fred cared for her alright. He goaded her about Billy's disappearance and then raped her, leaving her bruised, shaken, and sobbing her heart out.

'Ten weeks later, I realised I was pregnant. My parents assumed it was Fred's and insisted we marry. Had I not agreed, I would have ended up in a refuge for single mothers with my baby taken away for adoption.

'When the baby was born, I knew it was Billy's. Jacob had bright blue eyes, fair curly hair and was the spitting image of his father. Fred never said anything, nor did he once show the baby any affection during his short life.'

'Short life?' asked Amy.

Elsie's face crumpled again. Her grief still as raw as it had been all those years ago.

'Jacob died. Five months, two weeks, four days. The post-mortem said he had died of cot death. It was only the second time I'd left Fred in charge and will never forgive myself for going out that evening. When I left, he was sleeping peacefully. When I returned an hour later, he was dead. I'm convinced Fred, unable to accept that the baby was not his, smothered him out of pure spite.'

She told them she'd not let Fred touch her since Jacob's death and that he had more than enough lady friends to keep him out of her bed. He had, she said, abused her physically and mentally for over thirty years and had taken great pleasure in having her sectioned more times than she could remember.

'I've been in and out of the local mental health hospital for the past twenty years. Drink was my solace. But not anymore. I've been dry for sixty-one months and counting. I keep praying Fred will get what's coming to him. That he's locked up for a very long time so that I can live what's left of my life in peace.'

Anger burned deep inside Amy. Fury. Rage. She was more determined than ever now to find Ritter; to confront him; to find out what really happened to Uncle Billy and to Jacob. To make him pay for destroying their lives. For destroying Elsie's life.

Nick was seething.

'Did you ever hear Ritter speak about two of his wartime mates, Jimmy Knox and Ted Smithers?'

'Jimmy was a drinking pal of Fred's. He was killed in Normandy. Fred kept in touch with Ted but there was no love lost between them and Ted was known to have cursed him when he'd had one pint too many.'

'How did you find out about Amy and me?'

'A few days ago, I heard Fred shouting down the phone at some of his lackeys. He thought I was out at my AA meeting. But I couldn't face it that evening and stayed in my bedroom out of harm's way.'

She told them Fred was deaf in one ear and spoke very loudly when on the telephone. She'd heard him say something about a pot shot, tyres, and damaged body work.

'I wouldn't normally have taken any notice until he mentioned the words Yank, war and piss off home. I knew then this wasn't one of his usual tirades.'

She confessed she'd not thought any more about it until she saw the reward notice in the Grampus. The friend she was with knew of Amy.

'You helped stop her daughter Denise from being sacked. I took a chance and called the hotel on the off-chance Nick might be there with you. Small world, isn't it?'

Elsie smiled. Something Nick and Amy suspected was a rare occurrence. And probably had been for a very long time.

'Ritter obviously wanted to frighten us off,' said Nick.

Elsie nodded. 'He's hated Americans since they arrived

here in 1943. He must have found out you and Amy were asking questions about the war and became rattled when he discovered Amy's surname.'

Elsie looked around nervously. Her voice a mere whisper.

'Whatever you do, don't underestimate Fred Ritter. He may have found a way to drown Billy, probably murdered my baby boy and goaded me about what happened to his business partner. He's taunted me time and time again with *four's my favourite number.* The man's a psychopath.'

She stood up to leave, gave Amy a big hug and walked away, her eyes darting here, there, and everywhere. Checking, always checking.

They sat in silence, making sure Elsie had reached her car and driven away safely.

Amy was the first to speak.

'I believe every word of what she's told us.'

'So do I,' said Nick. 'And it's about time we did something about it.'

Chapter 18
Major Tom remembers

'COME IN, COME IN,' TOM SAID, WELCOMING NICK and Amy into his living room.

'It's about time you came back to see me, young Nick, and I'm looking forward to hearing how much progress you've made with your research, Miss Ridd.'

Tom insisted on making them all a cup of tea and produced some Rich Tea biscuits out of a tin that looked as if it had been around as long as Tom himself. Once they were settled, Nick came straight to the point.

'Tom, we wanted to see you because I have a confession to make and want to clear the air...'

'Let me stop you right there,' said Tom.

'You must think I was born yesterday. Just because my body's getting older, it doesn't mean my mind isn't as sharp as it's always been. I did some research of my own and here's what I think. Firstly, Nick, you're a private investigator, not a researcher. Secondly, Miss Ridd is American and as we all know, there were quite a lot of GIs here in the war, over ten-thousand in fact. Given your likely age Miss, I suspect you were born just before the war and your father spent some of his wartime service here. Thirdly, I called in some favours from the MOD.'

Tom told them how, being a recipient of the Victoria Cross had 'opened doors' and he'd discovered that a Lt Jim Ridd served in North Devon during the war as a public affairs officer, at the same time as his younger brother, Corporal Billy Ridd.

'I was told Billy was presumed drowned after a training exercise in Woolacombe Bay. I'm guessing that Jim is your father and Billy was your uncle. How am I doing so far?'

'Tom, please call me Amy. You're absolutely right. My father sadly passed away not long ago and I'm here at his behest, to discover what happened to my uncle that day. I asked Nick to concoct the cover story, and I apologise we misled you. We're trying hard to protect innocent people caught up in the investigation.'

Tom smiled, and sat down next to Amy.

'I'm sorry to hear about your father. From what I've learnt of his time here, he displayed great courage on a number of occasions. As to what you're trying to find out, I suspected something along those lines when Nick asked to see me. That's why, when I handed over my diary, I asked him to share anything worthwhile he found out with me first to protect all of us. Now that we've cleared that up, how can I help?'

Nick asked the question that had been puzzling him and Amy ever since they'd been shot at in the dunes.

'Tom, did many people know about the diary?'

Tom retrieved a key from behind the bookshelf and unlocked the top drawer of an old bureau and pulled out the front page of a newspaper. The 6 August 1962 headline of the North Devon Journal was blazoned across the front page.

Golf Club Captain's War Diary.

Underneath was a large photo of a much younger Tom holding his diary.

'It was my first time as Saunton Club Captain. The reporter who interviewed me claimed he was interested in local history and especially the war years. When we got on to my time in the war, I mentioned the diary.'

Tom told them the reporter had feigned interest, played to his ego, and that he'd told him far more than he should have done. He pointed to the reference in the article about the joint exercise and how he'd helped search for Amy's uncle.

'I regretted shooting my mouth off, but the harm was done. I was full of my own self-importance in those days. Too arrogant for my own good, you might say. The episode taught me a salutatory lesson. I've kept quiet about the diary ever since until Nick knocked on my door.

'So, to answer your question, lots of locals knew about the diary and about the reference to Corporal Ridd's death. When the club secretary told me Nick's office had been ransacked, I suspected the intruder was searching for the diary. It wouldn't take much for someone to work out the link between me, the club president and Nick Webber, our former club pro turned private investigator, working for an American client with a surname of Ridd.'

'Tom, why did you say the reporter feigned interest in your story?' Amy asked.

'I found out later the paper was struggling for news at the time. A friend of mine who worked there told me the reporter had been briefed to pad out the story of my appointment as club captain. They had little else to fill the front page. Ego can do funny things to a person and I've kept a low profile ever since. So, what now?'

Amy took some papers from her bag and arranged them on the coffee table in front of Tom.

'I've rewritten two extracts from your diary word for word. I want to see if they help you remember something important.'

Amy handed Tom the first extract – *Billy's fight at the Jubilee pub, the arrival of the military police and seeing a British soldier slink off into the night*. She asked him to read his words and visualise the scene in his head.

After a couple of minutes, Amy handed him the extract in which he described helping the coast guard search for the missing GI and *seeing a bedraggled British soldier coming out of the sea long after everyone else.*

She put Denise's sketch illustrating Tom's words on the table in front of him. It depicted a lone soldier wading ashore looking much the worse for wear, his clothing sodden; his body huddled in on itself from the cold.

She then handed him Denise's sketch of what the bogus hotel businessman's face could have looked like thirty years earlier. Tom stared at the face in front of him and then picked up the sea sketch. He re-read the two diary extracts and after several minutes put the papers back on the table.

'I couldn't place why the soldier wading out of the sea

looked familiar. There's no doubt in my mind. He's the one I saw staggering away from the pub after the fight with your uncle.'

Amy smiled and handed him Denise's sketch of the toupee-wearing intruder who'd ransacked her bedroom.

Tom scowled.

'That's him. All three sketches are of the same man. Fred Ritter. Our ignominious councillor a decade or so back, dismissed for corruption and a string of other offences. Nothing would surprise me about the misery that man's inflicted over the years. I'd give anything to see him brought to justice.'

Chapter 19
Peter Webber

Nick's father put the telephone down carefully. This was not a situation he had envisaged when he'd invited his partner over for their weekly rendezvous. Nick was on his way to see him and would arrive in twenty minutes.

'I'm sorry, Eileen, but you can't be here when my son arrives. He has an important client with him and it would be embarrassing if he found us here together, especially as he wants to discuss a case he's working on.'

Eileen paused. She couldn't decide. Should she play the compliant lover or make a stand?

'Sod it,' she thought.

'Embarrassing for whom? You still haven't told him about us, have you? You're happy to be seen out in my company and take me to your bed, but are panicking your son will find us together mid-afternoon and draw his own conclusions. Nick is mature enough to recognise you have a life to lead. I thought you were going to tell him about our relationship?'

'I will, I promise. And I'll make it up to you. I'll call you tomorrow. I'm sorry.'

Eileen drove off five minutes later and Peter heaved a sigh of relief. But there was no disguising the disgruntled look on her face after he'd ushered her out of the door and into her car.

Nick's call to say he and Amy would be with him in twenty minutes had caught him completely off-guard. *When was the last time Nick had called mid-afternoon?* It wasn't that he was ashamed of his lady friend. Not at all. But there was a time and place to share his personal life with his son and it was not today.

He still felt uneasy at his son knowing he shared his bed with another woman. Especially when that woman was the golf club lady captain; a divorcee who'd made no secret of the fact she'd taken a shine to the handsome ex-men's captain long before his wife became ill. Their relationship was the worst kept secret in the club.

Peter checked the house for any obvious signs of his recent tryst. He put the empty bottle in the kitchen bin and washed up the two flutes, unsure why he felt like a naughty schoolboy. He'd loved his wife and was devastated when she died. He missed her laughter; missed the intimacy; missed the sex. He'd strayed a couple of times during the marriage, but it was not something he was proud of and had never thought of himself as a ladies' man. But now, a widower in his early fifties, he was regularly propositioned by women of a certain age and – he had to admit – he relished the attention.

Even his housekeeper, who by his estimation had not yet reached forty, had started dropping not-so-subtle hints about staying the night as she put his supper on the table and poured him a glass of wine. And several of the eligible ladies at the club, and some of the ineligible ones, had made their intentions clear. Peter enjoyed sex. The lady he'd just said a hurried goodbye to was adept at satisfying his needs. They shared a penchant for sparkling wine and an afternoon in bed after their regular game of golf and lunch at the club.

Peter was still trying to get used to life without his wife. In their thirty years of marriage, he couldn't remember boiling an egg or ironing a shirt. Not unusual for men of his generation, especially men like him who lived to work not worked to live. He'd laboured hard around the clock when duty called; been ruthlessly ambitious; not hesitated to step on colleagues' toes when they challenged his cavalier methods, but consistently delivered the results his superiors demanded.

He'd never been a bent copper. But nor had he done everything *by the book*. The smell of his uniform hanging up in the wardrobe evoked images of the times due process had taken a back seat. The dozens of grasses he'd recruited over the years, the perpetual fag hanging out of their mouths, eager to snitch and earn another payday; the misfits he'd fitted up for petty crimes they'd not done because, by rights, they should still be behind bars; the number of times he'd turned a blind eye to one misdemeanour or another by local villains in order to focus on the bigger picture, be it drugs, prostitution or racketeering.

Promotion through the ranks to chief inspector had come quickly. It wasn't long before he'd become a highly-respected figure in the community, interviewed regularly by the local media on issues topical at the time. In the two years before his retirement, he'd been the star guest on a weekly crime programme for Westward TV. His opinion mattered. The limelight nurtured his pride.

And now he was just one in a long line of ex-coppers who missed the thrill of the chase; missed wielding the power that came with the rank and, if he was being brutally honest, missed being the centre of attention. He'd kidded himself that his eagerness to help Nick's business succeed was what any father would do for his son; altruistic, well-meaning. In truth, he knew it was, in part, because he craved the kudos that came with solving a major crime.

From the little Nick had explained to him on the phone, this case was the most challenging and high profile he'd taken on since setting up the agency. Peter wanted a share of the action; wanted to be back in the spotlight.

* * *

Nick drove towards their rendezvous. Amy sat beside him silently, hands clammy, biting her upper lip, trying her best to concentrate on her notes. She was fearful for everyone's safety in the light of Elsie's and Tom's warnings.

The man's a psychopath. The misery that man has inflicted over the years.

The words screamed out at her, and she was under no illusion. Fred Ritter killed people. He wouldn't hesitate to kill again.

The slow journey north around the coast gave Nick time to get his own thoughts in order. He wasn't immune to the sense of foreboding, nor the weight of responsibility to protect Amy. It crowded in on him. *What the hell had they got mixed up in?* Hopefully his father could steer them in the right direction as they closed the net on Ritter.

Amy must have read his thoughts. 'Do you think your dad *will* be able to help us?'

'We'll find out soon enough.' Nick pulled into the familiar drive and parked behind the Saab convertible that had been his father's pride and joy for more than twenty years.

Peter greeted them warmly and ushered them through the hallway to the table in his study. He'd taken in Amy's pretty face, and lingered a tad too long on her figure.

Amy looked at her surroundings; the simple but pleasing pine furniture, walls covered in golf etchings, shelf upon shelf of books – mostly on golf. In different circumstances, she'd have loved to browse through them with her host who, slim and casually dressed, was the spitting image of what she'd imagined Nick would look like in twenty years' time.

Peter was just about to say something about his collection when Nick's opener brought him back to the business at hand.

'Dad, I told you about the disappearance of Amy's Uncle Billy in 1944 and the growing evidence of foul play. We need to know if you can tell us anything about someone called Ritter. Fred Ritter?'

Peter stared at his son for a long time, then left the room without saying a word. Amy looked at Nick who shrugged his shoulders as if to say *don't ask me.* His father returned a couple of minutes later, a strained expression on his face, the earlier bonhomie long gone. He put several leather-bound notebooks on the table, and carefully opened one.

'I first arrested Ritter as a rooky police constable in the late 40's. He was charged with receiving stolen goods and was guilty as hell. But his sleazy solicitor and a street-wise barrister got him off on a technicality.'

Peter told them he'd never once managed to put Ritter behind bars where he belonged. 'Everyone knew he'd made his money on black-market goods during the war, and had been involved in a number of scams and petty crimes. Those crimes got more and more serious year on year.

'Ritter formed a business partnership in the mid-sixties with a local hotelier called Michael Lock. The pair would buy up run-down pubs and night clubs, do them up, put in good managers to turn them around and sell them on or add them to the expanding Lockman portfolio.'

'Did the partnership last?' asked Nick.

His father consulted another notebook. 'Lock was the brains behind the business. He had the right connections, knew the licensed trade inside out and was the majority shareholder. He died in mysterious circumstances. Lock supposedly fell down a steep flight of stone steps in a nightclub he and Ritter were looking to buy.'

'Supposedly?' quizzed Amy.

'The agent showing them round had gone off to find a set of keys. He heard a yell and ran back to find Lock at the bottom of the steps with Ritter beside him shouting for him to get an ambulance. The agent said it looked like Lock had broken his neck, and the ambulance crew confirmed this. The incident was investigated. Ritter, the only witness, claimed it was a tragic accident. He said Lock had tripped as he started down the stairs and had fallen headfirst to the bottom. The autopsy showed no sign of a struggle. The coroner ruled accidental death.'

'It sounds like you thought differently dad. But why would anyone think it suspicious? Surely Ritter wouldn't want to harm his partner and put the business at risk?'

'Well, here's the thing,' said Peter. 'Lock was a bachelor with no close family. It transpired he had left his estate to Ritter, *lock, stock and barrel* so to speak. During the investigation, we discovered Lock was gay and had strong feelings for Ritter. He'd hoped these feelings might one day be reciprocated and that the partnership would develop into more than just a business one.'

'And how did Ritter feel about this?' Amy asked.

'Let's just put it this way: people close to Ritter said he wouldn't have hesitated to lead Lock on and pretend to have feelings for him if it led to financial gain. They were right. He went from owning a minority stake to becoming the sole owner of the multi-million Lockman portfolio. Almost overnight, Ritter became Mr. Respectable; a legitimate local businessman heading up one of the largest businesses in North Devon.'

'What happened next?' asked Nick.

'Ritter sold the pubs and clubs and invested in caravan parks. He got elected onto the local council and joined the Masons to mix with the high and mighty, including some senior police officers.'

'Dad, if Lock's death wasn't an accident, that's another murder Ritter's got away with.'

'What do you mean *another* murder?'

The next hour passed quickly. Peter listened as Nick took him through their investigation. Amy summed up by explaining how Elsie had told them how Ritter would goad her when he was drunk or in one of his foul moods by saying *four's my favourite number*.

'Elsie told us Ritter had bragged about getting his own back on Billy and how she was convinced he'd smothered baby Jacob. She said that when he really wanted to frighten her, he would remind her of his business partner's demise, something that made little sense to us until now.'

Peter excused himself and came back holding an old newspaper. He showed them the front page of The North Devon Journal, the same paper Tom had shown them earlier.

Councillor's wife causes havoc at Town Hall

Yesterday's meeting of the Council's Planning Committee was interrupted when Cllr Fred Ritter's wife burst into the Council Chamber and accused her husband of murdering her baby son Jacob and of abusing her for years. Elsie Ritter appeared very drunk, and observers commented upon her mental health.

Peter told them the reporter who had written the story had been sacked and that Ritter had taken the paper to court for libel, winning thousands of pounds in damages and a front-page apology.

'He used his influence to have the paper's editor moved sideways to a smaller paper and was instrumental in getting one of his cronies appointed in her place. Since that day, there have rarely been anything but positive reports on Ritter and his business interests.

'This is the kind of man you're dealing with. A man who has evaded justice for thirty years and who has, time and time again, demonstrated he's prepared to take any steps necessary to destroy people who cross him. To make matters worse, it's well documented that Elsie has suffered mental health and alcohol problems for many years. She's hardly a credible witness. Finally, your Uncle Billy's disappearance happened a very long time ago. Cold cases are notoriously difficult to prove.'

'You think we're wasting our time?' Amy asked.

But Nick's father looked more determined than ever.

'On the contrary, Amy. I want nothing more than to put Ritter behind bars for the rest of his life. I'm hoping you'll let me join you in doing just that.'

Chapter 20
Burden of proof

'SO, WHO'S YOUR DAD'S LADY-FRIEND? NOT THAT IT'S any of my business!'

Amy and Nick were sitting outside The Ship Aground in Mortehoe. They'd gone over everything Nick's father had told them. The church clock struck seven and they were enjoying some downtime and a drink.

'Eileen from the golf club. She's been all over him since mum died. Dad thinks I don't know. But how did you know he was seeing somebody?'

'Your dad's bedroom door was ajar when I went to the restroom. There was the faintest hint of perfume in the air. I'd recognise it anywhere. It was one of my mum's favourites. Whatever else Eileen may be, she's got good taste in scent! Does it bother you him seeing someone?'

'Dad retired early so that he could caddy for me occasionally around Europe, so I'm in no position to begrudge him some fun with his lady friends. Even if he is having something of a mid-life crisis!'

'And what about you, Nick? Is there someone special in your life?'

The distant look in his eyes said all there was to say. Nick's right hand instinctively rubbed through his hair; a nervous habit he'd developed after his accident.

His voice quavered.

'Not anymore.' He took a long swig on his pint and looked up.

'Sally and I were to be engaged a week after my Ryder Cup debut. But when she came to the hospital after the accident and saw me in the wheelchair, all I saw on her face was pity. I couldn't let her commit herself to a life so far removed from the one she'd dreamt of. I broke it off.'

'Have you tried to get her back?'

'Too late. She married a guy on the tour; lives in Florida enjoying the good life and has a one-year-old daughter. I'm pleased for her.'

* * *

'Ok, let me see if I've got this right?' said Peter.

He sat in Nick's office, next to his son; Amy opposite them. The space was cramped but private. Motive, means and opportunity had focused their minds for the past hour. Peter reiterated that to secure Ritter's conviction, they needed solid proof that would stand up in court.

'Ted Smithers has gone AWOL, God knows where; one of our key witnesses is an alcoholic with a well-known history of mental illness over twenty years. Another is a retired major who would be credible if it weren't for the fact that he has early-onset Alzheimer's and has trouble remembering his own name, let alone the incident thirty plus years ago when Ritter injured Smithers and took his place on the landing craft.'

'But we can rely on Lady M and Major Tom,' interjected Nick. 'They *are* credible. And Bob Taylor, the retired landlord of the Jubilee Inn sounded lucid on the phone. He would testify about Ritter and Billy's fight in the pub.'

'Denise will testify it was Ritter who conned his way into my room,' added Amy. 'And I'm sure we could persuade Doris, Ted Smithers's twin, to tell the police all about Ritter's visit and the lies he told her about Ted's disappearance. She didn't take kindly to flash Harry.'

Peter applauded the information they'd uncovered so quickly, and their relentless search for the truth. But he knew it wasn't nearly enough.

'We probably have enough evidence to get Ritter convicted of breaking and entering and some other minor offences. But that's not what Amy flew across the Atlantic for. Nor why she hired you, Nick. It doesn't satisfy her father's dying wish. Nor does it give Elsie the justice she craves for the deaths of Billy and baby Jacob.

'We have to *prove* Ritter drowned Billy and somehow disposed of his body. Proof that's robust enough to withstand cross-examination by Ritter's scumbag defence lawyer. If we took what we have to the police now, they'd say it was all circumstantial. We need far more for Ritter to be convicted for murder.'

All that could be heard over the silence now was the low hum from the new fax machine. Peter had been in situations like this many times before. He knew exactly how they were feeling; morale on the floor; groping for that missing something that could unlock the impasse.

Nick refused to believe they'd reached a dead-end. Now was not the time to call a halt. And certainly not the time for Amy to cut her losses and head back to the States.

'There may be something we can use to our advantage,' said Amy. 'Ritter has an explosive temper, a very short fuse. He's delusional; convinced he's above the law; someone in the States we would call an untouchable. We need to find a way to exploit that weakness.'

Nick took a deep breath. *Now or never.*

'Ritter has so far made all the running; he's thwarted us from day one. The pot shot in the dunes, Amy's car vandalised, this office and Amy's room ransacked. He's put the wind up Ted Smithers and, worst of all, turned Elsie into a nervous wreck. Anything she might say against him in the future could be easily discredited.'

'And your point?' Peter asked.

'Amy's spot-on about Ritter's temper. Let's turn it to our advantage. Let's confront him face-to-face in his own home. Set out what we have about the deaths of Billy, baby Jacob and Michael Lock. Recount the evidence we have from 1944, from Lady M, Major Tom, and Bob Taylor Snr. And all that we know about Ted Smithers from Doris.

'Let's tell him Major Paulton remembered *everything* in fine detail about what happened on the day of the joint exercise. Goad him about failing to find Major Tom's diary. Tell him it contains evidence implicating him in Billy's death. Rile him and continue to rile him until, when he loses his temper, he admits something that proves decisive. Something that will get him convicted.'

'But,' said Amy, 'it'll just be our word against his?'

Nick looked across at his father, hoping he was thinking the same thing.

'Not if one of you is wearing a wire!' said Peter.

Peter kept his colleagues grounded by explaining the implications. Despite the earlier reality check, their mood lifted to anticipation, belief in their ability restored. They were disturbed by the loud ring of the office telephone. A rare occurrence that caught even Nick by surprise.

'Excuse me,' he said apologetically. 'I'd better take this.'

Amy stared at Nick, annoyed at the interruption. She understood he had other clients, other cases to investigate. She understood his business would not survive on her fees alone. And yet, it didn't stop her feeling frustrated he couldn't commit all his time to helping her.

She scolded herself for being so self-indulgent. *Stop acting like a spoiled brat. Get over yourself.*

Peter suggested he and Amy get some fresh air, leaving Nick to take the call. He walked her towards the first tee, pleased to be able to show off the course. They weren't alone for long. Nick appeared around the corner leaning heavily on his nine iron, breathless, hair dishevelled, shock ingrained on his face.

'You'd better come back inside.' His speech was laboured. Amy hadn't seen him look this concerned since the day they were shot at in the dunes.

They reconvened around Nick's desk, imagination working overtime.

'That was Martin. *Our* Martin. He's been taken to Barnstaple police station for questioning.' Nick paused, not quite believing what he was about to tell them.

'Jumble found a body washed up on Grunta Beach. Ted Smithers is dead.'

Chapter 21
Cold to hot

'MARTIN WAS ON HIS DAILY WALK AROUND MORTE Point when Jumble suddenly ran off down the cliffs and stood barking loudly by some rocks on the beach. It was low tide, the beach and rock pools exposed. Martin scrambled down, found a body and saw it was Ted.

'He quickly made his way home and called the police, telling them he worked for me and that he'd spoken to Ted a few days ago in the Grampus as part of an ongoing investigation. He also told them about Ted's sister Doris.'

Nick said the officer who interviewed Martin had reported the incident to the chief superintendent, David Short, and he made the link between Nick and his father.

'The chief super told Martin to phone me and get a message to you dad. You're to call him straight away.'

'David's an ex-colleague,' said Peter. 'We worked together for over twenty years. He's a damn good officer.' He took out his diary and dialled the number.

Nick and Amy waited patiently. Peter confirmed that he, Nick, and Ms Ridd would stay put and wait for David's arrival, and put the receiver down.

The police, Peter told them, had located Doris at the Grampus where she had a morning cleaning job. She'd apparently burst into tears on hearing the news. When the pub landlord overheard Martin had found the body, he made a point of telling the police Ted and Martin had been drinking together in the pub a few evenings before. He described Ted's strange behaviour, leaving his pint unfinished and scarpering out of the door like a frightened rabbit.

'The police had suspected suicide. Now they're not so sure. David wants to understand what our investigation is about, and will join us here shortly. Martin is likely to be with him in the squad car, no doubt accompanied by a couple of enthusiastic constables delighted to be involved in a potential murder enquiry.

'What was a cold case is now very hot. We need to bring David up to speed and take our lead from him. Ted's demise is part of a formal police enquiry. That means there's a real risk we could be side-lined.'

'Dad, there is no way we're going to step aside. We …' His father cut him short.

'The upside is that the chief super is as keen as we are to nail Ritter. He knows only too well how abysmal the police's record of convictions against him is. If there's a way of approaching this in a different, albeit unorthodox way, I'm confident that David will give it serious consideration.'

They agreed Peter should brief David. He'd recommend collaboration and push hard for Nick and Amy to confront Ritter in his home, just as they had been discussing before Martin's call.

'Then we will have to decide which one of you wears the wire. Something David will have a strong view on… *if* he agrees to our game plan.'

As the two men greeted each other, it was clear from the chief superintendent's body language that he had enormous respect for Peter. Nick, Amy, and Martin sat in on the briefing, with Martin instructed not to say anything unless prompted. That suited him just fine.

Peter was concise. No salient points missed. David listened intently and challenged constructively, obviously well versed in assimilating lots of information in a short space of time. His face gave nothing away when Peter had finished, and the two men walked briskly back to the squad car.

Martin was free to go, but warned not to leave the area. 'I'm not going anywhere!' He shot off, anxious not to have Jumble shut up in the house any longer than necessary.

Peter had a resolute look on his face when he re-joined them a few minutes later.

'We're on, but we have to do it by the book. If we *do* get to court, it will be up to the presiding judge whether he or she uses the recording or not. There are, however, a number of precedents David is aware of and these should act in our favour.'

'What does *by the book* mean?' asked Amy.

'You must not ask leading questions. And you *must* be able to demonstrate in court that you didn't force your way into the house but were invited in by Elsie. It's critical we don't give Ritter's counsel *any* opportunity to claim harassment and get the case thrown out before it's even started!'

Peter told them that they would normally be coached by a police officer for a task like this. But, with time not on their side, they'd have to make do with him.

'We need to act before the press hears about the body and before Ritter starts lawyering up. One of you should call Elsie now and suggest she invites you to her house tomorrow morning for a coffee and a chat when Ritter is out. You'll just happen to still be there when he returns.'

'And who did David say should be wired up?' Amy asked.

'He reckons Ritter will be much more suspicious of Nick. Being the misogynist he is, he's unlikely to consider a mere woman capable of going through with such a thing. So, Amy wears the wire; preferably attired in something as revealing as possible to put Ritter off his guard.'

'All in the line of duty!' said Amy.

Peter took Amy for a bite of lunch in the clubhouse, while Nick made the call to Elsie. She was eager to help and, despite being nervous, gave Nick a breakdown of Ritter's movements.

'He leaves the house in his jag at eleven o'clock every morning for his stint at the bookies, will expect his dinner on the table at half past twelve and be off again early afternoon to check up on his business interests. More often than not, he'll spend the evening with one of his whores.'

Elsie said she would make herself scarce when Ritter came home for dinner. She warned Nick he was likely to turn violent, especially if he lost his temper.

'You'd better bring something to defend yourselves.'

Nick looked down at the nine iron by his side.

Chapter 22
Not my first rodeo

ELSIE HAD LAST SEEN IT EIGHT YEARS AGO WHEN they moved into the ostentatious house with its grotesque pillars and 'look at me' front balcony. She hadn't been happy in their previous place, a modest former fisherman's terrace in the centre of the village. You can't be happy married to a monster. But she had felt more at one with her surroundings. Not that she was at home much. She'd spent most of her time in the mental hospital.

She remembered him carrying it aloft like some trophy, showing it off to the removal men. *Look what I stole from the GIs in the war.* She knew it was still there. He disappeared up to the loft every so often and she'd found traces of oil on his clothes from where he'd been cleaning it.

It wasn't hard to find. Hidden under an old blanket next to the box of black-market goods he'd been unable to sell after the war – stale tobacco, stockings, and packets of condoms, well past their sell-by date.

She cradled it in her arms. It was heavier than she'd imagined. But, to her untrained eye, it looked to be in good condition. Good enough for him at any rate. She opened it up and checked. It was as she'd expected, all ready to use, all ready to do its job. A job she should have done after Billy disappeared; should have done after he'd raped her; should have done after he'd smothered baby Jacob.

Why did I wait so long? The words reverberated around in her head. Guilt had eaten away at her for years. Now, thanks to her new-found friend Amy, she felt empowered to get the justice she deserved. At long last, she had the courage to take control of her own destiny.

What would tomorrow bring? Would the misery finally be over?

Elsie knew one way or another, it had to end.

* * *

'Are you sure about this?'

Nick and Amy were standing in the foyer of the Watersmeet Hotel looking out of the picture frame window at Ritter's house directly opposite. His red Jaguar XJC still parked on the driveway.

'You know how ruthless Ritter is. Why not let me wear the wire and you stay out of harm's way? You're the client. It should be me taking the risks. I'd never forgive myself if anything happened to you.'

Amy smiled. She knew Nick's suggestion made sense. But her parents had brought her up to never walk away from the challenges of life. She'd been in plenty of hairy situations interviewing unscrupulous people; people who turned nasty when faced with incriminating evidence. And she owed it to her father to see this through, whatever the consequences.

'Thanks for your concern, Nick, but Elsie is expecting me, and this ain't my first rodeo.'

Nick nodded. Her response came as no surprise. They turned their attention back to the road and saw a GPO van arrive on the Esplanade. The driver obviously had no problem locating Ritter's house, its vulgar architecture standing out against the more modest dwellings on either side.

The van drove thirty yards past and stopped next to a cable box. Two men, dressed in GPO overalls got out, put up a 'men at work' warning sign and began to attend to the wiring inside the box.

Just after eleven, Ritter got into his jag, swung recklessly into the road and sped away.

Ten minutes later, they made their way up the drive. Elsie was expecting them. She gave Amy a big hug and sat them down in the front room where coffee and biscuits were set out on the table. She had a calm expression, as if resigned to whatever outcome the day had in store. But there was no mistaking the tremor in her hands as she tried to pour the coffee. Amy stood up to help.

'It's the pills I'm on,' Elsie said. 'They make my hands shake sometimes; just one of the many horrid side-effects.'

She told them she couldn't remember the last time she'd entertained friends. 'Fred's business associates are the only people allowed in the house. He makes out I'm his housekeeper and I have to wait on them hand and foot. So, what happens now?'

Nick explained that when Ritter returned they would confront him with a barrage of allegations.

'We want to get him so badly riled that he loses his temper and says something incriminating enough for the police to intervene and arrest him.' He explained about Amy's wire, the telephone engineers in the road, and the police recording the discourse from the van.

'The telephone line for the houses in the road has been disconnected.' Amy said. 'Ritter won't be able to call on his lackeys to help him.'

They rehearsed how Elsie should introduce her new friends, saying they had met by chance in Putsborough a few days ago, and how she'd invited them here for a coffee.

'Once you've said your piece,' Nick said, 'get out of the house and go across to the hotel and wait in reception. We've told them to expect you. Stay there until, all being well, Ritter is handcuffed and led away.'

Elsie nodded, a defiant look on her face. She sat in an armchair near the door with Nick and Amy on the sofa facing the door. Ritter would see them as soon as he came in.

Whilst they waited, Elsie reminisced about her time with Billy and the short time they had together. 'I just know he would've been a loving husband and wonderful father.'

She told them about her love of walking and how she'd introduced Billy to the headland at Morte Point. 'He loved it when we spotted the seals on the rocks below. He said it reminded him of the coastline around Quincy.'

Her broad smile faded in an instant as they heard a car on the drive. Elsie looked at the clock above the mantelpiece.

'He'll be expecting his dinner on the table – so watch out for the fireworks.'

Amy's heart missed a beat as Ritter burst into the room. She *was* afraid. Who wouldn't be? But the thought that struck her, as he stood huffing and puffing, was that he was the spitting image of Denise's sketch. The likeness was uncanny. As good as any photograph.

Ritter's face was a picture of incredulity. *Were his eyes playing tricks on him?* For the briefest of moments he was lost for words, trying to take in the strange tableau before him. What the hell was going on? The Yankee tart. The crippled golfer. In *his* house with Elsie?

His unease grew as he switched his stare between the three of them. Was Elsie playing some kind of game? Only one way to find out. He took a menacing step further into the room. Amy's hand went instinctively to her handbag on the floor beside her to check it was open and within easy reach – just in case.

'Elsie, what the fuck are these two doing here?'

Chapter 23

Confrontation

'I MET NICK AND AMY IN THE CAFÉ AT PUTSBOROUGH and invited them to call in today for coffee. Amy's American. Her father and uncle were in Woolacombe during the war.'

The news didn't come as a surprise to Ritter who, ignoring Elsie, sneered at Nick and told him in no uncertain terms to get out of his house. 'And take your Yankee girlfriend with you.'

Nick and Amy sat perfectly still, saying nothing, not responding to Ritter's vitriolic outburst. Aiming to provoke him from the get-go. Finally, Amy turned to Nick and said, 'there's no disguising the likeness.'

She took out Denise's sketch and put it on the coffee table. Ritter glanced at it, contempt written all over his face.

Amy met Ritter's stare, defiance blazing in her eyes. 'We know it was you who arranged for us to be shot at in the dunes and my car vandalised. We know it was you who rifled Nick's office and broke into my hotel room. Did shredding my underwear turn you on? It was all a waste of time you know. All the incriminating evidence we have on you is in a much safer place. And there's a lot of it, believe me.'

Elsie slipped stealthily out of the room as Ritter focussed his attention on Nick, anger rising from the pit of his stomach.

'You can't confront me in my own home! Who the hell d'you think you are?'

'Two people determined to get answers,' replied Nick calmly.

Ritter's face was ablaze. Wild eyes narrowed as he clenched his fists, ready to lash out, ready to hurt someone badly – very badly.

Where was that slut of a wife? This is all her doing.

'I'll give you one minute to fuck off. If you don't go, I won't be responsible for the consequences. I could call the police and tell them you're trespassing, but I think a quick word to some of my less-desirable associates would be much more fun to watch.'

'Oh, didn't you know?' said Amy. 'Elsie says there's a problem with the phone lines. Didn't you see the GPO van in the road?'

Ritter moved to the sideboard and picked up the phone. The line was dead. He snarled and without taking his eyes off Nick, took something out of his inside jacket pocket and flicked it open. The menacing looking blade glinted in the morning sun reflecting through the large bay window. Nick stood up slowly. He picked up his nine iron and the two men stood facing each other, as if preparing for a duel.

'Did you know a golf professional can swing his short irons at seventy miles an hour? Just imagine the damage a club head could do to someone's face. Take out an eye perhaps? Break a nose? Certainly render an ear useless. How is your hearing by the way?'

Ritter stared at the club in Nick's hand and put the knife back in his pocket. He changed tack.

'You don't want to take any notice of Elsie. She lost the plot years ago and has been in the local nut house more often than she's been at home. She's on so many anti-depressants she doesn't know what day it is. If she's not doped up to the eyeballs, she's probably drunk soon after breakfast. She's quite a liability.'

'Actually,' Amy said, 'there doesn't appear to be much wrong with Elsie's memory. Her recollection from 1943 of you smashing up her face was particularly lucid. She remembers it taking weeks to recover.'

'It wasn't just Elsie who told us about that,' said Nick. 'A London journalist working here during the war told us about a local troublemaker who beat up women. But it seems he was pretty inept when it came to fighting men. I'm sure you haven't forgotten being humiliated by a GI in the Jubilee pub?'

Struggling to keep his anger in check, Ritter sat down on the arm of a chair.

'I know who you are,' he said pointing his finger at Nick. 'From what I hear, your career's as much a failure as your father's. You couldn't hack it as a golf pro, and you now play at being a crippled private dick, hiding behind bushes, spying on men cheating on their wives.

'Your father tried for years to put me inside but never succeeded. Neither will you. Like father, like son. Piss off back to the hut you call an office and take Faye Dunaway here with you.'

Nick and Amy ignored Ritter's vitriol. They stuck faithfully to the script they'd rehearsed the previous evening.

'Why don't you tell us about your ex-business partner Michael Lock?' said Nick. 'It must have taken real guts to push him to his death down those stone stairs. Was it a spur of the moment decision, or something you'd planned when you arranged the visit?'

'I was completely cleared of any wrong-doing on that score,' retorted Ritter. 'It's not my fault the poofter fancied me so much he left me his business. Perhaps I did lead him on a tad!'

'And then, there's Ted Smithers,' said Nick. 'Major Paulton was most helpful last week. He distinctly remembered Smithers turning up on the day of the joint exercise with a broken arm. And you just happening to be with him, kitted up for the exercise as if you knew Ted was going to be injured before the off. But you're not psychic, and there was nothing accidental about what happened. Not content with a clean break, your assault rendered his arm useless for the rest of his life. No wonder he hates you so much.'

The mention of Major Paulton and Smithers rattled Ritter. Nick sensed, for the first time they were starting to get under his skin. Amy tightened the screw.

'It was you, wasn't it, who told his landlady Ted had gone to see his brother in Southsea? Your toupee made a real impression on her by the way! It didn't take us long to track Ted down and he's given us chapter and verse about how you maimed him for life.'

Ritter jeered and stood up. 'You're talking bollocks. Ted can't have told you anything, you stupid bitch. He's fucking d...'

Ritter stopped mid-sentence, holding on to the mantelpiece, breathing heavily; faced flushed.

'He's what?' asked Nick. 'What *were* you were going to say?'

Ritter composed himself, his mouth curled up in a viscous snarl.

'You two are so much out of your depth. You've no idea how much influence I've got round these parts. This pantomime is over; get out now or you won't know what hit you. And I don't mean my fist. I mean a fuckin ten-ton lorry when you least expect it.'

'We'll go when we've got the information we came for,' said Amy, 'Why don't you tell us why you smothered baby Jacob?'

Ritter looked at her, his face incandescent.

'That baby died of natural causes. He'd been abandoned by his mother and it was just my luck the little sprog died on my watch. Elsie had no idea how to look after him. He was neglected from day one.

'Was I sorry about him dying? Was I hell! I wasn't going to let that fair-haired bastard live here a moment longer than necessary. Elsie didn't know I'd arranged with the council for him to be adopted. He saved me the trouble. Good riddance. Every time I looked at him, I saw that fuckin GI's face staring back at me.'

'That GI was my uncle.' said Amy. 'There was no way you were going to let him live was there? He was one of six innocent people you've killed. And that's just the ones *we* know about.'

Ritter looked at her, a perplexed expression on his face. 'You can't fuckin count darlin!'

Amy took a deep breath. She knew this was likely to be their last chance.

'You somehow caused the landing craft to capsize. You drowned my uncle.'

Amy paused, willing Ritter to respond.

Tempted; so very tempted. Keep quiet or show these two upstarts just how smart I'd been that day?

He kept quiet.

'And you're responsible for the deaths of the two soldiers who drowned inside the tank.'

Ritter had almost forgotten about Puglissi and Russo. He scowled at the image that flashed into his mind of the Sicilian GIs welching on his cigarette deal. He could see the knife across Jimmy Knox's throat; could hear the 'mother-fucker' insult. He'd vowed to get his own back. The scowl turned to a grin as he visualised freezing water getting higher and higher in their tank. *Good riddance you wop bastards.*

Nick seethed with anger and crockery went flying as he banged his fist down hard on the coffee table, a look of complete disgust on his face.

'What kind of man smirks at the deaths of innocent human beings?'

Vitriol spewed from Ritter's mouth. 'You're just like your wanker of a father, fuckin weak.'

'You smothered baby Jacob,' said Amy. 'You killed Michael Lock and had your lackeys murder Ted Smithers. And you physically and mentally abused Elsie for over thirty years. Elsie, who by rights, should have married my Uncle Billy.'

Spittle formed at the side of Ritter's mouth, red mist engulfed him, like a fireball about to explode. Hatred ingrained in his voice.

'Yeah, but she couldn't, could she? She married me and you know what darling? The one that gave me the most pleasure was taking out your fuckin' uncle!

'You amateurs are wasting your time. The police have never been able to get me. Do you really think they'd waste time investigating a GI's body missing since 1944? I've heard of cold cases but this one's fuckin frozen. No jury in the world would convict me!'

The door flew open. Elsie stood there, her eyes screwed up tight, Ritter's Enfield pointed straight at him. Her voice, when she spoke calm, collected, almost matter of fact; as if she'd been rehearsing this moment for decades.

'You're probably right, Fred. Why waste time going to court?'

The crack of the rifle rang in his ears; dark red patches spread like a tsunami across his chest and a cry of alarm emitted from his mouth as he slumped against the wall; a look of utter bewilderment on his face.

This can't be happening to me. I'm Fred Ritter. I always come out on top.

Not this time.

Chapter 24
Chapter and Verse

'IT'S ABOUT TIME YOU SAMPLED OUR NATIONAL DISH,' said Nick. 'And there's no better place to eat it than sitting on a sea wall at high tide.'

Nick and Amy had been first in the queue when Woolacombe's fish & chip shop had opened its doors to its hungry patrons at 5.45pm. This was their first taste of freedom in forty-eight hours. They'd been cooped up in Peter's bungalow with the ever-present Eileen waiting on them hand and foot, much to Peter's embarrassment.

Peter had come clean to Nick about his relationship. When Eileen heard Amy and Nick would be staying for a few days, she lost no time in installing herself as chief cook and bottle-washer; much to the chagrin of Peter's housekeeper who declared herself redundant and made her feelings very clear. *She'll soon get bored with playing the happy housewife. Don't come running back to me when she does!*

The telephone call they'd waited impatiently for had finally come that afternoon. They were to rendezvous with the chief superintendent in Barnstaple police station at

7 pm. His assistant promised them there would be a full debrief on Ritter and Elsie.

Chapter and verse.

Amy sat on the wall next to Nick, eating her cod and chips supper. A comfortable silence enveloped them, both lost in their own thoughts, transfixed by the seductive rhythm of the incoming tide.

The events that had happened two days ago were still something of a blur to Amy. She stared down at the waves. A melee of confused images flashed before her eyes as she tried once again to make sense of what had happened – Ritter's boast about getting rid of Billy; Elsie's potent words; the rifle's whip-like snap; Ritter clutching his chest; blood everywhere; the cavalry arriving with hordes of policemen and women, seemingly coming out of nowhere, followed closely by the ambulance crew, pushing everyone out of their way to attend to the prostrate body lying unconscious on the floor; the colour of Ritter's torso, a perfect match with the scarlet twirls of the living room carpet.

One image *was* horribly clear. Amy knew it would live with her forever. Elsie being handcuffed and led away to the black Mariah idling on the pavement outside, doors wide open, ready for the next incumbent. Was her nod to Amy one of resignation or relief, she wondered?

Shock had numbed Amy that day; frozen her mind; messed with her senses. She'd been unsure where she was or why she was there. She remembered her and Nick being guided into the kitchen, a woman constable steering her gently by the arm to where the chief superintendent was waiting; his words reverberating around her fuddled brain.

Congratulations ... we might just have enough ...
conviction for murder...say nothing to nobody...don't go
back to your hotel...soon be crawling with media...keep
your heads down ... stay at Peter's until I call you...might
be a couple of days... well done... well bloody done!

Nick's gentle tap on her arm disturbed Amy's musings. 'Well, what d'you think?'

She finished the last of her chips and washed them down with cola.

'Pretty good,' said Amy. 'But not a patch on New England lobster rolls! And only you Brits could get away with serving supper in an old newspaper!'

She rolled up the detritus and turned shamefaced to Nick.

'I've got something to show you.' She hesitated before taking a brown leather pouch out of her handbag and passing it gingerly to Nick.

'Lady M didn't send me lipstick!'

Nick's eyebrows raised high on a furrowed forehead when he saw what was inside.

'She thought her Derringer might come in useful. It was in my bag when we confronted Ritter. Primed and ready.'

Nick looked long and hard at Amy. 'Would you have used it?'

Amy didn't respond straight away. *Was this the time or place?* She'd been bottling up her feelings ever since Nick had told her he'd never forgive himself if she came to any harm.

She searched her head for the heartfelt words; her response, when it came, little more than a whisper as her impassioned voice did its best to be heard over the sound of waves breaking against the sea wall.

'Yes. Yes, I would, if it meant protecting two people who mean a great deal to me.'

'I don't follow.'

'Elsie and you of course!' Amy laughed nervously, a crimson blush spreading across her face like an aquarelle painting.

'Thank you.' Nick said quietly. He didn't know what else to say as a helter-skelter of confused emotions whirled around his insides, his eyes firmly fixed on his watch.

'It's almost 6:30. We'd better be on our way. We don't want to keep the chief super waiting. Dad will join us there. He's picking Martin up on the way.'

* * *

A constable showed Nick and Amy into the interview room where Peter and Martin were already waiting. Jumble was curled up in one corner fast asleep.

'The chief constable will be with you in just a few moments.'

David Short arrived five minutes later, a slim briefcase under his arm. His impassive expression gave nothing away. His tone, when he spoke, was business-like, almost curt. He was clearly not a man interested in small talk.

'Two things to kick-off. Everything you hear this evening is strictly confidential. The last thing we need is Ritter's lawyer getting wind of anything or any more interference from the media than we've had already.'

'And the second?' prompted Nick.

'Thank you for everything you've achieved. If it wasn't for the courage and determination you've all shown in exposing Ritter, we would not be in the favourable position we are now. But, from now on, this must be a police matter.

'Ms Ridd, I've no doubt you'll be keen to get back to the States. And Nick, you can get stuck into some new cases. I'm sure Peter and Martin will be eager to assist. So, and I mean this in the best possible way, leave Ritter, Elsie et al to me and mine. Understood?'

Amy didn't like being patronised. She eye-balled David, 'well, I guess that depends on what you're going to tell us.'

'Fair point,' said David. 'Let's start with Ritter. The operation to remove the bullet went well. He's in intensive care but conscious and off the critical list. We expect to interview him sometime tomorrow, matron permitting.'

'And Elsie?' asked Amy.

'Elsie has been remanded in custody. The shooting was clearly premeditated, so whatever we feel about the rights and wrongs of what she did, she will be charged with attempted murder. However...'

'No way!'

Amy's shout reverberated around the stark room; the anger in her voice reinforcing her Yankee dialect. Jumble, startled by the disturbance, took safety under the table beside his master.

'You can't let that happen. You just can't. After all Ritter did to her. After all she's suffered at his hands for over thirty years. That's not justice.'

The chief superintendent paused to let Amy's outburst have its moment. It was no less than he'd expected. He'd been here many times before.

'I was going to say: however, there *are* exceptional mitigating circumstances in this case. Provocation, physical and mental abuse and many more factors that Elsie's counsel will make abundantly clear during her trial.'

'Elsie's counsel!' Amy protested. 'How on earth is she expected to pay for expensive solicitors, barristers and God knows who else? She's hardly got a penny to her name!'

The chief superintendent smiled and looked across the table at Peter.

'I'm calling in some favours Amy. Elsie will be represented by the best legal team Devon has to offer and I'm footing the bill.'

Amy mouthed *thank you* to Peter as David continued.

'I'd expect her to receive a short sentence, most likely suspended for two years. She should walk out of court a free woman and, assuming she behaves herself, stay that way.

'Moving on, it's very unlikely that we will be able to reopen the Baby Jacob and Michael Lock cases.'

There was, he told them, insufficient evidence to have a realistic chance of securing a conviction. It was Nick's turn to protest but, anticipating the reaction, David held up his hand signalling Nick to listen.

'Hear me out. The best we can aim for, at this stage, is to charge Ritter with four murders: Billy, the two GIs in the tank and Ted Smithers. If he's convicted, he'll spend the rest of his days in Dartmoor.'

The chief turned his attention unexpectedly to Martin.

'Martin, after identifying Smithers's body on the beach, you said in your interview, you'd noticed something unusual when you were with him in the Grampus Inn.'

Martin shifted uneasily in his seat, never comfortable being centre stage. He cleared his throat and looked down at the table, as if for inspiration.

'Ted gripped his glass tightly. It was as if he was afraid someone might creep up and take it off him before he'd finished supping. That's when I noticed the fingernails on his right hand were extraordinarily long, unlike those on his left.'

'And the explanation you offered in your statement?' quizzed David.

'I assumed he was unable to cut them because he couldn't hold scissors or clippers in his damaged left hand. Maybe he had to rely on his sister to cut them for him?'

'Thank you.' said David. He told them the pathologist who carried out Ted's autopsy had found considerable amounts of black material under the long fingernails of Ted's right hand. Forensic analysis had revealed it to be Melton wool, the fabric used to make donkey jackets.

'The pathologist has described a possible scenario in which Ted grabbed his attacker's jacket with his right hand and hung on for dear life to try and stop his assailant hurling him over the cliff. Three of Ritter's close associates are being interviewed as I speak. One of them, a real thug with a long history of GBH, wears a black donkey jacket. It has a tear on the collar!'

'What about Billy and the two GIs who drowned in the tank?' Nick asked, trying not to let his impatience get the better of him. 'Do you have enough to convict Ritter?'

'Unfortunately, the prosecuting counsel doesn't consider Ritter's confession, such as it was, and the manner in which it was obtained, to be sufficient, on its own, to secure a conviction. I don't need to remind you the deaths occurred thirty-three years ago, and Billy's body has never been found.'

A stunned silence filled the room; disappointment hanging in the air like a 1950's London smog.

'However,' continued David, 'thanks to an enterprising young constable working on the case, further interesting items have come to light.'

David explained they'd been tearing Ted's digs apart for clues. They had found an old cardboard shoe box hidden away in the boarded-up chimney.

'Constable Wells will explain.'

All eyes turned to the constable who'd shown them into the room. Putting on a pair of latex gloves, he unlocked the cupboard and carried a small box to the table.

'I found this lodged on a small firebrick shelf just inside the chimney breast.' He opened the box for everyone to look inside at a broken wristwatch, a war medal, a pair of old silver-plate cufflinks, a pack of well-worn playing cards and two faded black & white erotic postcards of topless women (Amy mused they'd be considered art-deco today).

'I don't get it,' said Nick, speaking for all four of them. 'Am I missing something?'

'When Constable Wells examined the playing cards,'

said David, 'he found a message wedged firmly inside the pack. It looks like Ted glued paper to both sides of a playing card and wrote on it in tiny writing. The card is locked away waiting for verification by an expert. The writing is faded but there's no mistaking the content nor Ted Smithers' signature. The note is dated 12th June 1944.'

'That's ten days after Billy went missing,' said Nick. 'Ten days after the joint training exercise.'

'It is.' replied David. 'We think Ted wrote it on the day he was released from hospital. We found one of Ted's old business ledgers with customer names on it. If I were a betting man, I'd say it's odds on the writing on the note and the entries in the ledger were written by the same hand.'

'What did the note say?' asked Amy, as calmly as she could. Her heart was in her mouth, her mind working overtime.

David opened his briefcase and handed them each a page of A4.

'Ted's message typed, word for word. Take your time.'

If anything happens to me, hand this note to the police.

Private Ritter took my place on the Utah landing craft taking part in the training exercise in Woolacombe Bay on 2nd of June 1944. By agreeing to his plan, I was able to wipe off my £300 gambling debt to him. I would never have agreed if I'd known what he was going to do. He said he'd dislocate my shoulder on the morning of the exercise, and persuade Major Paulton that he should take my place. But he tied me to a post, put a rag in my mouth to muffle my screams and took a sledgehammer to my left arm, shattering the bones. He'd told me he was going to get even with some yanks and boasted about three bodies with one capsize. I've since heard a GI, Corporal Ridd is missing, and two yanks drowned in their tank when Utah capsized. Ritter is evil. One day, I hope to have the courage to confess what he made me do. One day, I hope to see him hang.

Edward (Ted) Smithers 12th June 1944.

'Now we *do* have enough to convict Ritter,' said David calmly.

The sweet taste of relief filled the room. Peter punched the air and shook David's hand; Martin lifted Jumble up towards the ceiling in delight; Amy and Nick hugged the life out of each other; their earlier tension evaporating like water in a spin dryer.

It was Nick who realised they had unfinished business.

'David, there must be something we can do to persuade Ritter to say what he did with Billy's body? Billy deserves a proper burial; Elsie and Amy deserve closure.'

'What do you suggest?'

'What if you tell Ritter he's going to be charged with six murders? And you let it be known to his solicitor the police would be prepared to drop the Baby Jacob and Michael Lock charges, if Ritter tells you what he did with Billy's body?'

David smiled. 'You're wasted as a PI Nick. You should get yourself off to Hendon! What you've suggested has already crossed our minds along with a couple of other potential deals we're looking at.

'I want you all to be assured of one thing. The police will do everything in its power, and I do mean *everything*, to persuade Ritter to tell us the whereabouts of Billy's body.'

Chapter 25

Message in a bottle

Nᴵᴄᴋ ʜᴀᴅ ᴀssᴜᴍᴇᴅ ʜᴇ'ᴅ ᴅʀɪᴠᴇ Aᴍʏ ʙᴀᴄᴋ ᴛᴏ Woolacombe, but she asked to be dropped off a mile or so from her hotel.

'A walk will help clear my head and the exercise will do me good. Let's catch up first thing in the morning.'

She needed to be on her own. Needed time and space to assimilate everything she'd heard in the past hour. Her initial elation at reading Ted's note had turned to melancholy. It enveloped her like a shroud. She wasn't subdued. Nor was she jumping for joy. She wondered if it was because Elsie was unlikely to get the justice she deserved for Jacob's death.

But she knew, deep down, it was more than that.

She'd come to Devon to solve the mystery of Uncle Billy's disappearance. To help right a wrong that had plagued her father for half his life. That task was almost over. And with it, her reason for being here. Her savings were running out and she'd need to head back to New England soon and pick up her journalism career. Her time here in Devon, working with Nick, was fast coming to an end.

Amy scolded herself for being selfish. Tonight was about Billy. Her pace accelerated as an idea formed in her head. On entering the hotel, she went off in search of Dan, the friendly barman. He was only too happy to oblige.

Fifteen minutes and much reflection later, Amy sat at the dressing table perched on the raised plinth in the bay window of her room, overlooking the bay. The room was in darkness save for the table lamp shining down on the blank page of hotel notepaper; her fountain pen poised, willing her to begin what she considered to be the most important prose of her life.

Words normally came easily to her. They were the tools of her trade. Not tonight. Amy looked out of the window at the sky. As the message became clear, her nib etched swiftly across the page.

30ᵗʰ September 1976

Dear Uncle Billy

We only met a few times before you and Dad went off to war and, as I was a 'babe in arms,' I know you'll forgive me not remembering you. But, having spent these last few weeks here in North Devon, I feel as if I've gotten to know you well, thanks to your lovely Elsie.

She's told me so much about you and about your beautiful baby boy, Jacob. I know how proud you would have been of him and how happy you all would have been living together in Quincy.

That was not to be. But I wanted you to know that Elsie is finally free of that evil man. I think, in time, she will be as content as she can be without you and Jacob by her side.

She still loves you as much as she ever did, and I know how much you loved her. This letter is not quite yet the closure my father hoped for, but be assured it won't be long before we can give you the burial you deserve.

And I promise I'll be there, holding Elsie's hand when she says her final goodbye.

God bless.

   Your loving niece
Amy Ridd

Tears welled as she opened the empty wine bottle Dan had found for her, rolled the note up tightly, pushed it in and replaced the cap.

Amy shivered in the night air as she stepped outside. She turned up the collar of her coat against the autumn chill, and gazed up in wonder at a crystal-clear sky overflowing with millions of tiny stars, dancing in harmony around a near full moon. It illuminated her path down to the beach, the torch in her pocket redundant.

One star stood out proudly on the black and silver canvas. Elsie had told Amy how she and Billy had adopted Sirius as their own. And there it was; glowing brightly in a fitting tribute to their short life together.

She headed out to the rocks on the western edge of the beach near to where Billy's craft had capsized. It was an ebb tide, advancing relentlessly towards America, equipped and ready for the task Amy had in store.

Her hiking boots provided good grip as she scrambled over the jagged granite rocks to where they dropped abruptly to the sea. Amy kissed the bottle goodbye, steadied herself and hurled it as far out as she could. The waves flicked it high into the air, as if rejecting the mission she'd asked of them. But not for long. They soon curled themselves around the precious cargo as it started its journey home.

As she stood motionless, staring out at the black sea, she saw her father's face as vividly as if he were standing, arm in arm, beside her. His mouth turned upwards in an appreciative smile.

'Job done dad.' she whispered. 'You can rest easy now.'

EPILOGUE
New beginnings

Ten days later

The Falcon Hotel, Bude.

Dear Lady M

I'm writing to you from what I'm told is the oldest coaching house hotel (established 1798) in North Cornwall at the end of my short 'fall' (I guess you would say autumn) break in this beautiful part of the world.

You asked me, when we spoke after the shooting, to update you with all the news.

Let's start with Ritter. Nick called me yesterday to say the police are building a strong case against him. The nasty piece of work he paid to throw Ted Smithers over the cliff has confessed. We should soon know what he did with Uncle Billy's body. The chief super (not someone prone to exaggeration) called it 'positive work in progress.'

I've managed to speak to Elsie a couple of times, and she's as ok as one can be in custody. She tells

303

me her defence team are kind, patient and working hard to prepare for her trial in three weeks' time. She's relieved to be free of Ritter at long last and is trying to stay positive by planning for her future. It seems Ritter put the house in her name as a tax dodge and she plans to sell, 'he's not going to need it where he's going,' and buy a small cottage, possibly in Putsborough.

She's also determined to find a job, her first in thirty years. Ritter forbade her from working, and kept her under virtual lock and key. She wants to train as a social worker and help young people with drug and alcohol-related problems. With her own experience to call upon and a heart of gold, I think she'll make a success of her new career, but we all recognise she's got a long way to go.

You might remember Lt Barry Frye. He was the American officer who, alongside my dad, tried to save the two GIs in the tank from drowning. He also risked his career by writing the damning report condemning the decision to proceed with the joint exercise in the prevailing black east wind.

The US Embassy in London found his contact details and I wrote to him in the States. He replied to say he has fond memories of my father and their time together in the West Country. We agreed we should work together to commemorate the hundreds of GIs who perished on the North Devon beaches before D-Day.

He suggested I ask the council and local

landowners for contributions to create a memorial. He'll liaise with key people Stateside and contact Commander Webb, the ex-CO of the Assault Training Centre to enlist his support. When I told Nick, he suggested Woolacombe Green, overlooking the beach and sea, as an ideal spot for a stone of remembrance.

I've got some good news about Denise. Her interview to study for a diploma in art and design at Plymouth College is in a few days' time, and I'm going to drive her and provide moral support. Thank you so much for showing her sketches to your contact in the art world and for agreeing to be her benefactor. Fingers crossed she'll begin her first term mid-October.

Martin and Jumble and Peter and Eileen, his now 'live-in' lady-friend, are all well. Peter is the toast of the golf club for helping to put Ritter behind bars. He revels in the attention, especially from the lady members!

That just leaves Nick and me. I'm driving back to Woolacombe tonight and we're together the day after tomorrow – on the golf course! Thanks so much for your advice. I'll let you know the outcome.

Fondest love,

Amy

* * *

Nick and Amy had an eleven am tee at Saunton. As they

were in good time, Nick pulled into the layby to savour the view after climbing the hill out of Croyde. The sun had broken through the clouds and slivers of silver flashed like swords in the surf. The wide expanse of Saunton Beach spread out before them, with Braunton Burrows just visible in the distance. The day the shots were fired was now a fading memory.

They sat for a while, lost in their own thoughts until Nick broke the silence.

'Strange to think, your uncle trained in the dunes where we're about to play golf – on what many consider to be two of the best links in the country.'

'I'm looking forward to playing,' said Amy. 'And to winning of course!'

Fifteen minutes later they were on the first tee of the West Course. Nick looked across the fairways and thought he'd rarely seen a more inviting vista. There was just the hint of wind, creating unusually benign conditions for links abutting the sea.

Nick soon saw how well Amy could play. Just under three hours later, she was one hole up with three to play. Her shots were crisp and accurate, as befitted her four handicap. Standing on the highly elevated par three 16th, Nick knew there was nowhere else in the world he'd rather be and few people he would rather be with. He was playing the game he loved with a talented young woman, with whom he'd solved what would surely be one of the landmark cases of his career.

Life was good.

Amy teed off first, her swing textbook perfect. The ball

soured high into the sky and landed some three feet in front of the pin. She turned and smiled at Nick with just the hint of a tear in her eyes and a quiver in her voice.

'That was for my dad. He would have loved playing these links.'

Nick's ball flew high and straight to land five feet past the pin, spin backwards and come to rest a few inches from the hole.

'And that one's for your Uncle Billy,' he said.

The match finished all square and they sat on the clubhouse balcony enjoying their drinks with the autumn sun dipping low in the sky. As the shadows got longer, they watched but did not really see the last players finishing their rounds. Amy shivered and Nick handed her his sweater to wrap around her shoulders.

'I'm not really cold. It just seems surreal sitting here, having solved something that plagued my father for most of his life. He never forgave himself for not returning to Devon. I hope he's looking down on us now, happy in the knowledge that retribution and justice have come out on top. Don't ever underestimate the contribution your agency can make to people's lives, Nick.'

'I won't. And thanks for helping out in the office yesterday. You being there was a godsend.'

'I hope you realise my receptionist skills were tested to the limit whilst you were out being a PI,' she teased. 'The telephone hardly stopped ringing. By five o'clock your diary was full of appointments for weeks ahead. The media interest surrounding Ritter's arrest has really put the agency on the map. They're calling you a hero a second time round. But did you notice the really interesting thing about the enquiries?'

'I did. I spent yesterday evening going through your synopses of the calls. Most of them relate to cold cases, some going back as far as your Uncle Billy's. That's why I've decided two things about the agency going forward.'

'I'm all ears,' said Amy.

'The Devon Constabulary closed its cold case unit six months ago to save costs. My Dad was angry because the two retired coppers who worked the cases had enjoyed considerable success. They're now tending their gardens, playing bridge and the occasional game of golf. It's such a waste.'

'So,' said Amy, quick on the uptake as ever, 'you're going to use their experience in the agency?'

'Yes, I am. I'm going to leave seedy divorce cases and fraud or corruption to others. From now on, we're going to specialise in cold cases, and I'll sign up those coppers as associates to work on an as-and-when needed basis.'

'That's logical.' replied Amy. 'It makes good business sense to differentiate the agency and focus on work you find most rewarding. What's the second decision?'

'This one won't be so easy. Martin is happy to carry on working on a casual basis but would run a mile from taking on any more responsibility. And my father will continue in a mentoring role, but he deserves to enjoy his retirement, play his golf and entertain his lady friends!'

'So, what have you concluded?'

'I need a business partner. Someone to share the workload with and help the business grow. Someone with strong investigative skills and the determination never to give up on a case.'

'Do you have anyone in mind?' asked Amy, unable to hide the tremor in her voice.

'I do. She's sitting next to me. All I have to do is persuade her not to go back to the States, to give up her journalism career and throw in her lot with this rookie PI with the gammy knee.'

Amy sat perfectly still, the sound of her heartbeat resonating in her head.

She'd hoped beyond hope he might ask her to stay. There was, after all, nothing to go home for. Her parents had passed away; the family home was empty. And she certainly didn't relish grovelling to her ex-boss for her old job back.

She had loved the buzz she used to get from chasing down a good story, but she'd really enjoyed working with Nick these past few weeks. It all felt so much more real somehow. She was about to respond when Nick's words clinched it.

'How does the Webber-Ridd Agency sound to you?'

The smile in her eyes said it all; joy radiated off her and she knew, in her heart and her head that this was the challenge she'd been looking for. A sense of calm embraced her, reinforcing the confidence she had in the agency's future.

'It sounds perfect Nick, just perfect. Thank you. It's a good job I applied for a new visa last week. Just on the off chance, of course, you'd ask me to stay!'

They burst out laughing.

'I can't wait to tell Lady M. And,' added Amy, 'you'll be pleased to know, I've got a lead on Peter, the missing boy case from the 1950s.'

Historical notes

THE TRAINING REGIME OF AMERICAN GIS IN NORTH Devon preparing for the D-Day landings in 1943/44 is well documented and the author has woven numerous authentic events into the fictional story of Jim and Billy Ridd.

The US military had little choice but to use this part of the coast for their amphibious training, despite the lethal undercurrents and strong waves after the British Army had rejected the area in favour of beaches in South Devon.

Over ten-thousand GIs did descend on the North Devon coast in September 1943. Their main encampment of 500 Nissen huts was based outside Braunton village, across the road from Braunton Burrows.

The Assault Training Centre was headquartered at the Woolacombe Bay Hotel, under the command of a Lt Colonel Paul Thompson.

Public affairs officers as depicted by Jim Ridd, were considered a vital part of the US war effort to keep the local community *on-side*, and to work with the world's media to portray morale-boosting news to the folks back home and around the world.

Much of the narrative in Jim Ridd's letters home describing life for the GIs and the locals in North Devon is based on real-life incidents recorded by local residents and American officers during 1943/44.

The *Tips for American Servicemen in Britain in World War Two* document was distributed to all GIs serving in the British Isles.

The Red Barn in Woolacombe was previously known as The Bungalow Café and became the American Red Cross Services Club during 1943/44. Today, it's a thriving pub/restaurant and very much a feature of village life for locals and visitors alike.

General Dwight Eisenhower visited the ATC and insisted upon the GIs using live ammunition during their training exercises to simulate what the troops would experience in Normandy. Several hundred GIs were killed in the ten months of training. The machine-gun incident, in which the guns sank into the sand lowering their field of fire resulting in troops being mown down whilst disembarking from their landing crafts, is authentic.

The Glenn Miller Band toured GI bases in Britain during 1943/44 and played to thousands of the US troops based in North Devon.

There were frequent visits to the ATC by British and US journalists, including one in 1943, by the aristocrat, Lady Margaret Frances Anne Vane-Tempest-Stewart. The Lady Margaret (Lady M) character portrayed in this novel is a figment of the author's imagination.

The *Jim Crow* segregation between white and black GIs was as strong in North Devon as it was in the USA.

Cardboard coffins were used for black GIs killed serving their country. The George Orwell quotation is authentic.

A Wellington bomber did crash on Morte Point but there were not, as far as the author can ascertain, any fatalities.

The capsizing of an assault landing craft, and the death by drowning of the tank crew members a few days before the D-Day landings is authentic.

There were not however, to the best of the author's knowledge, any joint training exercises on the North Devon Coast between US and British troops prior to the Normandy landings.

Many of the incidents recounted by the fictitious characters Major Tom in his diaries and by Elsie Ritter on the beach at Croyde and at Puttsborough Café are based upon real life events.

Saunton Golf Club was taken over by the US Military from 1939 to 1951 and tanks were parked on the course next to the sand dunes. By January 1952, club staff and German prisoners of war had the courses up and running again. The East and West courses feature regularly in the top 100 courses in the UK.

The American Road still exists today and provides a pathway through Braunton Burrows to the Taw and Torridge Estuary. The notice board in the car park features an old black and white photograph from 1944 of GIs on their amphibious landing craft.

Over sixty-thousand British women, many of them pregnant, left these shores for the States after the war to become GI brides.

A 1944 black and white photograph of tanks on the course at Saunton and the granite stone memorial, dedicated to American soldiers, erected on Woolacombe Green in 1992, were the catalysts for this novel.

Acknowledgements

A CONSIDERABLE NUMBER OF INDIVIDUALS AND organisations have assisted in the development of this novel. I owe them a debt of gratitude, especially those who contributed to the historical facts that underpin this work of fiction. Any inaccuracies are of my making and are my responsibility.

My sincere thanks are extended to you all and, in particular, to the following:

Richard T Bass, the military historian who has written several books on the American presence in North Devon and the US Assault Training Centre. Richard is a leading authority on this subject and his insights contributed to the factual backdrop to this novel

Richard Howse, a former police officer for his advice on police interviewing techniques and prosecution procedures

Christian Livermore and John Merivale from Blue Pencil Agency. Christian for her invaluable critique of my first draft and John for his robust copyedit

Brigadier General Allan G Pixton U.S. Army, Retired (deceased 2015). In 1944, he served as a Lt Colonel in the

ATC in Woolacombe in 1943/44 and wrote a compelling narrative of his time as an amphibious expert in North Devon. Several of the real-life incidents recorded in this narrative have been incorporated into Part One of this novel. My sincere gratitude to his family

Colin Thomas, a dear friend and colleague who's been with me for most of the *A Black East Wind* journey and whose editorial guidance helped shape my raw materials into the finished article

Independent booksellers – thank you for all your support and encouragement, especially those in the glorious South West of England

Edward Estlin Cummings (1894-1962) – the American poet, essayist, playwright and visual artist. His renowned *Tulips and Chimneys* poems typified the egalitarian spirit of the Jim Ridd character in Part One. Recognition also to his New York publisher Thomas Seltzer (1875-1943) for having the foresight to publish Cummings' radical work

Saunton Golf Club for the photo that inspired this novel and for allowing me to feature the club throughout Parts One and Two

The excellent team at Matador – 'partnership publishers' in the truest sense

Braunton Countryside Centre

Braunton and District Museum

Christie Devon Estates

Explore Braunton

Express Newspapers

Mortehoe Museum

Parkin Estates

Tales of Woolacombe at War by *Woolacombe Girl*
The BBC WW2 People's War Archives
The Guardian Newspaper
The Imperial War Museum
The Mail Online
The National WW11 Museum New Orleans
Traces of War
War Memorials Register.

Finally, sincere thanks to my wife Mary who patiently put up with me being locked away in my office in the barn for far longer than either of us anticipated!

———————————

News

Keep up to date with news from the author by checking out the following:

Website – www. jackgranfers.co.uk
Instagram – granfersjack
Facebook – jack granfers
Twitter – @JGranfers

You can also contact him by email at:
jackgranfers@gmail.com

The next Webber-Ridd Agency
cold-case investigation

If you enjoyed Jack's debut novel, here's an extract from his next novel featuring Nick Webber and Amy Ridd.

Bideford North Devon 1954

T HE THREE-YEAR OLD BOY WAS BEING PULLED along by his father, who seemed oblivious to the youngster's short legs having to work overtime to keep up with his long strides. And no wonder. The man was over six feet, ex-services and walked everywhere as if he was still on the parade ground at RAF Cranwell.

The boy was in his *Sunday best*, usually reserved for his weekly visit to the Sunday school at St. Mary's, the church his father attended. Tucked behind the town council building and close to the old bridge that crosses the Torridge River, St Mary's had been a haven of refuge for the father these past torrid months.

He'd dressed Peter in a cream woollen double-breasted coat with velvet collar, white shirt, dark grey shorts, and long black socks. The boy could see his reflection in his black Clarks leather shoes which contrasted vividly with his blond hair, cut the previous day in a short back and sides. National Health spectacles, as round as a one-penny coin, adorned his face, attached to uncomfortable wire frames. The right lens covered with a white patch to help correct a lazy eye.

But today was not a Sunday. It was a mid-October Wednesday afternoon. Slivers of sunlight from a cloudless sky filtered through the plane trees that lined their route, their leaves blowing every which way in the autumn wind. The temperature uncharacteristically warm.

Too warm for a long woollen coat, thought the father, but there wasn't time to go back and change. He wanted his son to look his very best for his mother. She'd not set eyes on her darling Peter for over four months. The father prayed that his wife, given the number of drugs she was on, would be alert enough to recognise him. And well enough, he hoped, to manage a long-overdue hug.

The father knew visiting hours at Bideford Hospital would be over in twenty minutes. He'd promised Peter he would find a way to smuggle him in, despite children under sixteen not being allowed on the cancer ward. *No ifs or buts.*

What the little boy didn't know, and couldn't possibly understand, was that his mother was dying. She had, at best, a few painful weeks before the cancer that ravaged her lungs finally got its way.

If the boy didn't see his mother today, the father believed his son's abiding memory, if young children did remember such things, would be her coffin being lowered into the ground and covered in the loamy earth of St. Mary's cemetery. He was determined not to let that happen.

The strict *no children in the wards* rule rankled him badly.

Why couldn't the officious matron show some compassion? She knew his wife could pass away at any moment. When he'd broached the subject with her, begging for Peter to be able to see his mother one last time, she'd pointed to the large notice displayed on the ward and walked away, stiffly muttering *rules are rules*.

Sod you, he said to himself as he reached the rear of the hospital building and the metal fire escape to the fourth floor. He lifted his son on to his shoulders and climbed the rusty steps as quickly as he could manage. Steps that looked as if they hadn't seen a coat of paint in fifty years.

His plan depended on the assistance of a young staff nurse who'd taken pity on his predicament and volunteered to push open the fire escape door a few inches for him and Peter to slip inside. He'd befriended the nurse over the course of the seventeen long weeks he'd visited his wife and appreciated the risk she was taking and the trouble she would be in if caught.

She'd shown him photographs of her three-year-old nephew and said she couldn't imagine, in similar circumstances, him not being allowed to visit his mother.

Once they were inside, the plan was for Peter's father to hide his son behind one of the large wicker laundry baskets adjacent to the fire doors. He would go and check on his wife and then, as the nurse kept matron distracted in her office, come back, collect Peter and scamper back to his wife's bedside, close the curtains and savour a few precious minutes together.

Breathing heavily as he reached the floor of his wife's ward, he lowered Peter to the ground and pushed gently against the fire door, hoping against hope it would open.

It did.

He peered inside to see the familiar scene – twenty patients with their visitors, sitting solemnly around their loved ones' beds, doing their best to make meaningful conversation.

He recognised the weary faces, exhausted by the daily ritual; worn down with hopelessness. A transient community that had got to know each other well; all grasping at lifelines that were not there and praying silently that the end, when it came, could be quick and pain free.

Time to get moving.

He had explained to Peter the 'game' they were about to play. *Hide behind the large basket and keep as quiet as a church mouse until I come to find you and we surprise mummy.*

Keen to please, the youngster crouched as low as he could. He put a finger to his lips.

I understand daddy, off you go.

There was ten minutes left before the bell sounded and the visitors made their way down the main staircase to the exit at the front of the hospital. Until tomorrow, same time, same wretched place.

He walked to his wife's bedside and pulled the curtain apart to squeeze in beside her. He'd often, on earlier visits, done a double take. *Am I at the right bedside?*

Sunken eyes looked up at him from a gaunt face, grey hair straggling down to thin shoulders above the tiny skeleton that was now her body.

Where was the beautiful fair-haired woman he'd married five years ago? Where was the smile that had stolen his heart? The smile that had made him the happiest man alive.

He took her hand in his and leant over to peck her on the cheek.

'Where's Peter?' she asked expectantly, her faint voice barely audible over the background hubbub of the surrounding beds.

'He's here. You're going to see your beloved son.'

The merest hint of a smile flickered across her face as if a sudden beam of sunlight had illuminated the darkest corner of her mind; her usual deadpan eyes alive once again as she savoured the thought of being re-united with Peter.

She loved her husband dearly. He was a good man, despite the demons of war that occasionally haunted him accompanied, more often than not, by the black dog of depression that left him paralysed with guilt for days on end.

He'd served his country as a Lancaster-bomber pilot, following orders against his better judgement and his Christian principles, in the relentless night missions over Germany, bombing the towns and cities along the Ruhr. And the civilians. A ruthless campaign orchestrated by Marshal of the Royal Air Force, Sir Arthur Travers Harris, 1st Baronet – *Bomber* Harris or, as the Lancaster crews, ushered out night after night, referred to him as *Butcher* Harris.

But Peter, her beautiful, beautiful boy, was her world. She loved him with a ferocity that had sometimes frightened her. He was, for her, the most precious gift a mother could have.

Especially given the circumstances by which he was conceived.

Peter's father re-traced his steps, pleased to see the matron and nurse deep in conversation in matron's office.

Peter had hidden himself well. There was no sign of him as Peter's father approached the basket, nor could he see him when he peered behind.

Perhaps he'd climbed inside?

The basket was empty. Nobody; no little boy. Nothing.

The father looked at the fire-escape door he'd closed carefully behind him a few minutes earlier. It was wide open. Bewildered as to why his son had not played the game they'd rehearsed, he stepped outside, fully expecting to see Peter sitting patiently on the metal platform.

The platform was empty. His son was not on the stairs and his heart missed a beat as he stared down at the ground fifty feet below. Please God no!

No sign of a crumpled body on the courtyard. No small boy; no smart cream coat; no shiny black shoes.

He shouted Peter's name as he ran back inside, jostling around the beds, trying desperately to find his son. All concerns about alerting matron, long forgotten.

Peter was nowhere to be found.

To be continued…